SHERLOCK
HOLMES
AND THE SERVANTS OF HELL

PAUL KANE

First published 2016 by Solaris
an imprint of Rebellion Publishing Ltd,
Riverside House, Osney Mead,
Oxford, OX2 0ES, UK

www.solarisbooks.com

UK ISBN: 978 1 78108 454 0
US ISBN: 978 1 78108 455 7

10 9 8 7 6 5 4 3 2 1

A CIP catalogue record for this book is available from the
British Library.

Designed & typeset by Rebellion Publishing

Printed in Denmark

SHERLOCK HOLMES
AND THE SERVANTS OF HELL

SOLARIS

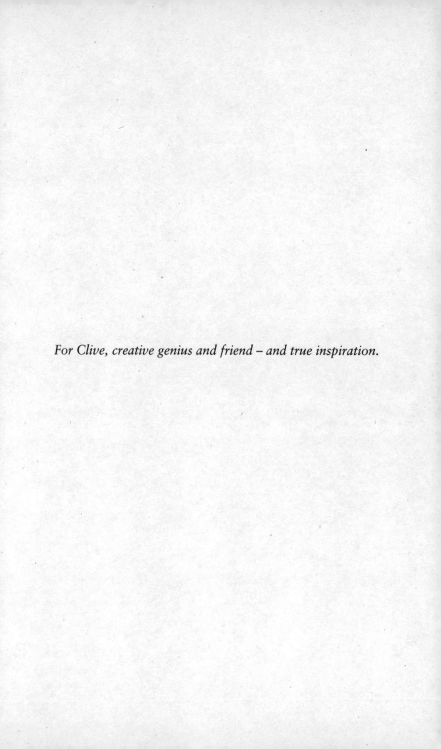

For Clive, creative genius and friend – and true inspiration.

INTRODUCTION
by Barbie Wilde

When Paul Kane first approached me about writing an introduction to his new novel, *Sherlock Holmes and the Servants of Hell*, my first thought was: "Egads! What kind of infernal 'mashup' is this?" Of course, my second thought was: "What a brilliant idea!"

When I was a little kid growing up in North America, my reading material was unconventional to say the least. Rather than the usual girlie stories, I raided my father's library of fantasy, science fiction, horror and last – but certainly not least – the entire canon of Sherlock Holmes. I read and reread all 56 stories and the four novels countless times, until my poor Dad's collection literally fell apart.

Fast forward to London, 1988. I'm introduced to the uniquely inventive world of Clive Barker when I'm cast as the Female Cenobite in his cult British horror movie, *Hellbound: Hellraiser II*, directed by Tony Randel.

Fast forward again to 2006. I'm contacted by award-winning author and (as coined by Clive himself) '*Hellraiser* expert' Paul Kane to be interviewed for his extensively researched and seminal book, *The Hellraiser Films and Their Legacy*. During the interview process, Paul took a generous interest in my own writing, which tended towards the real life horror of serial killers and crime fiction.

After meeting Paul, I began to delve into his books and subsequently discovered the wickedly visceral delights of *RED*, *The Gemini Factor*, *The Rainbow Man*, *Pain Cages*, *Lunar*, *Monsters*, *Blood RED* and more.

In 2009, Paul and his wife Marie O'Regan asked me to contribute a Female Cenobite story ('Sister Cilice') to their *Hellbound Hearts* anthology, which kick-started my career in writing horror. All the stories in the antho were based on the mythology created by Clive in his novella, *The Hellbound Heart*, the basis for the *Hellraiser* films franchise.

Well, I think the above establishes my credentials as not only a Holmes fanatic, but as a *Hellraiser* cognoscenti as well. So what did I think of Paul's "infernal mash-up" of Holmes and *Hellraiser*? As I certainly don't want to dangle too many spoilers in front of those eager readers out there, all I will say is what you have before you is a deliciously dark tale set in a demimonde of nineteenth-century London that bestrides not only the familiar and foggy Holmesian metropolis, but also the shadowy and perverse conurbation simmering beneath a Victorian world of frock coats, bustles and hansom cabs.

Paul masterfully creates an intricate puzzle(box) of crime, mysterious disappearances and the supernatural that initially confounds the greatest fictional detective of all time. However, Holmes, who had previously touched the darkness of the abyss at the Reichenbach Falls and survived, bravely decides to confront the diabolical challenge head on.

On this perilous journey, Holmes – accompanied by the ever-faithful Watson – encounters a new and powerful legion of Cenobites for a nail-biting showdown that will have you hanging on for dear life.

If you're a Holmes and Watson fan, you'll love this book.

If you're an admirer of Clive Barker's *Hellraiser* mythology of labyrinths, Cenobites and the exploration of the ultimate in sensual suffering, you'll also love this book. If you like vivid, imaginative and muscular writing, then, hell, you'll adore this book.

So, no more teasing. The game is afoot! Please find following, for your reading delectation, Paul Kane's *Sherlock Holmes and the Servants of Hell*.

Barbie Wilde
Actress (*Hellbound: Hellraiser II, Death Wish 3*)
and Author (*The Venus Complex, Voices of the Damned*)

PROLOGUE

THE BOX WAS full of possibilities; full of answers to questions he didn't even know he'd asked. It was a puzzle, yes, but so much more than that. The solving of this would bring forth not only solutions, but resolutions. It would provide him with the knowledge he'd been seeking all this time. And he had to see, he had to know...

The room he dwelled in was sparse. The walls bare, the floorboards dirty and littered with splinters. Such things did not trouble him. It was private; what more could he ask of the place? It did not even possess one solitary window, so there was no view to distract him – not that it would have done anyway. There was nothing outside to interest him that day; nothing else existed but the box. So there he sat cross-legged, stripped to the waist, body slick with sweat from his labours. The only light in the room emanated from the candles he'd arranged around himself, which caught the intricate golden panelling on the six sides of the box – broken up only by the obsidian blackness of the lacquered surface beneath – as it was turned over and over in his hands.

He had lost track of time in his quest to open the box.

Somewhere, at the back of his mind, he knew he had been working for hours; maybe even days. He felt neither hungry nor thirsty, however. His efforts, though they had yielded nought thus far, were sustenance enough.

Just when he thought he had it, the key to getting inside would – quite literally – slip through his fingers and he would have to start over again. It would all be worth it, he reminded himself. No more mystery, just enlightenment. Was that not worth however long it would take? Frustration nagged at him, though. On several occasions he had almost thrown the thing across the length of the room, hoping it would smash to pieces against the wall. Only the thought of what awaited him stayed his hand. But surely it should not be so difficult, if one were willing. If one had the... *desire* to open the box.

Was that it? Was that what he was lacking? The desire?

No – he wanted, *needed* this, more than he had ever craved anything in his entire life. It was a strange feeling, but the solving of the box was now the most important thing in the world to him, replacing all other concerns. All other obsessions. If only he could –

He cursed, something he was not generally inclined to do. The word and his voice sounded alien as it echoed off the walls. Others had achieved this, so why not he? What did they possess that he did not?

His eyes narrowed, tongue moistening his dry, cracked lips, and he concentrated once more. One last chance, that was all he would give the damned thing. One more opportunity. But he knew the threats were hollow. He would give the box all the time it deserved, all the attention he could muster. If it took until the end of time itself, he would sit here, and he would trace the lines of the cube, fingertips searching, ever searching.

He wiped first one hand on his trouser leg, then the other. Then he gave a determined nod and set to work again.

So intent was he on solving the puzzle that he did not notice the sound of the bell. A distant chiming at first, as if a church was calling the faithful to worship. *He* was worshipping at an altogether different altar. And he would give all the praise he could if only he might fathom its secrets. The solving was the first, and possibly most important, part. From that would come everything else, he just knew it.

Hold on to that thought, he told himself. *It will carry you through to victory*. Sure enough, just when he was absently considering giving up again, there was an audible *click*...

A smile broke across his face; more of a grin actually. This was it, the first step. Buoyed by his small success, his fingers worked harder, his eyes staring more intently at the ornamental shapes that were almost floating in front of him, swimming in his vision. He blinked, refocussed. Now was not the time to grow complacent, not when he was so near. He fought to control his excitement, slowing his breathing.

Another click... Then something whirring, a mechanism of some kind. *Yes, keep going*, he told himself, *you're almost there!* Closer than he ever had been since all this began, closer than –

A further click. And the sound of the tolling bell grew louder, not that he registered this fact. He was too energised by his triumph. So, imagine his disappointment when the clicks ceased. He waited for something else to happen... but it did not.

His fingers worked again, yet still there were no more noises from inside. Was the mechanism broken? He shook the box, then immediately regretted it. That could break the thing, if it were not broken already.

To have come this far, to have been given hope – only to have it snatched away from you... Well, it was torture: plain and simple.

He had managed to convince himself so utterly nothing else was going to happen that when the next click came he started and the box almost fell through fingers dripping with sweat. Luckily, he did not need them for the next stage of the box's transformation. For, now it was beyond a certain point, it took over, as he had always hoped it might. One of the corners turned, at a seemingly impossible angle. Then it rose, lifting itself and twisting.

At the same time there was movement on its opposite face, a wheel rotating. But that was not the end of it. More movement, above and below, tickling his palm, tiny changes to the box that created another, very different and less ordinary-looking object (not that the box had been mundane or commonplace before). With every twist and turn, he fancied he saw something inside, reflecting off the polished blacks and golds. Something at once spectacular, but more than a little terrifying. Something old, something unique.

A glimpse of another realm.

The sound of the bell had now been replaced by that of a tinkling tune played by the box itself. He marvelled at this, for he had not realised it was musical in nature. The rhythm was relaxed, at odds with the frantic motions of the box.

Then, though he did not feel any wind – and how could there be in here, inside? – the candles blew out. All of them, all at once. Yet he could still see. Light was filtering in from somewhere, cool shafts of cerulean blue. The room was shaking so hard he thought the walls might collapse. Indeed, the wall behind him was being torn apart. He could hear the wrenching of it, hear the footfalls of the figures as they entered, approached.

It was then, and only then, that Sherlock Holmes finally turned around.

PART ONE

Dr John Watson

CHAPTER ONE
Testing the Limits

LOOKING BACK UPON my career – or perhaps I should say *careers*, as I have had four worthy of mention (first doctor, then soldier, then investigator and author) – and indeed my whole life, I find there have been many occurrences of note. One such incident led directly to the taking up of two of those aforementioned occupations; callings that have become perhaps more important to me even than the profession for which I trained all those years ago, receiving my medical degree from the University of London, before serving as staff surgeon at St Bartholomew's (I suspect in part because even with all that training and experience I was still unable to save my beloved Mary). That incident was, of course, being introduced to my friend and companion of so many years, the world's greatest detective, Mr Sherlock Holmes.

I can still remember the day I first met him, not knowing at all what to make of the fellow. Abrupt yet brilliant, with dark, slicked-back hair and such an intense gaze it felt like he was seeing right into the heart of you, seeing your very soul. He gripped my hand in that chemical laboratory with a strength I would hardly have credited the man possessed. I had been warned by my friend Stamford that I might not get on with

Holmes, but right from the very start – during that conversation about haemoglobin, and the importance of blood (something that would take on even greater significance during the events I am reluctantly about to set down) – we had a connection. I felt it, and I like to think in his own way Holmes did as well.

It would be a meeting that saw me moving in to 221b Baker Street to share lodgings with him, whereupon I witnessed various visitors coming and going, including a distinctive Jewish peddler and a railway porter. Not long afterwards, I was drawn more fully into his world as we worked on our first cases together. It was a world I was at once excited by and eager to experience all the more. In time, I would begin to transfer my notes on the cases into stories – which Holmes would very often dismiss due to my embellishments, my use of what he called 'colour and life,' not to mention the more romanticised elements of the tales. More than once he chastened me for not keeping to the facts, for not simply presenting the instalments as aloof studies – something that I could never have done, because they involved people, they involved feelings and emotions; spheres of life that Holmes struggled with and could never fully understand. But there were more than enough clinical essays by the man himself on everything from tattoos to tobacco smoke, which he would often draw my attention to. What I was trying to do was present our exploits in a way that could be understood and – dare I say it – even *enjoyed* by the common man.

I have to admit, and I can do so honestly here, that in my pursuit of these literary goals I did embroider things a little. Something that became almost a necessity after Holmes' untimely –

But I have said too much already – and far too early. Suffice to say, it was not unknown for me to use 'artistic licence' in my detailing of our adventures, even including small jokes that I never for once thought would be taken seriously; a throwaway line about a giant rat, for example – something that did not exist, or that we certainly never encountered if it did. I wrote in that story, which detailed the debunking of the notion of a vampire in Sussex, that Holmes had said the world was not yet prepared for such tales. Again, this was not so much something the detective said as my own thoughts on other singular and more disturbing subjects.

Indeed, it took me some time to actually bring myself to write about particular cases: the terrifying Baskerville Hound, for one, a creature that I did not need to exaggerate about. Holmes' 'death,' as well – another pivotal occurrence in my life and work, something that so profoundly affected me it caused in the writing up of them to mistakenly set two of the entries in the period of those wilderness years that have come to be known as 'The Great Hiatus'; as if the very act of doing so would bring Holmes back to life. And, who knows, perhaps that was the case, because he *did* return to me, did he not? Returned with a story that was so fanciful I was hesitant to chronicle it at first for fear that, although true, it would be horribly derided.

Reality, fantasy. Truth, lies. The line between them is paper-thin. I have had the good fortune – or misfortune, depending on how you look at it – to live long enough to see Holmes make appearances on the silver screen, the most recent of which depict me as some sort of bumbling buffoon rather than reflecting the reality of the situation. I suppose I should be grateful that I appeared at all! And I know, for I left hints myself of so many uncollected stories, that others will take up the baton in years to come and continue to write about our adventures; some of which will be more outlandish and unbelievable than I ever could have imagined. I foresee a time when the fictional character of Holmes will time travel, just like H.G. Wells' character in his machine; when he will battle dinosaurs and alien creatures; when he will be just as at home in a future setting in the next century as he was in the fog-filled streets of nineteenth-century London. All this will come to pass, I am sure. But the truth will remain the truth.

Just as I was reluctant to put pen to paper when it came to chronicling some of our tales from the past, I have remained so about this tale for the longest of times. Not simply because I thought it might not be believed – such is the theme of the account – but also because I feared it might alter the way people saw Holmes. Actually, I *knew* it would change the way they perceived him; how could it not? It would also make them question what they knew about me, for do they not say the road to Hell is paved with good intentions? No matter how my friend and I arrived at some of our decisions, or the reasoning behind them, the results were still the same; the brush with darkness that cannot be denied. Therefore, although I am sharing my recollections of events – or at least those I was privy to – here, I cannot allow them to ever be published. In fact, the writings of this secret journal, once finished, will be destroyed; burned, actually, as would seem fitting. I have made arrangements for this to be so.

But, while I am still of sound mind, I will do what I do – yes, what I do *best*, for as accomplished as I like to think I have been in those other walks of life, I still regard this as the thing I put both my heart and soul into. And I shall do so again within these pages while I am still able.

I do not think it would be an understatement to comment that when Holmes returned from his watery grave in the Spring of 1894 (the only way, I was gravely assured, for Holmes to rid the world of the evil Professor Moriarty) I found him to be a much changed man. Everything that occurred in the story 'The Adventure of the Empty House' happened more or less as I described it, although again Holmes would have me apologise for the *way* in which it was described – something I was, and remain, unwilling to do.

I had been making use of myself aiding the police wherever possible – in this instance regarding the suspicious death of the Honourable Ronald Adair, son of the Earl of Maynooth – when

Holmes decided to reveal that he was still alive. He did this in typical theatrical fashion, by masquerading as a deformed book collector, then whipping off his disguise in my study – the shock of which on my part cannot be underestimated. His true self revealed, he then enlisted my help in capturing Moriarty's man, the crack-shot Colonel Moran; one of the factors preventing my friend from letting me know he was still very much alive.

It was his misguided way of keeping me safe, I understood that – feelings did not come into the equation as far as he was concerned – but there is a part of me that will forever remain angry at Holmes for this deception, especially in light of what I found out during this particular case... or succession of cases, as it turned out to be. Perhaps if he had warned me that there were still agents of Moriarty's on the prowl then –

But I digress. We captured Moran, by fooling him into thinking Holmes was at his window in Baker Street – when it was in fact a replica he'd had made – and the killer was promptly arrested. Even as the excitement died down, I could see something was different about my friend. He had always complained that without stimulus, without mysteries to solve – the kind of mysteries only *he* could solve, I should qualify – he soon grew bored. And when Holmes grew bored, it was usually only a matter of time before he took up his old habit of drug use, something I was forever attempting to dissuade him from with varying degrees of success.

However his penchant for his seven-percent solution of cocaine, administered via a needle he kept locked away in a polished Morocco box, was the least of my concerns after he returned, it transpired. Yes, there were conundrums to periodically keep him occupied between April '94 and the winter of 1895, such as his efforts to recover a famous stone, solving the murder of a young secretary and keeping a music teacher safe. All worthy causes and written up more or less as they unfolded, aside from a few changes to the character of Holmes, the reasons for which will soon become apparent.

In fact, we had only just cracked the case of the 'Bruce-Partington Plans' when we would be called upon to help the first family – that we knew of then – to be affected by the hidden forces at work in our world. In our very city! But before we come to that, it is essential I paint a picture of Holmes' state of mind at that time.

I wrote at the start of the Bruce-Partington affair that my friend was restless – even willing some criminal to take advantage of the thick fog that November in 1895 to commit an act that he might untangle. I confess I glossed over his mood in this respect.

You see, ever since the loss of Moriarty – the Napoleon of crime, responsible for countless interconnected unlawful and immoral deeds – Holmes had never really felt adequately challenged. It was as if he felt he'd reached his pinnacle with that struggle, and nothing afterwards was enough to fully engage him. The fact that he tackled all of the cases mentioned above, and more, when only partially invested in them, should tell you something about his abilities. For, in-between, he was distracted by another altogether more dangerous 'hobby.'

I, myself, have to admit to being preoccupied at the time – still suffering, as I was, from grief after the passing of my sweetheart Mary. As you can imagine, after Holmes' 'death', the loss of my wife, from a severe and virulent illness that yielded to neither diagnosis nor treatment, left me reeling. She slipped into a coma from which she would never wake, though I remained by her hospital bedside and prayed for her recovery – we never even got to say goodbye. There were some mornings during that time when I felt unable to even face the day, let alone any patients; I am afraid I let more than a few people down, and though they insisted that they understood, I was guilt-stricken for a long while afterwards. And though some even said they appreciated what I was going through, the pain I was enduring, I selfishly did not believe them – as if my own, personal hardships were any greater than other people's. Much later, I would wonder what

I was thinking, but I was far too close to it back then, too full of self-pity and Hell-bent on my own course of self-destruction.

I have always enjoyed a tipple and a bet or two, but both my drinking and my gambling got out of hand. If it had not been for the talking-to that Mrs Hudson gave me – a woman who had done such an incredible job of looking after me before Mary came along; looking after both Holmes and I, actually, God rest her soul – and for the police calling upon me from time to time to ask my opinion as a consultant, in lieu of Holmes' expertise, I might well have fallen into a hole out of which I would never have been able to climb. As it was, the terrible dreams I kept having about Mary and her death still persisted, even after Holmes' return; dreams that would often drift back into my time on the battlefield, the deaths of comrades and enemies alike blurring into one. Many's the night I woke up in a cold sweat, crying out for these visions to cease.

It is because of this, I suspect, that I thought I might understand what Holmes himself was going through; though to compare the loss of a wife to an arch-enemy sounds strange, I know. Nevertheless, I felt sure that they were two sides of the same coin, Holmes and Moriarty. As brilliant as each other, they balanced things out: good and evil. So when one was taken away...

Holmes said that after he left me at the Falls he went travelling, first to Florence, then to Tibet, and then Lhasa. Subsequently, under the adopted name of a Norwegian explorer called Sigerson, he visited Persia, entered Mecca, and enjoyed a brief stopover in Khartoum. He would finally end up doing chemical research on coal tar derivatives in France. These are the simple facts I presented, but there was so much more to it than that, as I found out when Holmes – at various points while he was under the influence – let more details slip.

I'll begin with Tibet, where Holmes told me he spent some time with the head Lama. Here my friend studied meditation and meditative states, in an effort to disconnect one's body from the mind: to disassociate yourself from the world and achieve higher levels of consciousness. In theory, using techniques like this, Holmes confided to me once, it was even possible to visit different planes of existence, though I found that hard, if not impossible, to believe. I have seen some strange things in my time, however, not least regarding the affair which I am about to relate – but before this even, in my time abroad, especially in Africa and India; the latter where meditation and prayer definitely go hand-in-hand.

His intention, I can only assume, was to learn how to push his body to its limits, while transferring his mind to another place. Of course, I did not realise this until I bore witness to some of the experiments he put himself through upon his return. It started off small; I would catch him holding his hand over a flame, focussed and unflinching as the flesh burned and cooked. Upon noticing me, he would sheepishly hide the blackened palm, tucking it away and retreating into his bedroom.

Once, on calling him and receiving no response, I found Holmes in the bathroom, submerged but fully clothed, eyes closed, no air bubbles rising to the surface of the water. I immediately feared the worst, leaping in to pull him out of danger – dragging him out of the bath and attempting to revive him. My thoughts, I have to admit, were that he was attempting suicide; something I had contemplated myself on a number of occasions during the dark days of the hiatus.

I slapped him across the face several times, but could elicit no response, and was about to forcibly breathe air into his lungs when he roused himself and asked what the Devil I was doing.

"Saving your life, Holmes!" said I, angrily, upon which he let out one of his laughs – the same tight chuckle he'd given when we first met, at my bemusement over his knowing I'd recently been in Afghanistan.

"My life," he replied, wiping water from his face, "was never in jeopardy, Watson!"

When I pointed out he'd not been breathing, he retaliated by saying that was the purpose of the whole exercise; to see how long he could remain under the surface after putting himself into a virtually comatose state.

I was far from happy, as you can probably imagine.

Even less so when I discovered – through a bit of detective work of my own – what he had actually been doing in Mecca and then France, dabbling not only with some of the most lethal drugs known to nature, but also various man-made ones, concocted by himself in those chemical laboratories. He had been dosing himself with assorted poisons, a practice which continued upon his return to Baker Street – I only discovered this after he spent a fortnight in bed, sicker than I had ever seen him before, as close to death as any man has ever been. Suffering from the after-effects of taking a poison derived from the fangs of the swamp adder we'd encountered a decade or more previously and which Holmes had stored for future use. He recovered from this, more or less, and actually berated me for causing a fuss!

If what was happening in front of my eyes was not enough, then what he was doing to himself behind closed doors – in any number of secret rooms he'd once told me he had across London, some of which I knew about, some I didn't – was so much worse. He would return with scars on his arms he tried to hide, and refused to explain; marks upon his person where I suspected he had been torturing himself – based upon obscure methods and techniques he had picked up during his visits to Italy and Egypt. I happened upon him once in his study after he had been missing for several days – nothing unusual if you knew Sherlock Holmes well – and he was in the process of pulling on his dressing gown. His back was a mess of puncture wounds, as if he'd been shot with something. He refused my attentions as his physician, and actually chased me out of the room! I knew well enough when to leave him be and the next time I saw him, the following weekend, he acted as if nothing had happened. Such was his changeable disposition.

Add to this, his original vice – that of the needle – and visits to the opium dens that he did not realise I knew about (I followed him on more than one occasion, asked questions of the owners in order to ascertain what he was taking – sometimes they would answer, if the price was right, but more often they would not). There had once been a rumour going around that had been the downfall of Dr Thomas Bond, a fine police surgeon of my acquaintance who was so pivotal in the case of the Torso Murders around the time the notorious 'Jack' was also operating on the streets of London. Well, there were other rumours, but those did not bear thinking about. I reminded Holmes of this, of how an upstanding man of the law might 'lose his way,' in an effort to perhaps make him see what he was doing to himself – as his friend and his doctor – but inevitably he would simply bat away my concerns with a flick of his hand.

"You are worse than a nanny, Watson!" he would declare, making light of the most serious of subjects. All fuelled by either his knowledge that he would never again be pitted against the likes of Moriarty, or maybe the realisation that perhaps he should have died at Reichenbach after all.

I am merely grateful that the incident in November, as close to Armageddon as it might have brought us, took his mind off these perilous notions for a least a short time. Time enough for another case to appear on the horizon; one that would tax his skills to the limits and beyond.

A seemingly ordinary case of a missing person, but something that would open up a puzzle which would find Holmes stretched to his capacity; that would uncover a conspiracy only whispered about, and inconceivable to anyone of a right mind. It was a few weeks before Christmas, 1895, when we received two visitors to Baker Street.

And I do not think I am putting it lightly when I say that life would never be the same again for any of us.

CHAPTER TWO
The Cottons

I WOKE THAT morning to find Holmes – rarely one to be dressed, let alone sitting in his study, at breakfast time – camped out in his chair by the hearth. Mrs Hudson had already prepared not only a roaring fire, but also one of her delicious breakfasts of bacon, sausage and scrambled eggs, the smell of which was enough to make my stomach rumble upon entering the room.

Holmes was studying a telegram, and barely seemed to notice I was in the room at first. Then, suddenly, as if a jolt of electricity had activated him, he rose and strode across the space to meet me. "Ah, Watson! What do you make of this?" said he, excitedly.

I looked at him, then down at the missive. "It is apparently something of the utmost importance, judging from the way you are brandishing it at me – and the fact it is keeping me from the delicious food Mrs Hudson has supplied."

I waited, expecting him to say something like, "Oh Watson, think of something other than your stomach for a change!" – which for Holmes himself was not difficult; he would very often go without food, and indeed sleep, for long periods of time (even more so since his return, which was – on reflection

– perhaps simply another way of testing himself). But he said nothing, so I took the telegram from him.

Mr Holmes, it said, *Assistance required. My brother has vanished. Could I visit? Sincerely Mr. L. Cotton.*

"It was delivered early this morning," Holmes added as I read the words.

"A missing person case?"

Holmes gave a curt nod. "I have already replied telling Mr Cotton that we will receive him at his earliest convenience."

I frowned, staring at Holmes and then back down at the telegram with an address not a million miles from Hampstead, on Lodovico Street. I had seen the man dismiss dozens, perhaps even hundreds, of cases such as this and could not for the life of me work out why this one had got him so fired up – especially in light of the absence of any kind of substantial information presented. It was as if he knew already what Cotton would have to tell us, what the investigation would eventually and inevitably lead to. But I have no idea how, and Holmes never did explain. As far as I knew, my friend was not familiar with Cotton or his family at the time – there was nothing remarkable whatsoever about the telegram, nor the message. Yet he paced about the room, never settling for more than a few minutes in one place or the other while I sat down and hurriedly ate.

Mrs Hudson had only just finished clearing away breakfast, sighing and tutting at Holmes' untouched plate, when there came the sound of a cab drawing up outside, followed by a sharp knock at the door. Just one rap, I noted, rather than the staccato rattle our visitors often favoured – in a state, as they tended to be, of anxiety or fear.

Next came the sound of footfalls on the stairs, not two sets – which would have been Mrs Hudson showing our guest up the stairs to the study – but three. In my time with Holmes, almost fifteen years by then, I had picked up a thing or two studying his methods. The other pair of feet were lighter, definitely a woman's.

Mr Cotton had brought a companion.

Then they were at the door to the study, Mrs Hudson announcing their presence. "A Mr and Mrs Cotton to see you," she said.

"Thank you, Mrs Hudson – that will be all!" I had often berated Holmes for the way he spoke to that woman, but he thought nothing of it. In his head, he simply required her to leave in order to hear what confidential information these people might wish to impart. And again, in his own way, he was probably keeping her safe in case said information should prove dangerous... which on this occasion it most definitely did.

Once Mrs Hudson had retreated, Holmes bid the couple enter, allowing me the opportunity to study them both quite carefully. Mr Cotton was dressed somewhat soberly, in a dark suit. He had brown, tousled hair and eyes that were intelligent but quite kindly. His complexion was pale, though positively healthy beside his wife's. She, for her part, had on a light grey dress that was taken in at the middle – with a modest hat atop her head. She had the most piercing grey-blue eyes and pale red lips; I thought straight away that this was a lady whose features had been soft in youth, but her expression was now quite severe. Undeniably a handsome woman, do not misunderstand me, but one who I imagined would not suffer fools gladly.

Both Holmes and I stood to greet them, my friend doing the honours. "I am Sherlock Holmes, and this is my friend and companion, Dr Watson," he stated, in what had become the customary way. I tipped my head first to Mr Cotton and then to his wife.

"Ah, yes," said the man. "I have read all your thrilling tales about Mr Holmes, Doctor. It is one of the reasons I decided to get in touch. Most entertaining I found them, too!" He smiled, as if remembering some of them. Then he appeared to choose a favourite. "That business with the Sign of the Four... most exhilarating!"

"I do hope Watson's little adventure stories haven't presented a false impression of us," said Holmes, gesturing for the couple to be seated on our settee, while we both settled down in our chairs opposite.

I bristled at this, but Mr Cotton simply continued to smile. "I'm quite sure they have not." I had to admit, for someone whose brother was missing, he did not seem unduly concerned or worried. If anything, it was Mrs Cotton who looked fretful, or perhaps she was just awkward in our company, I thought – something I dismissed when she opened her mouth and spoke.

"Laurence, perhaps you should get to the point and tell these good gentlemen why we are here." Her diction was clear and confident, her words telling us much about who actually was in charge in their relationship.

"Of course, of course," he said, patting her knee. It was obvious that the husband thought he was the wife's master, but he was clearly mistaken – or simply deluded. "My name is Laurence Cotton and this... this is my lovely wife, Juliet."

She regarded Holmes and then myself in turn. I felt a little like an animal at the zoo under her scrutiny; or, more accurately, a creature about to be dissected by a scientist. "You're here about your missing brother, I gather," I said to him, holding up my notebook and pencil – silently asking his permission to jot down details. He nodded twice, indicating yes to both.

"And you once worked for some time as a clerk in a counting house, did you not?" said Holmes. It wasn't really a question. They rarely were.

Cotton looked shocked, then his face broke into another grin. "Why, yes! Yes, I did. I would ask how you knew, but you *are* Sherlock Holmes, after all."

"Well, I'll ask, then," I said, more for my own satisfaction than anything.

Holmes closed his eyes, before opening them again and obliging me. "Your stooping frame was my first clue, Mr Cotton, developed from years hunched over a desk doing painstaking work, checking and re-checking. And though you have no doubt risen in the ranks since your five-year apprenticeship, you will never be able to fully lose the ink staining of your fingers from the meticulous keeping of ledgers in the court hand; somewhat old-fashioned in this day and age, but then your profession tends to be so. Coupled with your general colouring and slight squint, it was really no hardship to come to the one and only conclusion."

I thought Cotton was going to applaud at this point, but I had seen the trick before – indeed, I had noticed one or two of those clues myself. "Remarkable," said the man. "Isn't it, my love?"

Mrs Cotton said nothing, she merely offered the tightest of smiles.

"I did indeed end up in a more senior position, working for the firm of Henderson and Sons."

"And such a position would most likely have come about through a recommendation, say from a family member," Holmes went on.

"My father," Cotton replied.

"Who I would venture was a man of means after such a career, but wanted you to make your own way – starting from the ground up."

"Exactly, exactly," said Cotton, eyes turning downwards and brushing the carpet. "He passed away not long ago, a widower since his early fifties."

"Our condolences," I chipped in, knowing that Holmes would never offer them. People lived, people died – the mysteries they created during the period in-between were of greater interest to him.

Cotton looked up again, his eyes moist. "Thank you, gentlemen. That's very much appreciated. He has left us both well taken care of."

"Yourself and your brother," said Holmes.

"Indeed. The house, for example, where we set off from this morning, is now in both our names. It is a beautiful property, Mr Holmes – my family home – and one I should very much like to take up residence in permanently with my good lady, for it suits our needs perfectly. If Francis is agreeable, that is."

"Francis being your brother," I asked for clarity's sake and Laurence Cotton nodded once more. "Your missing brother."

"If he was simply missing, then I would not have come to enlist your help. For most of my life I have never really known where my sibling was, nor what he was doing... and perhaps that is all to the best."

"So you and your brother didn't get along?" I enquired.

"I would not say that; in fact, I think a part of me has always envied his freedom. He was the one who went off on his travels, who went exploring. Who turned his back on a conventional life – much to the disappointment of our parents, who nevertheless continued to love and think well of him."

It was in that moment I knew exactly why this man admired the stories of our adventures so much. Here was a fellow who lived his life vicariously through others. Who had a stable – some might even call boring – life, but lacked the courage to do anything else.

"No," Cotton continued. "It is the *way* in which he disappeared that is the most curious thing, and a puzzle I thought you gentlemen might appreciate."

Holmes leaned forward in his chair, steepling his fingers and urging Cotton to continue. "But please, do not leave a single detail out. Everything is relevant. Even the smallest aspect might be of the greatest significance."

"As I say, we returned to the family home with an aim to move in – compensating my brother for his half, of course, when he next made an appearance. He has never really been interested in the property market, Mr Holmes – not the kind of man to settle down in the one place. Nor with any one woman."

I noticed Mrs Cotton's lips pursing at that remark. Distaste at the absent man's appetites, I thought to myself, or something more?

"I am sure he would be willing... would have been, at any rate. Imagine our surprise, then, when we arrived back and found that Francis had already been there very recently. We'd missed him only by a day or so, apparently."

"He'd left by the time you returned?" I queried.

"Yes... no..." Cotton shook his head. "Not 'left' exactly. As I said in my telegram, he has vanished."

"I don't understand," I said honestly.

"Watson," Holmes said, rounding on me, "do let the man speak!" It was not uncommon for my friend to become exasperated with me during interviews, or at other times, come to that, but there was a brusqueness to his tone then that I had rarely seen before. A desperation to get to the facts of the case, to find out what we were dealing with and let nothing stand in his way. It was an augur of things to come, as I would later discover to my cost. I gave my friend a pointed look, but he either missed it or chose to ignore it. "Mr Cotton, pray continue."

Stunned, Laurence Cotton shook his head, and nodded again. "Since the death of our father, the house has been in the sole care of his housekeeper, Miss Ida Williams. Before that there was a small staff of servants to see to his needs, but he was always most fond of, and most trusted, Miss Williams. Now, before you say it, I know exactly what you are thinking. If she is in need of anything that might require a man's touch, she calls upon our neighbour, Mr Cecil Barbery – family friend and former groundskeeper to the Duke of Norfolk. Cecil also used to help my father with the gardens during the Spring and Summer months. Though retired, he still retains his strength – built through years of working in nature."

"I assure you I was thinking no such thing," Holmes replied. "I have known many capable women in my time, some who would put a man to shame in *every* department." And with this, his eyes drifted towards Mrs Cotton, returning her earlier scrutiny. Ever since Holmes came up against a certain Miss Irene Adler, he has never underestimated anyone of the feminine persuasion – in fact, I suspect he even admired her somewhat for outsmarting him.

Laurence Cotton coughed, partly I suspect to break up the tension that had formed in the room. "Of course. Nevertheless, you will soon see why I bring the matter up. We had barely set foot through the door when Miss Williams, in a state of some distress, rushed up to us and reported what had transpired. My brother, it would seem, returned home quite unexpectedly, and with no explanation whatsoever took himself off upstairs to the disused attic room, eschewing any food or drink that Miss Williams was kind enough to offer. He had with him a small leather Gladstone bag, she says, and he asked specifically not to be disturbed; even secured the door behind him. Oh, I should also mention that it can only be locked or unlocked from the inside.

"After several hours, Miss Williams was roused when she heard a terrible scream coming from upstairs. But when she went to the door and tried it, she found it was still locked. She called through the wood, but no-one answered. It was at this point she headed off to get Cecil, who returned and broke down the door. It was made from the strongest oak, you see, Mr Holmes. Miss Williams, as competent as she is in other departments, could never have gained entrance alone."

Holmes suddenly rose, causing all of us to start. He took out a cigarette from the silver holder in his pocket, which he waved around to offer the rest of us – with no takers. Then he bent and lit it in the fire, standing again to blow out a cloud of smoke, momentarily masking his face. "Tell me, what did they find inside?" Holmes asked finally.

"Well," Cotton replied, "that's just it, they found... nothing."

"The room was *completely* empty?" Holmes demanded.

Cotton nodded. "Save for Francis' empty bag, and a few candles that had gone out and been knocked over, yes. There wasn't anything really in there to start with – as I mentioned, Father had not used it in years."

"Vanished indeed..." Holmes said under his breath. "Are there any windows in the room?" he asked, after taking another drag on his cigarette. "Any way for Francis to have made his exit?"

"A very small window, certainly not big enough for a grown man to climb through – and my brother is no contortionist. It is one of the reasons why the room was left alone, because it was so dark up there. Mother always used to say it had a funny atmosphere, as if it were haunted."

"There are *no* such thing as ghosts, Mr Cotton!" Holmes pointed at him with the cigarette.

"No, of course not," said the man, shaking his head for a change. "I am simply telling you what my mother believed. It was more likely to be damp."

Holmes flashed a tight smile of his own.

"If I might say something," I interjected.

"By all means," said Holmes, his earlier admonishment completely forgotten about.

"The housekeeper... Miss Williams. She *did* leave the house unattended while she fetched help. Could your brother not have left then?"

Laurence shook his head once more, this time with complete conviction. "She was gone only a few moments. At any rate, if he had done so, the door would have been unlocked when she and Cecil returned, surely?".

Cotton had a point, but there again I had also seen Holmes himself escape from a prison once, from a locked cell. I couldn't help stating, "Stranger things have happened."

"And *what* of this friend, the neighbour Mr Barbery? What did he make of the situation?" asked Holmes.

Laurence let out a breath. "He believed it to be a prank on the part of my brother. He still remembers the days when Francis was a boy and used to tie his shoelaces together as a joke. I think he managed even to persuade Miss Williams this was the case. That was one of the reasons she did not go to the police, because she feared they would not believe her either."

"She is most likely correct in that assumption," Holmes informed him. "And as far as I can see, no real crime has been committed, save perhaps for the disruption caused to Mr Barbery."

"Quite so. However, by the time we returned home, she was again in a most agitated state – crying and asking over and over what could have happened to Francis." He looked across at his wife. "We did not have the faintest idea how to respond to her, as you can probably imagine."

"And that is what prompted you to contact me so early this morning," Holmes replied.

"That and my wife's insistence something needed to be done about the situation." He continued to look at Mrs Cotton, offering her a reassuring smile now. This was a man who would give his spouse anything she wanted, I felt certain – the woman only had to ask. "She has never really cared for my brother, have you, my dear? Not since meeting him at the wedding some four years ago. Juliet would like to see the matter settled, so that we will not have any... undue complications later on after having moved in."

"Understandable," said I.

"And this would be your second marriage," said Holmes, blowing out more smoke. Once more, it was not a question but a statement of fact.

Both parties turned and looked at my friend then in unison. "How did you..." Cotton shook his head, remembering the earlier explanation about his job, and just accepted Holmes' deduction (Holmes later told me privately that it was all in the way Cotton had introduced his wife, the hesitation almost an apology to his previous bride and the overcompensation of saying the current Mrs Cotton was 'lovely' to make up for this, not to mention his eagerness to please his bride; all things that I have to admit passed me by). "Yes, that is correct."

"Your previous wife having passed away," Holmes stated, then explained this one without having to even be asked. "The way you talked of your father's dilemma, it revealed a bond – and shared understanding – beyond mere father and son."

Cotton looked down again, another effort to avoid showing he was close to tears. He sniffed and looked up, looked over once more at his wife and took her hand, patting that instead of her knee. "Yes, some years ago. But I have been fortunate enough to be blessed again."

"It must have been a trying time, especially with a child to raise," said Holmes. "You must have envied your brother his freedom all the more because of that."

Laurence Cotton stood sharply, dropping his wife's hand. I thought for a moment he was going to lunge at Holmes (if he had, he would have been the loser) but then his breathing slowed down and his body relaxed.

"Please accept my sincerest apologies. I assure you, sir, I meant no offence," said my friend, extending his hand for a second time to indicate that Cotton should sit, which he eventually did. And of course he *hadn't* meant any offence, because Holmes had been testing this man – to see if there was a subject that would get his dander up.

"No, it is I who should apologise, Mr Holmes. I did not mean to... But my wife, my *late* wife, and Kirsten – they have no bearing on all this."

"Perhaps you did not hear me earlier. *Everything* is relevant, Mr Cotton."

"Holmes..." said I, and he relented.

"I... I did my best," said Cotton without any prompting.

"But after Helen passed away, it *was* difficult – even with help. My own mother had passed away, Father was growing older, and there was work..." The more I watched him, the more it seemed to me like Cotton was in a confessional, pouring out his sins. "In the end, even though I loved her more than words can... In the end, it was better that she go to be with her other grandparents, to finish her schooling."

"In Sweden," Holmes added for him. Cotton stared, open-mouthed, one final time. My friend stubbed out his cigarette, facing front, and put his hands in his pockets. "With your wife being of Swedish descent. Your daughter's name, Mr Cotton: a clear indication. And your late wife's own, a shortening of Helena, yes?"

Cotton nodded. "But the time is fast approaching when she will be able not only to visit, but to come and live with us for a little while. So that she might get to know her loving stepmother, and I might have my family with me again." He remembered the hand he had let go of and reached for it, but Mrs Cotton had since moved it out of the way. "Another reason why it is so important that we make the house on Lodovico Street our *home*. It will be a fresh start for everyone." Then Cotton looked at his wife with pleading eyes, as if to reassure her all would be well.

"But first, you need to know where your brother is," said Holmes. "And we shall endeavour to help you with your mystery. The room: it remains untouched?"

"It does," Cotton assured him.

"Then I would ask you to return to the house and prepare. We shall follow shortly, and will need to speak with both Miss Williams and Mr Barbery, after a cursory inspection of the room."

With that, we said goodbye for the time being to the Cottons – Laurence shaking our hands in turn (it was a very weak handshake, I have to confess) and Mrs Cotton merely tipping her head to us.

I could understand Holmes' desire to take the case more now that I had heard the full extent of it – a locked room mystery would always appeal to him – but still could not see what made it so special. I do not think even Holmes himself knew at that time, but we would both be enlightened soon enough.

And we would come to learn that the Cottons were only the tip of the iceberg. That their story, their problem, was just a tiny part of the puzzle.

A puzzle that went back centuries and was a threat to all of mankind.

CHAPTER THREE
A Faint Smell of Vanilla

THE DWELLING LAURENCE Cotton had told us about was indeed pleasant enough – a three-level brown affair with white window frames – but I would not have said it was particularly beautiful. But then, it had been his home growing up, and he was returning to it, with all the cherished memories that held.

If anything, I felt there was a distinct air of shabbiness about the place, which would have been in keeping with an elderly man like Laurence's father living with only a skeleton staff, and subsequently the housekeeper Miss Williams alone there to see to things. I could, however, see potential in the place for a family – though I did not think that it would be the most happy of environments for teenage daughter Kirsten to move into.

Holmes' thoughts on the subject, which he shared with me upon the Cottons' departure from Baker Street, as he gathered what he might need to begin our investigation, and as we travelled in our cab to that destination, chimed with my own on the subject.

"That woman would rather throw herself off London Bridge than become a 'loving stepmother' to Cotton's child," he said bluntly.

"I concur," said I. "More like a wicked stepmother from some sort of hideous fairytale. Did you notice the slight tic as he talked about the child's mother, and then Kirsten herself?"

"Of *course*," snapped Holmes, insulted. "It was obvious how much it pained her to be reminded about that. Almost as much as it pained Mr Cotton to part with his daughter, I should think – choosing instead to work hard and try to establish a life here that she could be a part of later on; a comfortable standard of living that they might enjoy together."

"Inheriting his father's home would definitely help reunite them," I pointed out. "Except in the meantime, Laurence met and fell in love with the second Mrs Cotton."

Holmes pulled a face. "She was never meant for children, that one."

I did not know whether he was talking about her temperament, or if he suspected that she might not be capable of bearing a child, but in the end it mattered little. His next sentence spun the conversation off into a completely different topic, anyway. "Furthermore, I suspect that the new Mrs Cotton had an affair with Laurence's brother, Francis. Quite possibly only short-lived, especially given his attitude towards women, but nevertheless passionate. It is partly the reason she was so strident about engaging us in the search for Francis."

"Good Lord, really?" I spluttered. "But Laurence said that she couldn't abide the man!"

Holmes slowly nodded. "There is a fine line between love and hate, Watson. In all our time investigating crimes, many of which have revolved around both, you should have come to realise that. Nevertheless, I do not think for one moment Juliet Cotton hates Francis. If anything, the opposite is true. She adores the man beyond measure, Watson. It is the very absence of him that Laurence has picked up on – the hatred of *that* rather than the person – and she would give anything to be with the fellow again. It is a dangerous kind of obsession."

We had alighted from the cab, walked up the path to the house, and were about to knock on the door when it opened suddenly, revealing Laurence Cotton. Glancing across, I saw his wife moving away from the downstairs window, which I would discover – upon entering – belonged to the parlour. Just as Holmes had been eagerly awaiting them earlier, so too had she been watching for our arrival – ready to dispatch Laurence to greet us.

"Mr Holmes, Dr Watson, please come in," said the man, stepping out of the way so we could cross the threshold. There were rooms on the left and the right, a hallway stretching out in front of us, and a set of narrow stairs that, I presumed, led up to the second and third floors. A funnelling space which could easily carry sound, I thought as we divested ourselves of our coats and hats; little wonder the screams of Francis Cotton could be heard so easily throughout the house with acoustics like that. "Miss Williams and Cecil – Mr Barbery – are waiting in the –"

"The attic room, Mr Cotton," said Holmes. "If you would be so kind."

Again, there was method to this – as he wished to carry out an assessment of the room in which Francis had 'vanished' before speaking to those who had tried to aid him. Hearing their stories beforehand would only serve to cloud his judgment, to contaminate his thoughts. There had been enough contamination already, as we saw when we were escorted upstairs to the room, past the second level that contained the bedrooms.

"Not even the Scotland Yard brigade themselves could have done a finer job of blundering about the place," Holmes muttered with a weary sigh after Cotton flung the door wide, careful not to catch himself on the damaged frame. Standing just behind him, I cast my eyes around the room, which was indeed clear, apart from an empty packing box or two, Francis' open case – which I noted had his initials on the side – and the candles Laurence had spoken of. There was also the small window he had told us about and I saw now what he meant; it could not have been more than a foot square, designed more for ventilation than anything – although judging from the state of the paintwork, it was probably stuck shut; more than likely the reason for the damp. The room was also dusty, and it was obvious even to me that Miss Williams and Mr Barbery's forced entry and subsequent search had obliterated any traces of other footprints we might have found.

Nevertheless, Holmes got down to examine the floorboards – scrutinising what evidence might be left with his magnifying glass. Then he began to examine the candles, touching the top of one, measuring the distance between another two – no doubt to try to establish where they had been positioned before their fall. I had seen him like this on many occasions, and described him as such – the most frenzied, I believe, being a time when he needed to find a secret compartment at a crime scene before the police returned to it. Was that how Francis might have exited? I wondered. Some sort of hidden compartment in the floor or walls, perhaps? A secret compartment, like the one a certain Mr Jonas Oldacre had hidden himself in during a previous affair? Holmes was running his fingers along the walls, frowning, which did nothing to dissuade me from my hypothesis.

It would prove not to be the case, of course. There were no rooms on either side of this one, so no space in which to hide – although there was a smaller storage room opposite – and the window wall overlooked the side of the house. Even if Laurence's brother *had* been some sort of carnival contortionist, he would still have had to negotiate the drop, and would no doubt have been seen by the returning Miss Williams and Mr Barbery, as they raced back to help.

Holmes then began sniffing the air. I have so often commented on his keen sense of smell, indeed the man has written papers on the subject of both that and the use of other senses in detective work. But when he spoke again, even I could discern the scent he was talking about.

"There is a faint smell of vanilla in this room," he said finally to no-one in particular.

And yes, there was. Faint, because whatever had caused it was long gone (and we would later rule out any sort of perfume, for Miss Williams was not one to partake of such a luxury). Faint, but lingering, as if to leave a trace of whatever had happened here behind. I certainly did not know what to make of it.

Once all his explorations were concluded, and with an examination of the lock on the inside of the door on the way out – broken to gain entry – he told Laurence Cotton that he was ready to interview the witnesses, separately if that was at all possible, starting with Cecil Barbery.

"We can use Father's old study," Laurence said. "For privacy." After showing us where that was on the ground floor – a room full of books with numbers on their spines rather than titles, marking them as ledgers, and also containing a desk and two wooden chairs – the man went to fetch his neighbour.

Holmes insisted I take one of the chairs, and I did not argue for I could see he was full of nervous energy and would not be able to sit still even if he took the spare seat. When Cecil Barbery entered the room, he had to bend so as not to catch his head on the top of the door frame. He had grey hair, but a young face, and his open-necked shirt and jacket strained to contain his chest and shoulders. Miss Williams had been quite correct to enlist him in the breaking down of the attic room door.

When he shook my hand, I felt him squeeze it – as if testing my strength – but he stopped when he saw me wince. Holmes barely twitched at the man's grip, however, and Barbery soon let go after a few moments of staring squarely into my friend's eyes. When I came to start writing in my notebook, I had to flex my fingers a few times, still cramping from Barbery's attentions, but I managed to catch up with the exchange fairly swiftly after that.

"All this fuss," growled Barbery, taking a seat and causing the wood to protest. "He's just playin' silly beggers, is little Frank." I daresay *everyone* was little to Barbery, but he had known the brothers when they were just children and so still thought of them that way on some level. The use of an abbreviated form of Francis also gave the man we were looking for a much harder edge. "He'll turn up when he's good and ready, with a sly grin on his face and a woman in tow."

"So, it's your evaluation that Francis Cotton is the mischievous sort," said Holmes, standing with his back to us, hands clasped behind him.

"Oh, aye. Never been anythin' but. Black sheep of the family, that one," grumbled Barbery. "Not like Laurence. Fine upstandin' gentleman he is, just like his father. Always time for people."

"How did you come to know the family?" I asked.

"Through Mr Cotton's dealings with the Duke. He had business affairs with him and used to visit quite frequently, and we just got friendly. That was the kind of man he was. When I heard about his wife, and I had retirement myself coming up, I moved in nearby so I could keep an eye on him. Help out where I could."

"Most kind of you," I said.

"Aye, well, that's just the sort of man *I* am."

Holmes spun around. "Please, if you would – the evening in question. When Miss Williams called upon you, from the beginning..."

Barbery related what he could remember, which tallied with what Miss Williams had told Laurence: she'd banged on his front door for help, shouting something about an intruder and an attack – which is what it must have sounded like to her. He'd gone with the housekeeper and shouldered the door open, but they'd found no trace of Francis Cotton inside, in spite of all their 'stomping around' – as Holmes had called it – searching for him.

"You heard no screaming?" asked Holmes when the man was finally finished with his account.

Barbery thought about this for a little while. "I... No, I don't recall any screamin'. But he will be when I get hold of him for all this trouble," the large man promised. I was beginning to see that Francis Cotton was a person that not many people liked; unless, of course, you were of the female persuasion.

That opinion was enforced when we talked to the housekeeper, Miss Williams herself. She was a lot younger than I thought she would be, with auburn hair and green eyes – that were also reddened and sore-looking from her tears.

"Oh, please, Mr Holmes, Dr Watson, if there's anything you can do to help us find Francis... Mr Cotton, I mean..."

"How long have you known the gentleman in question?" Holmes folded his arms, then slipped out his left hand to tap a finger against his lips.

"Off and on, ten years or more, since I came into Mr Cotton's – the late Mr Cotton's – employ as a maid, sir."

"So, since you were nineteen, twenty?"

The woman nodded.

"And have you been in love with him all that time, or is that more of a recent development?" Holmes said suddenly, and Miss Williams looked at him as if she'd just been caught stealing something.

"In love?" she replied. "I-I don't under –"

"Oh come now," Holmes said, drawing closer and taking up a stance that would have intimidated the most hardened of criminals, let alone a young woman. "You're not very good at concealing your feelings for him, Miss Williams. Francis, indeed!"

"I am just concerned about his welfare, and that is all," she argued, growing angry.

Holmes batted her words away with a wave of his hand. "As you wish. You might also be concerned for your position in this household, though – especially if Mr and Mrs Cotton move in as they plan to."

I watched her as Holmes said these words and their true meaning was not lost on Miss Williams, I could see. Perhaps it was common knowledge about Juliet Cotton and her brother-in-law (common, that is, to all but her husband), or maybe she had noticed the agitated state Laurence's wife had also been in since the man went missing and the steps she had insisted upon to find him – regardless of whether it involved her infidelity coming to light.

Even I could see that Miss Williams' days in this house were numbered, if Mrs Cotton had anything to do with it.

"I intend to move on anyway, Mr Holmes – once the mystery of where... Mr Cotton is can be solved." She said it like she was issuing a challenge to him, and I also had to wonder whether Miss Williams thought – or hoped – that when she moved on it would be with Francis Cotton by her side. The more I heard about the chap, the less likely it seemed, I had to admit.

Once we were finished with the witnesses, Laurence escorted us to the parlour where Juliet Cotton was still waiting. "Well?" she demanded, rising from her chair as we stepped through the door. "What do you make of it all?"

"It is difficult to say," Holmes admitted.

"You do not even have a theory?"

"Oh, I have a theory, Mrs Cotton," said Holmes. "I have several, in fact; but none that I wish to share at this moment in time."

"Mr Holmes," said Laurence, looking from his wife to my friend. "Do you or do you not know what happened to my brother? I have seen – read – tales where you have solved cases in much less time than this! Tell us!"

Holmes sighed. "Very well. I believe your brother to be deceased, Mr Cotton."

Mrs Cotton staggered sideways a little and I thought she was going to faint. Laurence immediately rushed over to the woman to steady her. "Mr Holmes, that is a cruel thing to say, even in jest."

"I assure you, I never make light of such matters," Holmes told him. "Your brother *is* dead."

Not even I knew what Holmes was playing at, saying such a thing. "Holmes, how can you be sure that –" I began, but he held up a hand to silence me.

"I would rather not say any more," Holmes stated.

"This is preposterous!" shouted Mrs Cotton, baring her teeth as her husband settled her back down on her seat. "How can you say such a thing? I will not have it! Laurence, would you escort these men out – immediately!"

He looked unsure for a moment, then nodded; he was never going to refuse her. But Holmes was already backing out through the door, retrieving our coats and hats.

"I *am* sorry to be the bearer of such news," he said to Laurence Cotton as he followed. "Nevertheless, you wished to know."

"I think it would be best if you do not return," said the man who had been so keen to hire us that morning. He looked back over his shoulder, through to his wife – who appeared on the verge of tears.

I expected Holmes to argue with him, given the fact he had been just as eager to take on the case, but he simply nodded. It was as if, having come here and seen what he'd seen, talked with the witnesses, he had found out what he needed to know and could leave this place – if not the mystery itself – be.

Breathing in the bitter early evening air, we hailed a cab and, once safely inside, I asked what my colleague had discovered.

"Another person visited that room aside from Mr Barbery, Miss Williams and, of course, Mr Cotton himself," said Holmes. "I do not know how they gained entry or exited again, but they were there."

"And you believe this person was responsible for the death of Francis Cotton?"

Holmes held up a finger. "Now, I did not say that, Watson. But I do believe they were there to retrieve the murder weapon."

"The murder..." I was stunned into silence; I had absolutely no idea what Holmes was talking about.

"Something Cotton took out of his bag, along with the candles he'd brought with him which – before they were disturbed – had been lit and arranged about him in a perfect square. A square that mirrored the shape of the object which was taken, that had been on the floor during the slaughter of Mr Cotton: I found markings in the dust at the back of the room which suggested it might have been box-shaped. Precise dimensions, three inches to a side. And solid, Watson."

"Something Cotton might have been struck with, you think?"

"Blood had been spilled in that room, most definitely – a lot of blood – although it had also been cleaned up again, more efficiently than I have ever seen in my entire career. So well, I almost missed the tiny specks of it between the floorboards, in the cracks of the walls. And the distinctive smell of copper, underneath the vanilla." Holmes paused and I thought he'd forgotten my original enquiry altogether, until he said, "But I cannot say for sure that it was the murder weapon that spilt the blood."

"Holmes, you're not making any sense, man," I told him. It was something he admitted himself with a cock of his head.

"Yet that is what I saw, Watson. That is what I *detected*." He sat back in the cab's seat and held up his hand again, a signal that he would talk no more – and we rode the rest of the way home in silence.

I wondered then if this was to be simply one of those mysteries which was destined never to be explained, not by Holmes nor anyone else, regardless of his best efforts. Indeed, if Holmes could not put his finger on what had occurred, what hope was there for anyone else? Moreover, the authorities were unlikely to investigate a death – or murder, as Holmes insisted – the existence of which could not even be proved. Where was the body, for one thing?

No, I felt sure that this was one story I would never, ever get to write up, let alone finish; my readers would think me mad. Indeed, in the months ahead, I would come to question my *own* sanity.

And I would begin to wish the mystery had remained unresolved.

CHAPTER FOUR

Further Disappearances

THE HOLIDAY SEASON came and went, and I did my best to put the events of Lodovico Street from my mind.

Holmes was his usual irritable self around this time of year, reflected in arguments with Mrs Hudson that would have put Scrooge to shame: about the decorations, the tree, Christmas dinner and such. It was not that Holmes hated Christmas, for he could understand the notion of religion well enough – and the comfort it gave people who had precious little the rest of the year. He had also, on occasion, spoken about a higher power – and once, at length about how something as wonderful but unnecessary as a rose gave us hope in such a divine being – although I know that he much preferred the evidence of his eyes to faith in things that could not be explained or proven (another reason why the case we had just investigated remained such a frustration – especially to him, which did little to help with his disposition).

But he saw the benefit of a period in which folk were encouraged to be generally kinder to each other. In fact, had Holmes himself not been lenient with the thief Ryder after he had taken the Blue Carbuncle during a moment of madness and secreted it in that goose – my friend claiming then that to have him arrested would create a more hardened criminal later on; although I could see it was more than simple foresight. It was in keeping with the spirit of Christmas, whether Holmes believed in this or not.

That adventure seemed a long time in the past. During the month of December 1895, Holmes' mood swings grew increasingly worse, punctuated by long intervals where he would simply disappear again – vanish off the face of the Earth, as surely as Francis Cotton before him – only to return in some sort of stupor, or wounded, or both. I had no hope of tracing him on these occasions; he was just too proficient at avoiding being followed.

As the end of the old year rapidly approached, I even attempted to coax Holmes out for a drink to see in the new one, but his answer to that was, "One year is very much like the next, Watson. It does not expect a welcome, it merely is!" Then added, somewhat morbidly, "The passage of time waits for no man!"

All the more reason to celebrate while you still could, was my reasoning. Although on the one hand, I was very glad of that night with a mixture of old friends, mostly former-military pals, especially when I looked back on it in the months to come; at the same time – looking around me at the revellers, the singing and the drinking – I was incredibly aware that this would have been Holmes' idea of Hell itself.

Little did I know that one of those people at the New Year's Eve gathering would be in touch with me not a month later, as January marched into February. I had served with Alfie 'Gunner' Harris during my time in India with the 5th Northumberland Fusiliers and we had kept in touch ever since. He always called me by my middle name of Hamish, and had the annoying habit of ruffling my hair whenever he saw me, as an uncle might do to a younger nephew he hadn't visited in a while.

I received a letter from Alfie, telling me about a quandary that the cousin of another friend of his was in – and they wondered if he might speak to me on their behalf with the intention of seeking the advice of Mr Sherlock Holmes.

I know this might be something of an imposition, Alfie wrote, *but I don't think she has anyone else to turn to.* It was a line we heard all too often, but not even I was sure whether Holmes would respond positively to such a request at the moment. I was already gearing myself up to go alone, and employ his methods as best I could in his stead, when I read about the nature of the case.

I immediately showed the letter to Holmes and waited for him to finish it. "It is remarkably similar, do you not think?" said I when he was done.

He rubbed his chin and read through the letter one more time. "There are parallels, certainly. But without investigating further..." He paused. "Yes. Yes, I believe we will look into this one, Watson."

We telegraphed ahead and the very next day were on our way to Essex, to the home of Alfie's friend's cousin. When we arrived, I saw that this was a smaller abode than that of the Cottons: a manor house with only two floors, but in leafy surroundings. There was a white gate set between two posts at the entrance, and a small drive leading to the front door.

It was the lady herself who answered our knock, a thin woman with a plain dress and her hair tied back. "Please, do come in, gentlemen. Thank you so much for making the trip," she said, the relief palpable. "Can I get you something: tea, coffee?"

"Tea would be most welcome," I told her, with Holmes himself plumping for the other option. She bid us follow her through to the kitchen, where she explained there was just her in the house. "I've always preferred to do for myself," she stated. "Perhaps it's my upbringing, the work ethic instilled in me by my parents. In any event, keeping the household running occupies – *occupied* me when Howard was abroad."

Through the kitchen window, I could see out into quite a long garden, with a summerhouse at the end of it. It was not a big structure, more like a hut, but it would be the focal point of both our conversation and our enquiries that day. She served us the beverages as we took our seats at the table, then the woman joined us.

"Mrs Spencer," said I. "Perhaps you could tell us in your own words what happened on the day of your husband's disappearance?"

She blinked a few times, bit her lip, and began. "As Alfred might have already told you, Howard has not long been back home. He was injured in the line of duty, fighting in the Jandamarra Guerrilla War. As a lieutenant, he did not want to return before the conflict was over, to leave his comrades, but was left with no choice due to his leg wound."

I saw flashes then of the Battle of Maiwand, where I had received a wound of my own akin to Lieutenant Spencer's. Scenes that still haunted my dreams, along with Mary...

"...the same since he returned," the woman was saying when I snapped to.

"I'm sorry, could you repeat that?" I said, ignoring Holmes rolling his eyes.

Mrs Spencer just nodded and said again: "Howard has not been the same since he was forced to come home eight months ago. It was obviously not his first time in combat – and I fretted so on every single occasion – but there was something very different about his mood upon his return. It was... it was as if he was still back there, still fighting. As if without that, he was nothing. *Had* nothing. Some days he would just stare right through me, as if I were a ghost."

I thought about Holmes after he came back to me, the loss of Moriarty too much for him to bear. How the absence of a thing exposes how important it was to you when you had it.

"It was as if I was not enough for him. Ellie was not enough for him."

"You have a child?" I asked. "Alfie never mentioned... Ellie; a daughter?"

She gave a small laugh. "A son, just turned twelve. Ellie's a shortening of his name, it's just what we... what I call him. Thank goodness he is away at boarding school at present, and was not here to see all this." Mrs Spencer put a shaking hand to her mouth. "I haven't told him yet. I do not even know how to! He idolises his father, wants to follow him into the military one day – become a decorated soldier himself. Given what has happened, I am not altogether sure that is the right path for him."

"People must find their own way in life," Holmes told her sombrely, taking a sip of his coffee. "No matter where it leads them. Do continue, Mrs Spencer."

Composing herself, the woman carried on with her story. "He would be distant with me, with both of us. And... and there would be nightmares, horrible nightmares. Howard would thrash about so in the bed, screaming and shouting out. Once I tried to wake him from one of these night terrors, for I could stand the pain he was going through no more. My reward was to almost be struck by Howard's fist." She looked up at us both, tears collecting in the corners of her eyes as she described the stranger that had once been her loving husband. "Sometimes he would take himself off, I know not where – and he would provide no kind of explanation when he returned."

Once again, I was reminded of Holmes and the times, even recently, when he went missing without telling anyone where he was going. He could have been lying dead in a gutter somewhere, for all we knew of it!

"I did not have the heart to follow him, in case I should find out there was someone else. I do not think I could have coped with that on top of everything. Either he would go out, or he would retreat to our summerhouse, regardless of the fact it is winter. I tried to get him to come indoors, but he ignored me;

as if I wasn't there. I would watch him from here, through the window – just sitting inside and staring into space. Or looking down as if he'd fallen asleep."

"And that was where he was on the day he..." I let the sentence tail off.

Mrs Spencer nodded. "I could see him from the window here." She rose and pointed at the view. If Lieutenant Spencer had been sitting in there, his wife would certainly have been able to witness the fact. But the man must have been freezing! Holmes got up and went to look through the window himself, and I joined the pair just as Mrs Spencer carried on with her tale.

"On this particular afternoon, less than a week ago, I was getting things together to start preparing dinner – although Howard has not had much of an appetite of late, I still liked to put a nice plate of food in front of him, to tempt him. Anyway, I was in here tenderising some steak, watching Howard through the window once more. He looked to have nodded off in the summerhouse, head down – eyes closed. But then the strangest thing happened."

Holmes looked sideways at the woman, eager to hear the rest. "Go on."

Her brow furrowed as she remembered. "Everything went dark."

"You mean overcast?" I asked. "About to storm?"

Mrs Spencer shook her head. "I do not mean the weather, Doctor. I mean inside the summerhouse itself."

I glanced through the window at the hut. "It looks to be quite shadowy inside there anyway."

"This was different. It was like when the moon passes over the sun, only inside the summerhouse itself. Completely black – but tinged with blueness. A sort of... black light. Yes, that's the only way I can describe it to you. A black light."

No-one said anything for a few moments; I think we were trying to digest the information.

Then Mrs Spencer took up her story again: "It did not last very long, and during this time I could not see any sign of Howard at all – but I could hear his screaming, plain enough. Just like when he was having his nightmares. Then it was brighter in there again, and my husband was gone."

"Are... are you saying that this darkness *took* him?" I was trying very hard to hide the disbelief in my voice.

"I know how it sounds, Doctor – but I swear to you that was what happened."

"And next?" asked Holmes.

"Well, I rushed out of the house, naturally, rushed into the garden and towards the summerhouse. The closer I came, the more it was apparent that Howard was gone. The summerhouse was completely empty, his chair overturned."

"Is it not possible that he might simply have climbed out of one of the side windows?" I enquired, putting forward the obvious question.

Mrs Spencer shook her head again, more vehemently this time. "I was watching the summerhouse the whole time, I would have seen it. No, one minute he was there – then came the blackness and the screams – and the next he was gone."

"But that's not all, is it?" Holmes said.

"No. As I was looking in through the front of the summerhouse, I heard a noise off to my left – a rustling. I ran around the side, thinking perhaps it was Howard, though how he would have gotten around there is anyone's guess. But it was not him at all – it was another man. His coat was ragged, shabby, and he was hunched over as if he could barely walk, let alone run. He had gloves that were cut off at the fingers; I noticed that because he was in the process of putting something in his pocket... I thought he must be some sort of a vagabond, here to steal something. It was at that particular moment he noticed me and turned, looked right at me. I remember shivering under that gaze. Those cold, blue eyes."

"Could you describe him more fully to us?" Holmes was shifting about on the spot, agitated.

"He had a beard, which was unkempt. Wild hair and dirty skin... I thought about giving chase, even though I was scared for my very life – but in the moment that I thought about it, the man was gone too."

"You mean he climbed over the back wall?" I said, nodding past the summerhouse to the brick barrier that ran along the rear of the garden.

"No, I..." Mrs Spencer shook her head, this time in bewilderment. "I do not know where he went, and that is the truth as well." Then she seemed to go into a trance herself, mirroring her husband. "I recall hearing the sound of a bird's wings flapping, but that is all. I was alone after that and have remained so ever since."

Holmes asked to see the garden and the summerhouse, so Mrs Spencer took us outside, through the back door she had used when rushing to get to her husband. "Is it possible...?" began Holmes, then he stopped and stood still on the lawn.

"Yes?" asked Mrs Spencer.

Holmes looked up and down the garden, back towards the window, then ahead to the summerhouse. "I was just wondering... Well, the angle you were observing your husband from. Is it possible that he was not asleep, but rather looking down at something?"

"Something on the floor?" asked a baffled Mrs Spencer.

"Something in his hands," Holmes corrected. "What was his expression like?"

She thought for a moment. "Serious, but then it always is of late. Nothing like the man I used to know."

"Could it have been a look of concentration?" my friend enquired, but then didn't even wait for an answer – he was striding off towards the summerhouse to carry out another survey.

"You went to the police, I gather?" said I to Mrs Spencer as we headed to join Holmes.

"Yes, but they were not very sympathetic. They did not believe Howard simply vanished... was taken. But rather he wandered off of his own accord – something that I can see would make sense, given his recent state of mind."

I was not surprised. Miss Williams had been right not to contact them about Francis Cotton's disappearance; they would have been of no use whatsoever.

"Oh, Doctor, I know something is wrong with him – but Howard is still my husband, and all I have apart from my son. Do you really think you and Mr Holmes will be able to help me get him back?"

I thought Mrs Spencer was going to break down right there and then on the lawn.

"We will do our best, as always," I told her, but there was little or no assurance in my voice. We had got nowhere with the Cotton case – indeed, our clients had practically thrown us out. I hoped Holmes had learnt from this, and that if he suspected Howard Spencer to be dead as well, he might spare the poor man's wife that knowledge; at least for the time being.

We reached him as he was emerging from the summerhouse, searching the area around it. "A pity we were not called in sooner," he observed, staring at the ground, apparently following a trail to where Mrs Spencer said she'd seen the interloper. "But there is sufficient evidence remaining to corroborate your version of events, Mrs Spencer. The man's tracks definitely end here, well before the wall."

The relief was palpable on Mrs Spencer's face. "Thank God someone believes me."

"Then he must have covered up his tracks before getting away." I have to admit, I myself was having trouble believing Mrs Spencer, as I had Miss Williams before her. People did not just disappear into thin air. Cotton, Spencer... the vagabond.

Then I thought of a solution myself, thought about the trance both Howard Spencer seemed to be in and then how his wife had looked when remembering the event. "Is it possible that this man, this intruder, put both Mr and Mrs Spencer into some kind of hypnotic state? She mentioned his eyes..."

Holmes pondered this for a few moments. "It is certainly a theory worth exploring more fully. Mrs Spencer," he said then, turning to her, "thank you for your hospitality – we will be in touch in due course."

Holmes was already ushering me away from the summerhouse, towards the main house, and then – after we had said our goodbyes – to the street. "Holmes, why the sudden rush?" I asked my companion as we were hailing another cab, but he did not answer. Once again, it was as if he had gotten everything from the scene he needed and did not want to be around it one moment longer. Had there been an atmosphere about the place, as there had supposedly been about the room in the house on Lodovico Street? "What about Lieutenant Spencer?"

"He has suffered the same fate as Francis Cotton, I fear," Holmes said coldly, and without a shred of doubt in his voice. So he *had* learned from his last outburst, after all, I thought to myself. "You were right to bring this to my attention, for it has all the same hallmarks: the smell of vanilla was present again, with an underlying scent of copper. Minute traces of blood, the scream. Lieutenant Spencer's vanishment... and our friend from the attic room, the one who managed to get in and out of the place without unlocking the door. Here to retrieve the same item as before, I trust."

"The 'murder' weapon," I said.

"Indeed!" Holmes replied. "The two cases are definitely connected, I just don't know how yet. Or why."

But then a cab arrived, and he would speak about the summerhouse and Spencer no more that day.

All I could think about was that young boy; because if Holmes was right, he would grow up without a father now. Grow up and probably enlist in the Army for all the wrong reasons. I had to wonder about his fate.

About what would become of little Ellie.

CHAPTER FIVE
The Summons

As far as I could determine, Holmes made as much headway with the Spencer case after our visit to Essex as he had with the Cotton case previously. And although I pressed him on it in the month or so after we'd visited Mrs Spencer – largely because she herself had been in touch to ask about progress, as had Alfie who made the original request – he could furnish me with no answers. So I could, in turn, give them none (and again, my thoughts turned to the Spencer boy – who must surely have been told his father was missing by now; a puzzle that looked like it would never be solved... I wondered if he himself might even take up the mantle later on in life).

All I knew was I would walk into the study on occasion to find books scattered about the place – as well as papers and drawings – and Holmes still in his robe, sitting cross-legged in the middle of it all, as I admit I'd seen him do before when deep into a problem. But nothing seemed to come of it this time; Cotton and Spencer themselves were not connected in any way.

There were no sudden revelations about the vagabond, about hypnosis – which I would still have bet on at that time – about 'black light' or the flapping of wings. I even ventured another theory, that perhaps some form of hallucinogen – similar to the one Holmes had told me about that a certain Egyptian cult favoured, delivered by means of a thorn and blowpipe – might be involved. But I knew myself I was just clutching at straws.

We appeared, for once, to have come across a case that stopped Holmes dead in his tracks.

To be fair, he was not at the top of his game at this point in his career. He was still going missing from time to time, although now I suspected it was to get away from the mystery surrounding these cases as much out of sheer boredom or to test himself. He was spotted, however, according to one of our mutual informants – a lad called Sam, part of the group of street urchins Holmes sometimes relied upon for data, the so-called Baker Street Irregulars – visiting a corner of London known to be rife with the sick and the plague-ridden. I have visited such parts of the city myself – taking every precaution, naturally – to do my bit as a medical man and try and comfort those dying from consumption. Holmes, it would seem, took no precautions whatsoever. According to Sam (who approached me not only because he thought the information might be worth a shilling, but also out of a concern for Holmes' welfare), my companion was walking about amongst the worst cases without even a mask on; bending and talking to some of them as they lay in their cots. It was almost as if he was *trying* to catch the disease that had proved so rampant of late. Or maybe it was just another way of tempting fate?

I said nothing to Holmes about all this, but it was clear to me that his malaise was gaining momentum. That if these were in fact efforts to feel something, to feel *alive*, then they might well kill the man instead.

It wasn't long after this that Holmes received a summons from his brother Mycroft, to come to the Diogenes Club – he wished to speak to him about a most urgent and delicate matter. Such a 'request' was not a common thing, and it had only been a few months since we had last aided Mycroft, so this came as something of a surprise. It was during that former affair Holmes finally felt able to confide in me about what his older brother really did; about his crucial role in the British Government (about how, at times, he *was* the British Government). Imagine my amazement to discover that the conclusions of every single department were passed on to him, that Mycroft was the central exchange, the clearing house which makes out the balance. Before that, when investigating the curious case of Mr Melas, Holmes had told me only that his sibling audited books for some government departments; and before that, I had no idea at all that Holmes even *had* a brother, for he had never mentioned him – nor any other member of his family, come to that.

If Mycroft was calling for us again so soon, it could only mean trouble – and within an hour of the telegram arriving we were at the door of the Diogenes, a club on Pall Mall that Mycroft actually co-founded and appropriately named after the Greek philosopher who was one of the founders of Cynicism: the moral being to trust nothing and nobody. It was an odd place, the Diogenes, where you had to be as quiet as a mouse unless you were in the 'Stranger's Room,' which was where we were taken upon our arrival: past lots of ancient-looking gentlemen all sitting in leather chairs, smoking cigars and reading their periodicals – and up the winding staircase.

I had visited the Stranger's Room before, but it never failed to impress me. More books lived here than in most libraries, and this time they were not ledgers like those that lined the walls of Mr Cotton, Sr's study. Instead they were more interesting volumes on history, on science, on... indeed, on every subject you cared to name; in addition to the fiction volumes that I would love to have spent a year sitting and reading in the comfort of this place.

Mycroft was seated by the window, looking out. Holmes had said once that the man lacked energy (the two brothers were exact opposites, much like the Cottons), and this is how I will always remember him until the day I die: in a seated position, watching the world go by outside – and content in the knowledge that he had a major say in how it was run. A large gentleman with a rapidly receding hairline, Mycroft said nothing in greeting: he merely waited for Holmes to join him at the window.

Then, and only then, did Mycroft raise a chubby finger and point down into the street. "Those two, Sherlock."

Holmes raised a hand to his chin and I drew closer, in an effort to also see the pair Mycroft had singled out. A man of about thirty, with what I assumed to be his partner – a slightly older woman – linked arm in arm.

"I'm sure to the casual bystander they might appear to be a couple, but there is more to it than that. Observe the way she is pulling him in, directing him. And look now, how they stop at the edge of the road – a ritual since the man was a boy. She is quite clearly his mother, though she had him early in life. She was widowed early, too, and transferred her affections – and obsessions – to her son, quite possibly in a most unhealthy way, that will have seen a number of suitors run a mile in the opposite direction."

As I watched, the more I could see the controlling nature of the woman, the way she was looking left and right before almost dragging the poor man across the road. Then, at the other side, adjusting his coat lapels, brushing him down and bidding him stand up straight. A domineering mother, who had never wanted her 'boy' to grow up.

"They are returning home having just visited the travelling fair which has set up camp in Hyde Park," said Mycroft. "Note the traces of pink on the edges of his sleeves, where she bought him a strawberry penny-lick ice cream – an enforcement of the mother-son relationship she has encouraged over the years. He attempted to win a stuffed animal for her at the coconut shy, but was unsuccessful, hence their sour faces after coming away from such a place of merriment; not to mention the rough handling and lack of patience of a parent disappointed in her child."

I'd witnessed this game a few times now, something – I deduced myself – that started when these two were little, but was still astounded by it. Holmes had told me before that Mycroft's analytical skills even outstripped his own, but would never put it to the same use because of his lack of energy and ambition (though I had to wonder, how much more ambitious could a man be whose word was taken as Gospel at even the highest of levels?). Nevertheless, you could see the rivalry between them in these mental jousts. Though it was hard to picture either of them as boys, I had an image in my mind of them doing this at home or at school.

Holmes also said that Mycroft lacked the imagination to make leaps of deduction that he was able to. I wondered now what the fellow might have made of our last two unsolved cases: the missing men, the bearded vagabond and the smell of vanilla. Would he dismiss them as nonsensical, as I was inclined to do myself? But we were not here to pick his brains about such things.

Mycroft turned to look at me then, obviously satisfied by a palpable hit – I wasn't sure how these things were scored – and said, "Dr Watson, how pleasant to see you. I do hope you've gotten over your little bout of jealousy. The grudge you've been holding against me since I helped facilitate Sherlock's ruse?"

Nothing had ever been said openly about this, and I omitted the atmosphere between us when writing up our last meeting, but I should have known that something as obvious as my feelings about the deception would have been picked up on by a brain such as Mycroft's.

"I do not blame you for that, I assure you."

Mycroft gazed at me and smiled. "Nor should you blame

Sherlock. He was just trying to do what was best for all concerned, to keep you out of harm's way, Doctor. We do not have the luxury of choosing our family, but we do choose our friends. If anything, that should tell you more about how much Sherlock –"

"Mycroft!" snapped Holmes.

Until that moment, I hadn't thought about the situation that way. Over the previous years, I'd spent so much time with Holmes – come to know him better than anyone else, even his own brother. Come to think of him almost *as* a brother. And I felt sorry for Mycroft, for although Holmes had confided in him when he needed to lay low, there would never be the same bond that my friend and I shared. Whether that was intentional or not, I cannot say. Holmes wasn't to know what the effects of his actions would be, the consequences inflicted upon myself and –

But it also made me sad that Holmes had changed so much in the time since his return; that he was shutting me out now as well. That he had his own private little world I was no part of, his own demons to battle.

"And you, Sherlock," said Mycroft, turning to face his younger sibling. "You are looking thin and drawn. Is there something I should be concerned about?"

"Nothing that warrants serious consideration," replied Holmes rather too quickly. "You, brother of mine, on the other hand, appear quite the opposite – you've put on several pounds since I last saw you. A consequence, no doubt, of too many potted shrimp consumed here at the Diogenes. When you are worried, you eat more – I take it our summons here today and your expanding waistline are related?"

Mycroft remained silent for a moment or two before nodding. "As grave as the situation was when I called upon you over the missing plans last November, circumstances have arisen that might even put that debacle in the shade."

"Good Lord – what could possibly be worse than the start of a war?" I asked.

"The complete disintegration of the infrastructure of the British Government," Mycroft announced without missing a beat.

While I took that statement in, Holmes said, "Explain."

Mycroft laced his hands together over his considerable girth. "Have you heard of a fellow by the name of James Philip Monroe?"

"*I* have," I stated. "Owner of a gentleman's club called the Vulcania, I believe."

"After the Roman God of Fire and Forge," added Holmes.

"Not the sort of place you'd expect to see members of the Diogenes," I remarked.

"You would be surprised," replied Mycroft. "And one of the youngest owners of such a club in England's history. I knew his parents much better, before they passed away. His father came into money abroad and made a bit of a name for himself, although, it is said, not altogether legally. It is also rumoured that Mr Monroe, Jr did not want to wait for nature to take its course as regards to his inheritance." He let that settle before continuing. "The Vulcania – above which Mr Monroe has lodgings – caters to all kinds of needs, from gambling to more... uncouth practices. Certainly some pleasures of the flesh, so I hear. But discreetly."

"Hardly that, Mycroft. Parties at the Vulcania are legendary," I assured him. "They almost rival those of the Hellfire Club!"

"Legends are myths, Doctor. And myths are very hard to prove – especially when you have certain members of the police force on your payroll. One Inspector Thorndyke, for example; who, it is said, clears up a lot of the messes that inevitably ensue after said parties.

"Mr Monroe has the ear of some very important people, something that has consequently led to my keeping an eye on the lad for some time. He is a collector, you see."

"Of antiquities?" I asked, settling myself down into one of the other leather chairs in the Stranger's Room.

"Of a sort, ones that come with quite an expensive price tag. But he is also a collector of people, and of secrets. It is how he is able to further fund his expensive lifestyle. His secrets, gained when guests are at their most vulnerable, ensure that he has their full co-operation – and access to their wealth."

We had come across another scoundrel like this already only four years previously: Charles Augustus Milverton, who demanded as much as seven thousand pounds for letters the owners of which would not want exposed. He came to a very sticky end when one of his former victims shot him; hoist by his own petard.

Holmes could see what I was thinking, the obvious comparison, and said, "These... guests knew full well what they were entering into. They weren't the dalliances of youth come back to haunt them. Moreover, I suspect they even paid a hefty sum to place themselves *in* such positions."

"True," said Mycroft. "Quite true."

"So, I fail to see that it is any concern of ours!" Holmes concluded.

"It is now that James Philip Monroe has gone missing," Mycroft countered, then pursed his lips.

"Missing?" repeated Holmes. He looked back at me, then found a seat himself. "*Missing*, you say?"

"I do indeed. No-one has seen him in close to three days."

Perhaps someone had done the same to him that the woman with the famous husband did to Milverton, I thought to myself. And good riddance, too!

"The man rarely leaves his chambers, nor sets foot outside of his club," Mycroft continued. "Yet there doesn't appear to be a sign of him anywhere. The last anyone saw of him, he was heading back to his bedroom late at night with a lady, which is not at all unusual for him; and they are nearly always ladies from an unsavoury background, with no family or friends to speak of. But nobody saw her leave, and neither of them were present when his servants brought breakfast the next morning."

"I presume this is not something that was reported to the authorities," Holmes said.

"Hardly – although I think you'll find Inspector Thorndyke *has* looked into it, privately, probably more to make sure his own nose is clean than anything else. You see, Monroe disappeared without letting anyone know where he keeps his stockpile of secrets. He definitely would not have entrusted them to a bank – you, of all people, should recognise how unreliable they are, Sherlock. Look what almost happened regarding that business with the Red-Headed League!

"Monroe never struck me as the trusting sort anyway," Mycroft went on. "Which leads me to conclude that what we're looking for is still somewhere in his chambers. And if ever they were to get into the wrong hands, Sherlock..." Mycroft visibly shuddered.

"So you want us to find his hiding place, rather than the man himself – and the unfortunate woman he was with?" I asked.

"If one is a consequence of the other, then all the better. I'm sure it is not something that Thorndyke will be looking into all that closely. Ah, but from what I hear you've become a bit of a missing persons' agency of late, isn't that correct?"

Holmes said nothing in reply.

"You know exactly what's at stake here, Sherlock," said Mycroft, using a kind of blackmail of his own. "Besides, I thought it would be a... diversion you'd find interesting."

"Wait a moment, just how exactly are we expected to search his chambers?" I asked. "Climb inside like common burglars?"

"Not at all. The club and its activities have continued unabated, hosted by Monroe's right-hand man – a former barman by the name of Richard. They are trying to maintain the illusion that Monroe is in charge; he has been absent for days at a time before, recovering from particularly lengthy entertainments. There is a private party tonight, in fact, and you two gentlemen are on the guest list – under assumed names, naturally. Your credentials have been vouched for, all you need to do is show up."

I swallowed dryly, not relishing the prospect at all. "What if we are recognised?"

"Recognised?" Mycroft began to laugh out loud. "Recognised?" His chuckles were so loud I feared he might disturb the rest of the members of the Diogenes below us. "Oh, Doctor, I never realised what a wit you have."

"I'm quite serious," I said sternly. After all, I had a reputation to maintain, not only as an agent of the law, but also a practising physician. I didn't care who might be venturing to the Vulcania, nor for what reason; I did not want to be seen to be there myself.

"My good fellow, I do believe you are. Why, are you not lodging with one of the great masters of disguise of our generation? If my brother can conceal his true identity well enough to fool the Napoleon of Crime and his cohorts, then I'm sure you pose no challenge whatsoever to him."

And so, the meeting was over. It only remained for us to return to Baker Street and prepare for the evening's adventures. But no matter what form they took, they would not prove to be any preparation for what lay ahead.

No preparation at all.

CHAPTER SIX
Pleasure and Pain

My inaugural experiences at the Vulcania Club were bad enough at the time, however.

I saw things there that I would not wish to repeat in good company, although as no-one will ever see this journal I will share them here. If nothing else it will serve as some form of catharsis, like the rest of this account.

By the time Holmes was finished with us both, and I looked in the mirror, I no longer recognised myself, let alone him. Mycroft had been right, of course, and we could have strolled past a parade of people we had helped incarcerate over the years and not a one would have been able to pick us out. Holmes' skills in this department – as with many of his talents – were exemplary.

My friend had donned a false nose and padded out his mouth with wadding. A bit of rouge on his cheeks, a monocle, a wildly different hairstyle and the result was incredible. Turning his attentions to me, he extended my moustache to a trimmed fake beard and added bushy eyebrows with actor's glue. A false set of yellowing, crooked teeth were the only things necessary to complete the illusion. It even changed the way I spoke!

"There," he said, once we were done. "Not even Mrs Hudson will recognise us!" As if on cue, the woman knocked and entered the study without waiting for a 'come.' She set down the pot of tea she'd made for us and said hello to both myself and Holmes in turn.

"I'll leave you boys to it," she said as she retreated.

Now, for one thing she knew we were both in residence upstairs – she had taken our coats and hats after visiting Mycroft – and for another she was well used to seeing Holmes dressed up in a variety of disguises after all this time; but all the same...

"Well, perhaps not Mrs Hudson," Holmes admitted, and I thought he was going to laugh then, but he caught himself and turned more serious again – as he was wont to do these days. "I think perhaps we should be on our way, don't you?"

"Holmes, I –"

But he was already heading for the door, leaving me behind.

As I followed and went down the stairs, feeling sorry for Mrs Hudson as she looked from us to the study above where her tea had been left, ignored, I wanted to say more to my friend – but, as always, the timing just wasn't right.

What Mycroft had hinted at back at the Diogenes was still on my mind. What he'd said about friends and family. The more I thought about it, the more I wanted to do something to help Holmes – to steer him away somehow from this dangerous road he was heading down: this terrible testing of himself. I simply could not fathom the reasoning behind it all.

But my mind was soon occupied by other things, feeling the trepidation at visiting this place which was – by all accounts – one step off Sodom and Gomorrah. "What do you think we can expect to see in there?" I asked Holmes in the brougham that was speeding us partway to our destination.

"You're a man of the world, Watson," was all he would offer in reply.

"I'm not a man of *that* kind of world," was my response. I

asked him again what I should expect and Holmes, as enigmatic as usual, came back with:

"The unexpected, Watson. Nothing more than the unexpected."

It should have been a mantra for this whole episode, for nobody could have expected – or even suspected – what was ahead of us.

After switching cabs to mask our intentions, we were greeted upon our arrival at the Vulcania Club – which was situated off the main road, in a secluded square of buildings in St. Marylebone – by two large men, who barely fit into their suits (in fact, they would have given Cecil Barbery a run for his money). One had a ragged scar down his face, across a completely white eye, and the other had horribly burned skin at his collar. I wouldn't have fancied tackling either of them, even if I'd been armed – and it was a good job I wasn't: as Holmes had anticipated, we were searched before being allowed entrance. A necessary precaution in a place where things could go horribly wrong within the space of a few moments.

Our new monikers were Cook and Gibb, for myself and Holmes respectively; simple and easy to remember. And, once it had been established we were not carrying weapons – Holmes was allowed to keep his cane, however, thanks to the show he made of relying upon it to walk – we were escorted through into the lobby of the large house, filled with paintings depicting classical scenarios. Most seemingly involved women in loose-fitting togas, but there were also pillars and statues, including a replica of Michelangelo's David and a less famous one of Tacita, Roman Goddess of Silence (Holmes later informed me), which was rather appropriate. Paintings lined both sides of a horseshoe-shaped staircase, which itself was covered with red carpeting. I peered into the smoky room on our right, to see people drinking and gambling at tables: cards, roulette... games I was familiar with from a time when I displayed less restraint than I did at that point. The more 'respectable' side of the club, I warranted.

It wasn't long before we were shown the other side. A man wearing a tuxedo introduced himself to us as the 'Host' – keeping his actual name out of the proceedings, though this had to be the fellow Mycroft had referred to as 'Richard' – and led us through the rooms at the back of the house, some filled with people, others with just a handful inside.

Now, as Holmes said to me earlier, I am a man of the world. I've travelled, seen lots of strange – and, yes, even depraved – things in my time, but what was going on in those back portions of the Vulcania was enough to make the most experienced abbess at a brothel blush. Men – some, those not wearing masks or hoods, I fancied I recognised from the higher echelons of society, even a Judge – were doing the most outrageous things to the prostitutes provided, of both sexes. Either that, or having things done *to them*.

One fellow I saw was chained up against a wall, being struck with a stick – the only thing protecting his modesty a small undergarment made from leather. Someone else was riding a virtually naked woman like a horse, holding on to her hair like a rein and whipping her violently as she spurred him on. In yet another instance, I saw a woman wearing only her corsetry, barking orders to a man lying on the ground – someone who quite obviously craved to be dominated. All this, while other acts of a more intimate nature were taking place that I won't go into; suffice to say some of it still haunts my nightmares to this day.

Our host was holding out his hand. "Gentlemen, feel free to... express yourselves in any way you see fit. Everything that happens at the Vulcania remains strictly confidential."

It was the only way these people would participate in the first place, and with other like-minded individuals around them. No doubt that simply served to excite them more, the atmosphere tinged with lust and desire. But it was only confidential as long as you did as the master of this place said, holding such things over their heads – perhaps even taking photographs with hidden cameras, I thought to myself. It was the kind of material we had been discharged to find, I reminded myself, and I looked across at Holmes pleadingly. Hoping against hope that we would not have to carry this charade on any further.

"Thank you," my friend said to Richard. "I think we are happy enough observing for the time being, though, before we..."

The host smirked. "Of course, of course. First time is always a little awkward. But once you throw yourselves into it, I'm sure you'll experience pleasures the like of which you've never encountered before."

There was a loud crack of a whip at that moment, and my attention was drawn to a man bent over a table, being lashed severely. And pain as well, I thought, wincing – though they were seemingly one and the same here.

We spent altogether too much time in those back rooms for my liking – witnessing far too much. What Mary, God rest her soul, would have said to it all – to me – I had no idea. She would probably have just hung her head in shame. Again, I had to remind myself it was for the greater good; for the country. Though if it was being run by 'gentlemen' such as this, then I feared for the future of our Great Empire.

We were approached a few times while we were there. On one occasion a young woman, dressed only in a robe open at the front, with gawdy make-up covering her face which I thought gave her the appearance of a clown, brushed up against me – her leg raised high and her arm across my shoulders. "Want me to show you a good time, sir?" she asked.

I smiled as best I could and replied. "P-perhaps later, my good woman." It was the only thing I could think of, but seemed to work and she smiled back, disentangling herself from me with a sigh. I tried not to show my relief.

Once Holmes was sure we were no longer under Richard's scrutiny, free to pick our way through the carpet of undulating flesh in room after room – each painted a different colour, which reminded me a little of those parties described by Poe in 'The Masque of the Red Death' (and look where that got them) – he tapped me on the shoulder.

"Mr Cook," he said. "Shall we?"

"Not before time, Mr Gibb," I replied. "I doubt anyone here will miss us."

We slipped out silently, heading back in the direction of the staircase – which would take us up to Monroe's chambers on the second floor. Holmes reached across at one point, pushing me back against the wall when he heard someone walking through the lobby area, but they did not spot us. In fact, it was relatively easy to sneak around and up the stairs, as most of the staff and guests alike were occupied with their own tasks or amusements.

Upon reaching the uppermost floor, my friend glanced left and right, making sure the coast was clear, and we made our way along the landing. "How will we know which door leads to Monroe's room?" I whispered to Holmes.

But he was already answering my question, heading towards an ornate set of double doors; an entryway fit for a king... well, the king of this particular castle at any rate.

They were also locked.

"What now?" I asked. "I can't think you've brought your lock-picking equipment, Holmes, else you'd have lost it when we were searched."

He grinned, then, dropping the monocle from his eye socket and tracing the chain back to the pocket of his waistcoat. He pulled on it, so that the end came free – and attached to it was a small length of metal. Holmes used his fingernail to flip open the sides of this, so that by the time he was finished it resembled a key.

"A skeleton key," Holmes elucidated. Looking left and right

one last time, he slotted it in the lock. At first I thought it would not work, but there was finally a click and we were in.

Holmes slid sideways through the crack he'd made in the door, then closed it after me. I took in the chambers, my mouth falling open. The walls up here were also covered with paintings, but they were more overtly erotic in nature than those in the lobby or along the stairs. There were antique Japanese silk paintings of various couples, and while I could appreciate the quality of the artwork itself, not to mention its historical value, I was taken aback by some of the acts they depicted: more explicit and intrusive than those happening beneath our feet downstairs, if you can believe that.

There were scenes from that well-known Indian handbook on the subject, the *Kama Sutra* – depicting all manner of positions – sited along the far wall running towards the back. And while I recognised the style of Caravaggio – one could not be a friend of Holmes' and not have a grounding in all the arts – these were paintings I did not recognise of his, perhaps even some that had been kept hidden? They certainly made works like his *Amor Vincit Omnia* look modest by comparison. Holmes pointed to a far corner of the room.

"It looks to be an exact recreation of Catherine the Great's 'erotic cabinet,'" he informed me, "from her palace at Gatchina." As I looked, I saw furniture – tables and chairs – that had men and women's private parts carved into them.

Here and there, though, were more primal works, including phallic African fetishes – although what fascinated me the most were the ones of figures with what looked to be nails banged into them. One was covered in the things, from head to foot – including, or perhaps that should be *especially*, at the groin. There were also representations of ancient gods... These competed for space with graphic engravings from Egypt, some of a more bestial nature, as well as those from ancient Greece and Rome: in one, some sort of horned half-man, half-animal creature (perhaps another god or even a demon?) was forcing itself upon a naked young maiden, her mouth a rictus of terror.

Worryingly, that wasn't the only reference to the Satanic – as Monroe's chambers were also littered with images from Bosch (including his 'musical hell'), Goya (where giants ate human limbs and witches held their Sabbats), and the more recent William Blake (there was a huge depiction of the Great Red Dragon – its wings unfurled, tail curling around beneath its bulk – hanging over Monroe's gigantic bed).

His reading matter also reflected this interest, from copies of Bolingbroke and Gilles de Rais' diaries, to the German book the *Malleus Maleficarum*. There was simply too much to take in at a cursory glance.

I think Holmes could see the state of shock I was in, and placed a comforting hand on my arm; it was like having the old Sherlock back for a moment. "Hold steady, Watson. We may yet see much more disturbing things before the night is over... and we have work to do."

Of course – the records we'd come here to secure. If we managed to obtain those, and avert catastrophe, I would at least feel a little better about what we'd gone through that evening. But Holmes, as he inevitably – and sometimes frustratingly – tended to be, was right. There were still more horrors to face.

I began searching the place, but there appeared to be no obvious safes behind paintings, no hidden panels. It was Holmes, again, who struck upon the solution, using his famous methods of deduction: "Where else would a man so obsessed with hedonism hide something, but his very bed!"

There was nothing beneath the piece of furniture, nor in the mattress or pillows, save for the feathers they'd been stuffed with. We got more than we bargained for, however, when Holmes triggered a mechanism by twisting one of the knobs at the foot of Monroe's bed counter-clockwise. The wardrobe to our right, which we had also searched, finding nothing but clothing – both conventional and specialist – rumbled forward and sideways on a concealed track. The hole it left revealed what we had been looking for back at the Cottons' attic room and were denied: a secret chamber *within* Monroe's chambers.

Or a passageway, at least.

"Come, Watson," said Holmes beckoning me, lighting the gas-lamps along the stone-clad walls through a narrow, snaking corridor to a small opening. In this room, somewhere within the heart of the house, were rows of drawers, seemingly set into the walls. None of them were locked, as we discovered when we tugged on their golden handles, so we began rifling through papers, photographs, receipts... soon realising that these were the very items we'd been sent here to recover. "Cram as much as you can into your pockets," said Holmes, taking off his jacket and making a sack out of it, which he filled and tied up at the sleeves.

"I think we're almost there," I said, suddenly noticing Holmes wasn't beside me anymore. He was at the wall ahead of us, touching its surface. Then he began rapping on it with his stick. The noise sounded hollow rather than solid. Could it be that –

I was no sooner thinking it than Holmes had found the trigger for yet another hidden door, which ground slowly sideways. It appeared we were only standing in an antechamber, and the real hidden room lay beyond.

There was light coming from inside, a sort of faint glow. "Stay back, Watson," said my friend, "let me go first."

I did as he wished, then waited a few moments. When there was no 'all is well' sign from Holmes, I followed him – and immediately wished that I hadn't. He was standing, staring at what was in the room, as *I* soon found myself doing. I wanted to close my eyes, shut out the sights, but it was already too late.

Huge candles on intricately carved stands provided the light, still burning brightly away – but I would have given anything at that moment for it to have been pitch black in there. Or would I? Perhaps that might have made it worse.

x

83

There was blood, a lot of it. Spilt on the floor, used to paint markings that had a ritualistic air about them – although there were footprints in it as well.

"Our friend again," Holmes said through gritted teeth, and I knew he meant the vagabond from Spencer's garden – for the prints seemed to tail off and stop. And even I could smell it this time; that strong, almost overpowering scent of vanilla blended with copper.

I also saw that on several plates on the floor were the severed heads of birds – doves, if I remember rightly – plus a jug of yellow liquid that stank like urine.

But it was the objects arranged in jars about the place that really unnerved me. Human organs in some kind of preservative: a liver here, a kidney there... and a heart, which looked to still be beating, though I put it down to a trick of the light.

"Monroe?" I asked finally, and Holmes shook his head. It was then that I realised these must be the remains of the poor girl he'd brought with him to his chambers. Used as some kind of sacrifice; an offering of sorts to someone... or some*thing*. Of Monroe himself there was no sign, as with Spencer and Cotton before him.

I hadn't seen the likes of this since we stopped a monstrously evil Lord who was bent on using his cult affiliations to take over Parliament.

My eyes were drawn to the front of the room, to a pillar that stood there. Unlike the elegant classical designs of those in the lobby, this one had an odd shape about it, due to the carvings on its trunk: bodies formed out of stone, naked, with limbs flowing into each other, ribs straining and faces framing each top corner. It was almost as if it was stone and flesh at the same time, and I fancied I saw those bodies moving, writhing, as if trapped beneath its surface. I blinked and the scene righted itself.

As natural and flowing as the pillar appeared to be, there was a small hole in the centre of the design, where it looked like something had been removed.

Holmes moved to step forward, dropping his 'sack' and stick – drifting as if pulled by invisible strings. He apparently could not help himself; when I placed a hand on his arm, to try to stop him, he shrugged it off. In moments he was there, trampling through evidence in a way that would have had him screaming with rage if anyone else had done it. He had his right hand up, fingers out and reaching towards the statue just as he had done with that false wall moments earlier. He was inches away, fingers of both hands brushing against the surface, touching the carven body parts.

"It... it feels warm," he uttered absently, his voice sounding strange, disconnected. Then his right hand moved sideways towards the cavity, fingers about to inch their way inside.

I was all set to lunge forward and yank him back, out of what I felt strongly was harm's way, when a voice shouted, "What the *Hell* is all this?"

When I turned to discover the source of the cry, I saw our host Richard in the doorway – alongside one of the men from the entrance, the fellow with the unfortunate scar across his eye. Someone had noticed our absence from the party, after all. I wasn't sure at first – for the man in the tuxedo was glancing about the place at the candles, the jar, the blood – whether he was talking about the secret room, its purpose, or the interlopers they'd caught snooping around inside it. In the end it mattered not, because they didn't pause to wait for an answer.

They simply attacked.

The reflex in Holmes that manifested itself whenever he was in danger suddenly took hold and he turned his back on the pillar – snatching up his stick in the process. The larger man was heading in my direction, but Holmes propelled himself forward and sideways, into the giant's path. "You take the barman, Watson!" he called back to me, ducking a swing from the larger man and striking him in the side with the stick.

Richard, evidently taking exception to being called a mere

'barman,' raised his fists and engaged me. Now, I'm no stranger to the fine art of boxing, but the man clearly had no regard for the Marquess of Queensberry rules. A swift kick to my shin taught me the measure of him, but I retaliated by dealing him a jab to the face with my left fist, following it swiftly with an uppercut from my right that sent him reeling into one of the organ jars.

I risked a look to see how Holmes was getting on, only to witness him holding up his cane like a staff, the scarred man bringing down his heavy hand to break the thing in half. Not missing a trick, Holmes smashed his two splintered sticks against both sides of the fellow's head simultaneously. The giant staggered backwards, clutching his ears.

Distracted, I barely avoided a left cross from our host, managing to pull back just at the last moment. Off balance, he plunged forward – helped on his way by a push from myself – and smacked into the floor, sliding across the slick blood and sending more of the jars flying. If the crime scene had been contaminated before, it was well on its way to becoming useless now.

Holmes, for his part, was busy dodging a lumbering lunge – sidestepping the brute and striking him across the back with both parts of the broken stick he was still holding. The scarred man pulled over a candle, then fell sideways into the pillar at the head of the room.

The column dropped heavily, cracking across the middle.

A lot of what happened next is a bit of a blur, I'm afraid. It seemed to me that the pillar virtually exploded, bits of stone flying everywhere at once. But at the same time one of the candles connected with the preservative fluid seeping out of the organ jars, catching light with a mighty *whoosh*. I cannot say for certain, especially knowing what I know now, whether the sudden light that filled the place came from the fire or the pillar's demise – or perhaps it was a combination of both? Either way, the sacrifice room was alight in seconds, engulfing the scarred man first, lapping over him like waves against the shore as he screamed and screamed. I remember thinking, even if he did survive, he would look even worse than his burned partner from the doorstep. Nevertheless, Holmes – having discarded his makeshift weapons – attempted to help him, only to be driven back by the flames.

So, instead, he motioned for me to grab one of the unconscious Richard's arms, taking the other himself. I was about to ask about the 'sack' Holmes had also dropped, then noted the flames had taken that as well. It was time to get out of there, and between us we did our best to wrestle our charge through the anteroom full of drawers and up along the corridors, towards the exit – all the while looking back to gauge the progress of the fire, which was rapidly gaining on us.

After what felt like an eternity, we finally broke free of the corridor and virtually fell out into Monroe's chambers. "Watson, we can't afford to falter now," Holmes shouted, nodding back down the shaft at the approaching blaze, which was stalking us as a hound chases the fox.

We again took up the barman's weight, pulling him past Monroe's collection towards the door we'd unlocked not half an hour ago. Out onto the landing, where we saw smoke and flames affecting other areas of the house; it hadn't gone unnoticed below either.

"*Fire!*" barked my friend and we did our best to carry our unconscious load down the right-hand side of those curving stairs. "Everyone out!"

But he needn't have bothered. People were fleeing of their own accord, panicking and clambering for the exit: first those who'd been in the gambling section; then the half-naked pleasure-seekers who hadn't bargained on their entertainment being curtailed in such a way. Those who couldn't wait to see a break in the crowds were even smashing windows and jumping through them.

Holmes and I kept our heads down and practically had to ram our way out, the host in tow. Once we got into the open air, we saw people scattering – many of them not wishing to be found on the premises in their current state. I couldn't say I blamed them, after what they'd been up to. But at the very least it seemed like most of the inhabitants of the Vulcania managed to get out before the conflagration spread.

A fire that only took the club building, and left its neighbours be.

A fire that, looking back, was akin to those from the very pits of Hell itself.

CHAPTER SEVEN
Order and Law

WE MADE IT back to our lodgings in Baker Street in the wee small hours of the morning. After waiting for the fire brigade to arrive and ascertaining as best we could that nobody was still inside the burning wreck of the house, we were on our way before any untoward questions could be asked.

The intense heat that had ravaged the club house burned itself out almost as quickly as it began, leaving our brave men from the brigade with little to do in the end. And leaving nothing by way of evidence.

We removed our disguises en route, so that no-one would ever know it was us who'd been at the Vulcania, and after walking much of the way on foot we finally hailed a cab to ferry us the rest of the way home. A quick clean up, and I told Holmes that I was heading to bed, for the excitements of the evening had exhausted me.

I rose late, oversleeping, having had terrible nightmares again – not of the fire, but of my time in Afghanistan, of Mary – and when I queried Mrs Hudson about the lateness of the hour she said, "Mr Holmes left specific instructions that I should let you rest."

"Left instructions? So Holmes is out, then?"

She nodded. "Said he had some errands to run, and then he was off to see that brother of his."

No doubt reporting on the events of the previous evening. I discovered much later from Holmes that the conversation had essentially consisted of Mycroft saying, "When I asked for your help, Sherlock, I did not imagine your solution to our little problem would be so... extreme. Nevertheless, can I assume that our house is now in order?"

It wasn't clear to me whether by 'house' Mycroft meant the Vulcania building itself or Great Britain, but either way Holmes assured him that all was indeed in order. Only one body had been found in the burnt-out ruins, which we both took to be the scarred doorman – but which the police and rumour-mongers alike were assuming was James Philip Monroe. Two men – one chubby-cheeked and wearing a monocle, the other bearded with protruding teeth, according to the acting manager of the club, who was now recovering in hospital – were being sought in connection with the fire, which was believed to be arson.

As far as I was concerned, however, matters were anything *but* in order. For one thing, when I entered the study, I found our table had been covered in my haul from the previous evening; that Holmes had fished it all out of my pockets and begun sifting through it (no doubt to satisfy his own curiosity that we had done the right thing in going to the club and inadvertently causing the fire). I had a cursory rummage through it myself, not really wanting to know more than I did already about the situation. Nevertheless, my eye was drawn to a handful of receipts I had gathered up in my haste. They apparently had nothing whatsoever to do with what had been going on at the Vulcania, but pertained to purchases Monroe had made for his collection. Sundry items, mostly, but one which was certainly of interest: a receipt for an ornate decorative pillar.

I held it up and read the name of the shop out loud to myself.

It was called simply, 'The Gallery.'

"Now then, Dr Watson," said Mrs Hudson, who had appeared behind me while I was distracted by my thoughts. "Let's clear some of this away, shall we, and get you fed." She was carrying a tray of kippers and a fresh pot of tea, nodding at the papers on the table; I had to admit my hunger got the better of me, for it had been a long night and I hadn't eaten since before we set out to see Mycroft. I doubted Holmes had, either, but that was out of our hands.

I shoved the receipts into the pocket of my dressing gown and transferred handfuls of documents to the couch, careful not to let Mrs Hudson see any of the photographs, then sat down eagerly to her delicious meal.

In fact, I wouldn't see Holmes again for a day or so – when he glossed over his other so-called 'errands' – by which time the fire was all over London's papers.

But so was something else.

"What did Mycroft say the name of that corrupt inspector was?" I asked Holmes, as he was flitting about looking for his Ship's tobacco to fill his pipe.

"Hmm?" he asked, not really paying any attention at all.

"Mycroft. The other day..."

"Oh, look at all this!" said Holmes suddenly, seeing the papers that I'd moved onto the couch. "It really must be disposed of, Watson!"

"I wasn't the one who left it lying about," I retorted, as he began ripping up the items and putting them on the fire.

"There!" he said when he was finished. "Consigned to the flames, just like its brethren. My brother will be able to sleep soundly. Now, what were you saying, Watson?" Holmes spied the tobacco finally, for once not in the toe-end of his Persian slipper, and proceeded to tip some into the end of his pipe.

I walked over, showing him the page of the newspaper I was holding. "It's right here, look – a piece by Summersby & Kline."

"The mark of quality," said Holmes, and if he'd been referring to any other members of Fleet Street's fraternity you would have heard the sarcasm in his tone. But the duo were fast becoming a name to be reckoned with in the field of investigative reporting. He peered at the piece I was pointing out, almost overshadowed by the Vulcania blaze.

"It *was* Inspector Thorndyke, wasn't it?" I asked. "The man in Monroe's pocket?" Holmes said nothing, but read the article:

> *Fears are growing for the officer, a family man with a wife and daughter, as his whereabouts still remain unknown. At the time of his disappearance, he was involved in several cases, one of which revolved around the hunt for a missing child – thought to have been abducted. Scotland Yard have yet to make an official statement, but it is believed they will be doing so in due course.*

"It surely can't be a coincidence," I said to Holmes. "Yet another person who has vanished from the face of the Earth – and a policeman this time, no less!"

Holmes put his pipe down on the mantelpiece without even lighting it. "It definitely warrants further attention," he told me. "Watson, let us pay our good friend Inspector Lestrade a visit."

WHEN HOLMES SAID 'our good friend' he was being generous indeed. Lestrade was an acquaintance, at best, and remained so up until his death a few years ago at the coast where he was living out his retirement years. Indeed, now I think of it, I never even learned his first name, just the initial 'G.'

I have described Lestrade before as being sallow, rat-faced and dark-eyed; unkind though this may have been, I nevertheless stand by my sketch of the man. For those characteristics also reflected his nature, devious and arrogant even though he remained on the right side of the law at all times. He thought nothing about taking credit for the crimes Holmes solved – in fact, I often thought that he somehow managed to convince himself he *had* cracked the cases, in spite of Holmes' 'interference.' But had it not been for my friend, I doubt Lestrade would have retired with as many honours as he did.

Of all the officers we encountered and dealt with on our cases, from Inspector Bradstreet – that tall, stout official – to Baynes of the Surrey police force, who Holmes congratulated on his methods, I believe my friend 'liked' (if I can use such a word), or perhaps favoured Inspector Gregson the most. Perhaps that goes back to him being the inspector assigned to our very first case together, but I believe it was more than that. Nevertheless, Lestrade was the inspector best-known for having worked alongside us – and *definitely* the man we worked with most often, for better or for worse.

As I took a seat in the waiting area of Scotland Yard – or the relatively new building with that name, on the Embankment – and as Holmes joined me after telling the desk sergeant who we were here to see, I began to ponder the events that had led us here, and how they were apparently linked.

There were the disappearances, all – from Cotton to Monroe – marked by that odd smell of vanilla at the scene. And the man Mrs Spencer had called a vagabond, with those hypnotic eyes. We'd even tracked his footprints into Monroe's secret lair, where they seemingly began as abruptly as they ended; though admittedly we hadn't had the time to examine the area properly. There, if Holmes' theory was to be believed, to retrieve something every time – the murder weapon, except it hadn't actually been used to kill, according to Holmes. And what had been inside that crevice in the pillar? None of it made any sense. But now here we were chasing up a lead on a policeman whom Monroe was paying to look after his interests.

It was at that particular moment Lestrade chose to break into my thoughts. "Ah, Mr Holmes, Dr Watson." My friend rose and grudgingly shook the Inspector's outstretched hand, as did I. "I was wondering when you might put in an appearance."

"You were?" I asked.

"Oh, yes," said the man, with a considerable degree of certainty. He sniffed then, and apologised, telling us he was starting to come down with a cold. "Spring must be just around the corner, eh?"

I smiled through gritted teeth, looking down at the hand I'd used to shake his. Holmes paid it no heed, but then he had been exposing himself to much worse of late.

When I continued to look puzzled, the Inspector said, "The fire. I assume you're here about that? I have to concede, I considered darkening your doorway yesterday but, well, you know how busy things get. I knew you wouldn't be able to stay away from this one, at any rate. Now, the two fellows we're looking for go by the names of Cook and Gibb and –"

Holmes held up a hand to stop him. "Inspector, Inspector. We're here to offer our services with regards to a very different matter altogether."

"Oh?"

"Yes. The fire wasn't arson, Lestrade – it was caused by someone knocking over a lit flame."

I looked at Holmes, thinking he'd gone mad and was about to confess. Was he trying to get us both thrown in jail? Meanwhile, Lestrade's eyes were narrowing. "And how exactly would you know that, Mr Holmes?"

"Elementary, Inspector," said my friend. "For the fire to have spread so quickly, it must have bloomed outwards from the centre – from where the reports say you found the remains of Monroe's body, am I correct?"

Lestrade gazed at me then, sucking in a breath through his teeth – which made him cough – before saying, "In a terrible state he was as well, Doctor. Not even you could have done anything with him."

"But did your investigators find any candle holders at all?"

"Well... I'll have to check, but yes, I believe they might have come across something like that. It still doesn't prove –"

"Mr Monroe, known hellraiser that he was – perhaps entertaining someone of the opposite sex? A little alcohol involved as an accelerant... His employee covering for him by making up a pair of fictitious culprits. I'm surprised you didn't think of it yourself."

Lestrade coughed again; actually it was more like a hack this time. "Yes, well, I'll have someone look into all that. Give it some consideration."

"I'd be happy to talk to your... witness myself, get to the bottom of it," said Holmes, the corners of his mouth rising, "if you so wish?"

It was Lestrade's turn to hold up his hand now. "No, no. That won't be necessary, Mr Holmes. I know my job." I almost broke into a grin myself at that; the clever way my friend had covered up *our* part in it all. "Now, you mentioned something about another case you might be able to assist us with..." Lestrade always put it like that, as if Holmes was merely a concerned citizen who could help with a little information – rather than the key person who would, more often than not, tie up the entire investigation with a bow.

"Indeed. We have just read about Inspector Thorndyke in the paper, and –"

The hand was up again. "Let me stop you right there, Mr Holmes. What the papers are reporting is nothing more than hearsay; rumour. There is nothing to substantiate it at all."

"But Inspector Thorndyke is missing, is he not?" I pressed.

"Well... yes, technically, I suppose you could call him 'missing.' But then that is nothing unusual in itself. He tends to be a bit of a law unto himself, that one, if I'm honest with you." I thought again about Holmes' mysterious wanderings, his tendency to be gone for days on end. "Into some funny business, if you ask me."

"I don't believe we've ever come into contact with Inspector Thorndyke," Holmes mused.

"I'm not at all surprised. He doesn't tend to be offered the high-profile cases. Those are more my territory, as you know." Lestrade's capacity for blowing his own trumpet never did cease to amaze me.

"What of this missing child that he was looking for? Might there be a connection there to his... absence?" I asked.

Lestrade coughed again, took out a handkerchief and sneezed into it. "Oh, I really must apologise, gentlemen. No, I shouldn't think there would be any correlation at all. From what I gather, the child was an orphan – he probably wandered off somewhere and got lost."

"Wandered off and –" This was a child, we were talking about; a *missing* child – and Lestrade was talking about him as though he was a pet that had run off and left its owner.

"Would you have any objection to our looking into the issue?" Holmes got in before I could say anything more.

Lestrade stared at him blankly. "It's your own affair if you want to waste your time. But I wouldn't be at all surprised if Thorndyke wasn't to walk through that door at any moment, whistling and acting as if nothing had happened."

Holmes nodded slowly and touched the rim of his hat. "You've been most obliging, as always, Inspector. I won't hold you up any longer. I know how busy you are."

"Oh, yes, indeed. But never too busy for my old friends Sherlock Holmes and Dr Watson." He smiled, genuinely believing in that friendship, I think – and I felt quite sorry for the man, even though I knew relatively little about his private life. But then his capacity for self-delusion was incredible and I suppose that's what buoyed him up.

We left the inspector coughing and spluttering, and exited the premises. "Most enlightening," said Holmes as we stepped out onto the street.

"It was?"

"Definitely," stated Holmes. "Come along, Watson – I think our next port of call has to be the man's family, don't you? They must be worried sick about him!"

"But Holmes, how do you know where he – where they live?"

"That I gleaned from Sergeant Clark back there before Lestrade was even informed we had arrived," he told me matter-of-factly. "I once got his brother-in-law out of a fix. I knew that we would need it, once we had spoken with Lestrade, so I took the liberty of dispatching two birds with the one stone."

And I thought then that the Inspector was wrong about Holmes.

He never, ever wasted his time.

HOLMES WAS ALSO – more often than not – right.

Thorndyke's spouse was very worried about her husband, and incredibly happy to see us.

"Of course I know who you are, gentlemen!" she said as she bid us welcome into her home, and her sitting room. "There is not a policeman's wife who doesn't, I should think. The famous Sherlock Holmes and his colleague Dr Watson. I thought it may be the press again, for I contacted them when my concerns grew... Please gentlemen, please tell me you come with news of my Joss."

Mrs Thorndyke was a pretty young woman with blonde, wavy hair, and she lived in a modest house – a little too modest for an inspector, which made me wonder where all the money had gone that Monroe had been supplying.

"We're... certainly here to help," I told her, trying to calm her nerves.

Holmes had wandered over to a nearby table, crowned with a chess set. "Your husband plays?"

"Oh, yes. He loves games; puzzles of all kinds," the woman informed us.

"I see," said Holmes, finally taking a seat beside me and opposite her. "And when was the last time you saw or heard from him?"

"It has been a good few days," she said. "I have known Joss to be away for a night or so before, working." Mrs Thorndyke looked down and then up again, tears in her eyes. "But never this long. Something is wrong; very wrong. I just know it."

"This 'work,' as you call it – you know of its true nature?"

She sighed. "I do. I also know of his habits, what goes on at that club he visits from time to time. I'm glad it burnt down!" Mrs Thorndyke put a hand to her mouth. "Oh, no, you don't think Joss was in there when –"

"He was not. Of that you can be certain," Holmes assured her, but she didn't press him as to how he knew. Instead, my friend asked how she knew about his other 'activities.'

"Joss talks in his sleep, Mr Holmes." The tears were breaking free now, rolling down her cheeks and I offered her my handkerchief, for which she thanked me. "I know there have been others, and I know that sometimes he partook of substances stronger than a whisky or two. But he's my husband, and I love him. I always have."

"Of that I am certain," said I.

"He didn't used to be this way, Doctor. He... changed over the years. Perhaps it was the pressures of his job?" She shook her head, as though not really believing it herself. "People do change, as time goes on."

"They can," I replied, looking sideways at Holmes. I took in Mrs Thorndyke once more, thinking what a strong woman she was for putting up with so much. She and Laurence Cotton should have been a pair – they would have been a match made in Heaven, in fact – instead of which they were both partnered with the cruellest of people.

It was at that point I heard someone bounding down the narrow stairs outside the room, and a little girl – no more than seven or eight years of age – came rushing into the room. "I heard the door!" she yelled. "Is Daddy back?" She looked excitedly around and when she saw only us, her face fell.

Mrs Thorndyke wiped away her remaining tears, not letting the girl see how upset she was, and rose to meet her. "No, sweetheart. Not yet. These gentlemen are friends of his." We both stood as well and I waved in greeting.

"But I thought..." The sentence tailed off. She was so adorable, the absolute image of her mother, with the same golden hair. It made me wish again that Mary and I had been able to have children. Then again, perhaps in my line of work that was a blessing.

"I'm sorry, Claire darling." She hugged the girl to her, stroking that hair. "He'll be back, soon. I promise." It was not an assurance I would have given to the child, personally. "Now why don't you run along back upstairs and finish your jigsaw before bedtime? Then I'll come and read you more of Alice's adventures."

Reluctantly, the little girl turned and made her way back towards the door. But not before stopping, casting a glance over her shoulder, and returning my original wave. I couldn't help smiling and gave her another one in return. Once again, I felt a pang. I would love to have read the Alice books to my own daughter – or son, even – for I had loved them so myself growing up (I read the first, devouring Carroll's every line and word, when I was just twelve years of age).

"She's very sweet," I told her mother, who nodded.

"Joss dotes on her, calls her his Little Princess. He rarely misses saying goodnight to her himself, which leads me to conclude something terrible has happened. He does love her so, would do anything for her."

"His affection for little ones extends to the case he was working, I'm led to believe," mused Holmes, who had remained markedly silent all the while Claire had been in the room.

"The little boy?" said Mrs Thorndyke. "Yes, he spoke about that. Awful business. I know the conditions at the establishment he disappeared from were not wonderful, but even so... You think the two are related, Joss going missing and the child?"

"That is yet to be established," Holmes informed her. "Before we go on our way again, is there anything else you think might be relevant? Anything that could help us trace your husband?"

The woman thought hard, her brow creasing. Then something came to her and her face lit up. "Gallery," she said. "He said something about a gallery!"

"What gallery?" I asked, stepping forward.

"Oh, he did not tell me about it as such. It was another night-time conversation with himself, Doctor. But I did make that out. Is it important?"

"Quite possibly," I told her, and Holmes shot me a quizzical look.

We said our goodbyes, promising that we would be in touch with Mrs Thorndyke should there be any developments; should we find her husband.

"It does not seem likely," Holmes advised me as we travelled back to Baker Street again in the cab.

"Oh?"

"Surely you must have worked out by now that he shared the same fate as Monroe?"

"The same fate as Cotton and Spencer, too?" I reminded him. "He is dead, then?"

"I believe so, yes."

We did not talk anymore until we returned to our lodgings, but once we were upstairs and Holmes was pouring us brandies, he asked, "The gallery, what makes you think it is significant?"

"Ah, yes." I went off and retrieved the receipts from my

dressing gown. By the time I returned, he had also retrieved his abandoned pipe from the mantel and finally lit it. "I'd almost forgotten about these – but it can't be a coincidence, Holmes. It really can't."

"And they are?" he asked, puffing on the pipe. He took them from me and began perusing them.

"I'm astonished you didn't come across them yourself while you were looking through Monroe's papers on the table back there."

He looked up at me, still waiting for an answer.

"They're a lead, dear fellow. Our first real lead."

CHAPTER EIGHT
The Missing Piece

THE GALLERY WE were seeking was not far from Piccadilly, so we set off the very next morning to visit it.

Located down a sidestreet, it was tucked away – where seemingly only those who knew about it would find the place. It also looked deserted, as if it had closed down in the time since Monroe had frequented it – or perhaps he had sent Thorndyke in his stead? The front was all glass, tiny pyramids etched onto it and separating the lettering that announced what this shop was. I commented then about the Egyptian connection again; after all, Monroe had had pictures originating from that culture in his chambers. However, there had been many works of 'art,' from various cultures, in that depraved man's quarters.

When we found the door to be locked, I peered in through one of the windows, shielding my eyes so I could see.

The inside was empty, no paintings on the walls, no sculptures taking up space on the floor. "It would appear that we are too late," I said. "They've shut up shop – forever, by the looks of things."

"A pity," offered Holmes, stepping back and taking in the gallery again.

"Or not, depending on whether they've cleared *everything* out.

There are always back entrances to places such as these – and you do have your lock-picking equipment now." I looked about me to make sure we were not being observed, then made my way down the right-hand side of the shop.

The lock on the wooden back door proved no match at all for Holmes – though he appeared somewhat hesitant – and moments later we were inside. There was an entire back room that had receipts and records in it that had been left behind, although it was all in a bit of a muddle. We spent a good while going through these, looking for something, anything that might be of use. Finally, I found a record of where the pillar had originated.

"Here we are, Holmes – look. It was bought from a place in France, just outside Paris: the Malahide Institute. Originally the property of someone called... Le... it's quite hard to make out; the handwriting is atrocious. Lemarchand, it looks like."

"Curious," said my friend, taking the record from me and reading it himself.

"Do you think he might be the owner of this institute place?"

"Possibly..."

"There's a photograph of the pillar as well," I told him, examining it. I squinted, trying to make out what was in its centre: the object that had been absent when we discovered it in Monroe's secret lair. "It looks very much to me like the missing piece is some sort of box." Holmes snatched the photograph from my hands and began to peruse it himself; I scowled at his rudeness, folding my arms, but he took no notice. "It would certainly be in keeping with the dimensions of whatever it was Cotton had with him in the attic room, wouldn't you say? Though what it was doing embedded in a statue, I have no clue. Perhaps this Lemarchand fellow might be able to tell us more?"

Holmes said nothing, lost in his scrutiny of the statue – or more accurately what it had contained. The object that Monroe had obviously detached from it; the same object, Holmes seemed to believe, that was missing from the hidden room, that had been missing from the scenes of Cotton's and Lieutenant Spencer's disappearances, that had been retrieved by the vagabond.

"Holmes, are you even listening to me?"

He snapped out of his daze and looked me in the eye. "Of course, Watson. I'm always keenly aware of everything that is going on around me at any given time."

"Then what do you think is going on *here*?" I unfolded my arms, tapping the photograph. "What is that and why have so many people died because of it?"

He opened his mouth, as if about to say something of great import – then closed it again and shook his head. "You are quite correct, Watson. This Lemarchand character might well have the answers we are looking for. That is why I need you to go and see him."

"You need me to..." It was my turn to open my mouth, gaping at him in disbelief. When I'd recovered my composure, I said, "Go to France, you mean? On my own?"

Holmes nodded.

"What exactly will you be doing in the meantime?" I asked.

"Continuing with my investigations," he said directly.

"But Holmes, this is –"

"Please, Watson, do not argue." With his free hand, he rubbed his forehead, then fixed me with a stare. "I need someone I can trust to look into this. You have done so before, without question."

"Yes, and on that occasion you followed me and hid in a cave. Will I get to Paris, only to find you there, too, disguised as a Frenchman?"

"No," stated Holmes. "You will not. I shall remain here and look for the missing boy; the orphan. It is my belief that *he*, at any rate, is still alive. Who else is there to find him? Lestrade?"

I couldn't really take issue with that. I gave a nod and told Holmes that I would do as he wished.

And by the beginning of the next week, I would find myself abroad – heading to the Malahide Institute in search of answers.

CHAPTER NINE
The Institute

I TOOK THE earliest train in the morning I could find to Dover, having already booked the steam ship to Calais. The surgery was fairly quiet at that time, but I arranged for what patients I did have to see another doctor in my absence; sometimes I wonder why they stayed with me as long as they did, when I kept deserting them like this at the drop of a hat.

Mrs Hudson fussed about me while I packed, as was her wont: asking if I had this and that. When the pantomime was concluded, I went to Holmes in his study and told him I was off – for he had already notified me he would not be coming to the station himself. I suppose I was lucky he was around to even say goodbye.

He had a book in one hand, held out at a distance, and a cigarette in the other, and barely looked up when I said, "Right then – I shall see you later."

"Yes. Do let me know when you find anything out, won't you?"

"Naturally," I replied. "I will keep you informed every step of the way."

"Very well, then."

"Holmes." I walked over to where he was sitting so he

couldn't really ignore me. "Holmes, you will be all right while I'm gone, won't you?"

He did look up then. "All right? Whatever do you mean, Watson? Of course I shall be all right."

"Only..." Now that I had started, I found I did not really know what to say. How does one approach a topic as sensitive as this? The changes in personality; the abuse he was putting his body through; his dalliances with death. In the end I said, "Just be careful, won't you?"

He nodded. "You too, old friend." I was almost at the door again when he added, "I do appreciate what you're doing, you know, Watson."

"I know," said I.

"There is a pattern to all this, but I am at a loss to see it yet. You will be playing a vital role in helping me to do so, providing critical intelligence."

I nodded. "See you when I get back."

Then I left him, not looking back once; only asking Mrs Hudson upon my departure from Barker Street to, "Keep an eye on him, please."

"I will do my level best, Doctor – but he does not make such things easy for me."

I could never have imagined the circumstances in which we would meet again; not having the *capacity* to imagine it back then. Nor what it would result in for my friend.

And I could never have predicted what was waiting for me, either, across the water in France.

I ARRIVED AT the docks in good time, and my journey to Calais was smooth enough. From there, it was another train ride to Paris itself, passing the Eiffel Tower as I went: a marvel of modern design and engineering. I was desperate to visit, but reminded myself I was here on very serious business. There would be no time on this occasion for sight-seeing. I had been booked into an impressive establishment called the Hôtel Meurice – free of any charge, a consequence of another service Holmes had done someone in the past, although he did not go into details. It was characterised by a row of arches along the front, and a platform for terraces on the first floor. The inside was no less awe-inspiring: a huge, high-ceiling lobby crowded with people. I had been in some remarkable hotels in my time with Holmes (from the Ritz to the Savoy) and this was no exception.

"Monsieur Watson," said the manager, his English almost perfect, as he arranged for my luggage to be taken to my room. "We have been expecting you. How was your trip?"

"Very pleasant," I told him, once again wishing that I was here for pleasure rather than information-gathering.

"And Monsieur Holmes, he is well?"

I nodded.

"Good, good. His family, they are remembered and still well respected in the area, you know."

I knew that Holmes' grandmother was French, the sister of the artist Vernet, but did not know his family was so well thought of in particular. "I'm sure he will be delighted to hear it," I told the man. It had been a long journey, however, and the day was wearing on, so I decided to take dinner (which was superb, I have to say: the finest filet mignon I have ever tasted) and try to get a decent night's sleep – before setting out early the next morning for the Institute.

Holmes and I had discovered that the place was in fact a facility – a sanatorium, if you will – for those afflicted with and recovering from problems of the mind. Privately run, from what we could ascertain, it had once been the home of some kind of nobleman – an aristocrat, possibly one of the Lemarchands? – at the end of the eighteenth century, but after he disappeared it fell into disrepair. It had been bought fifteen years previously by one Dr Malahide in order to serve its new purpose. I was expected there, having telegraphed ahead to request a day visit, under the pretext both of professional curiosity – I was 'thinking of moving sideways into that area of medicine' – and of observing the Institute and its methods for a possible paper. Flattery very often grants one access to places that otherwise would remain out of bounds.

Perhaps the pillar had been part of the house, left over from the aristocrat's time? I wondered as I lay in bed, my stomach full, staring at the ceiling and trying to get to sleep. Maybe he was the key to all this; the fact that he'd disappeared as well was definitely suspicious. Had he been the first person to whom this had happened? All questions for the morning, but it did not prevent me from asking them over and over that night, with no possible hope of getting any answers.

The one thing I could be thankful for was that, when I did eventually drop off, I did not dream. There were no nightmares that I can recall.

Those were waiting for me when I arrived at the Institute itself.

THE DOORMAN OF the hotel hailed a cab for me the next morning, and I told the driver before I got in where I wished to go. He did not set off immediately, but looked at me as if I were mad. I repeated my destination, thinking he might not have understood me – though place names surely needed no translation – but he had grasped my meaning all too well.

"You are quite certain, Monsieur?" he asked me, his accent much thicker than the manager's.

"Yes. Why?"

He did not answer at first, but then he said: "That is not a... nice place."

"Oh? How so?" Holmes had always told me that locals were the best source of information, so I fancied I could learn something even before I departed.

"There are stories, legends about the house..."

"What kind of stories?"

I caught him exchanging a look with the doorman, and my driver suddenly fell silent. "Never mind. I will take you there." It was all I would get out of him, even after pressing the fellow for more information along the way. The Institute was located on the outskirts of the city, surrounded by open land – I imagined so that if any of the 'residents' should wander away from the place (allowing patients outside their wards was already becoming common in facilities like this), there would be nowhere for them to go. Nothing for miles in any direction but greenery, so they could be easily spotted and escorted back.

I saw this as I was driven up the long, winding path towards the estate: towards the house itself, a faded tan mansion with massive doors, huge square windows on its first two floors and smaller, arched windows in the roof. A structure no less impressive than the Hôtel Meurice in its own way, it was nevertheless in far worse condition, with cracks in the walls and ivy climbing the sides. It reminded me, in a lot of ways, of the imposing Baskerville Hall, where I'd stayed the last time I had been information-gathering for Holmes. I hoped I would have better luck here than I did there.

My driver dropped me off at the door, but did not dawdle once he had been paid – with instructions to return around six – for already there were men venturing out to meet me dressed in the navy-coloured smocks and loose trousers of orderlies. One had long, dark hair that came to his shoulders; the other had much shorter hair and tattoos on his arms, where his sleeves were rolled up to the elbow. Of the two, the latter had the kindlier face.

"I'm Dr Lane," I called to them, holding up my hand in greeting. "I have an appointment." The long-haired one examined my (fake) papers and then looked at me, as if expecting to see some sign of my deception. Luckily, I was well-versed in pretence by then – and the best lie is always the one closest to the truth. I was a doctor and I have always had an interest in places such as those, ever since an uncle of mine was placed in one when I was in my twenties. The same man then searched me, but found nothing other than a fresh, blank notebook and pencil.

"Dr Malahide will be pleased to see you," he muttered gruffly, in tones that said *he* was anything but. "Henri, show our guest to the Doctor's office."

"*Bien sûr*, Gerard," said the tattooed man. "If you would come with me..."

"Thank you," I told the orderly, following him into the Institute.

It was actually very similar inside to the Vulcania, only much larger. A single set of stairs rose ahead of us, and corridors ran away on the left and right. Here and there, I spotted more men dressed in the same uniform as Gerard and Henri. I was desperate to see what lay along those halls, but Henri was already bidding me to follow him. There had been attempts to renovate inside, more so than the outer part of the mansion, but they were largely superficial. When we paused at a set of double-doors, I saw where the most modern 'improvement' had been made. When Henri pressed a button, the doors opened into what looked like a small room, but was in fact a lift – or, as the Americans called them, elevators. He got inside, then beckoned me to do the same, assuring me it was quite safe; I wasn't convinced at all. There was only enough room in that thing for three or four people, I surmised, but even with two it felt cramped as the doors closed. Henri pressed the top button and the carriage rocked as it began to ascend.

"Have... have you been working here long?" I asked my guide, more to take my mind off it all than anything.

He looked over and shook his head. "Not long, *monsieur*. But long enough."

"I see... and before that, a sailor?"

The fellow frowned. "How could you know this?" I realised I had slipped up. Too used to being around Holmes and his methods, I had just come out with the deduction without thinking – through sheer force of habit.

"Oh... er, your..." I pointed to the tattoos on his lean, but well-muscled forearms. He followed my gaze down to first one arm, then the other. "They indicate a person who is well-travelled. And on the underside there: that one especially, suggests someone with nautical leanings."

He turned over his left arm, which had a small mermaid on the underside. "You see a lot, Doctor," he stated.

"It helps in my line of work."

"I was once a sailor, *oui*. A ship's cook."

"Ah," said I. "A noble profession." I thought I saw a smile then, the corners of his lips rising. He nodded and I felt confident that I had extricated myself from what could have been a very troublesome situation.

The lift ground to a halt and I thought for a moment we were stuck; but the doors opened once more and allowed us to exit. We hadn't walked much further when Henri paused at a large oak door.

"Here we are," he said, giving a rap on the wood.

There was a muffled, "Come."

My guide opened the door for me and held out his hand. "Thank you, Henri." Even as I was stepping over the threshold, and taking in the room – wall-to-wall with bookcases and tomes I would have loved to read at my leisure, punctuated here and there with human skulls and models of the brain – a man with slicked-back hair and spectacles rose from his seat behind the desk.

"Dr Lane, I presume?" His accent bore only the slightest trace of French. He held out his hand for me to shake across that well-ordered desk. The handshake itself was limper than Laurence Cotton's, which Holmes would no doubt have said belied Malahide's position at the hospital. Either that, or he was holding something back. "Please, please – take a seat. Can I get you something? A little morning tea, perhaps?"

"That would be lovely," I told him.

"Henri," said Malahide, shifting his gaze back to the orderly as I settled down in the chair in front of the desk. "If you would be so kind?"

Henri nodded and withdrew from the room.

"So, Doctor, you are here to do some research?" Malahide sat back down again – a more smartly turned-out gentleman I had yet to meet – and regarded me over the rims of his glasses.

"And possibly write a paper – with your permission, naturally."

"Naturally," he replied, as if I could not even leave my chair, let alone publish a thing, without his express say-so. His handshake might have been weak, but his will clearly was not. "Well, you couldn't have picked a better facility to observe, Doctor. Our methods are quite unique, modelled – I should add – in part on some of the more progressive therapies at Charenton."

The name rang a bell with me, and it was only later I remembered it was the asylum that had once counted the Marquis de Sade as one of its inmates.

"They favour the more humanitarian treatment of patients – as do we." He steepled his fingers in a way I'd only ever seen Holmes do before. Indeed, there was much about this man that reminded me of my old friend, not least in his detached demeanour. "Where did you say this paper would be published again, Doctor? Your telegram was rather vague."

"Oh, the *British Medical Journal*," I said quickly, thinking it was broad enough an answer to satisfy Malahide. "I have friends who work there."

"Ah – and you've been published by them before?"

"This would be my first time... if I am successful."

"Hmm," Malahide leaned back and I got the feeling I was being studied, even mentally dissected. He shook his head. "A pity. I was hoping for perhaps the *Journal of Mental Science*, or the *Asylum Journal*."

"I'm sorry to disappoint," I replied. "But I felt that your endeavours here might benefit from being presented to a wider audience." Again, if nothing else is working, try flattery.

"Quite so," Malahide agreed. "Quite so. And how is it, again, you came across us? We are more than a little bit off the beaten track. Literally," he added, with a chilling grin.

"By reputation," I informed him. "Word of mouth."

"I see," said Malahide. "It is of little consequence, you are here now. Perhaps a dialogue first and then an inspection?"

I nodded. "That sounds most agreeable. Thank you, Doctor."

And then we began.

OUR 'DIALOGUE' TOOK up most of the morning, with my taking notes (pausing briefly to sharpen my pencil) and Malahide offering the broad strokes of his work with patients at the Institute – the fundamental principles being that of rehabilitation rather than remedy through punishment.

"As you're no doubt aware yourself, Doctor, the days of induced vomiting, of the swinging chair and water torture are long gone. We are not here to drive out the demons that were once thought to inhabit the bodies and minds of the sick. Our patients are not shackled, they are free to move around the place – under the watchful eye of staff, it goes without saying. They are medicated, but in most cases not to extremes and only for their own protection. At the Institute we are more concerned about quality of life rather than curing through heavy-handed approaches. This isn't the Spanish Inquisition," he added with a chuckle.

He talked at length about the mind, about studies ranging from the ever-increasing field of psychiatry to the marvels of the brain itself. "I wonder, Doctor, if we shall ever solve its mysteries," Malahide mused, standing and stretching his legs – before taking down one of the model brains from the bookcase and turning it over and over in his hands. I felt very much as if he was never granted the opportunity to talk about all of this with other medical men; that he was unburdening himself, almost, as I jotted down notes. I was very glad of the tea and sandwiches that Henri provided, for I fear by the end my flagging interest was showing.

"What about the history of this place?" I asked, for a change of pace more than anything.

"What about it?" Malahide retorted, seated once more. "Is that relevant to what we are doing now?"

"I suppose not," I admitted. "But readers are always interested in background."

"I thought you said that this was your first piece, Doctor. You talk like someone who has been published before." It wasn't the first time I'd felt like he was trying to trip me up.

I touched my hand to my chest. "I meant as a reader myself. And although it will be my first time published by the *British Medical Journal* – hopefully – I did not say it was my first time published." I smiled. "I am a little too long in the tooth for that. My work has appeared in smaller, less prestigious publications over the years, but I am hopeful this will lead to bigger and better things." Another lie that was close to the truth, enough to satisfy Malahide anyway, as he noticeably relaxed. "I just thought maybe something about how this place used to belong to an aristocrat, a Lemarchand –"

If he'd relaxed before then he visibly stiffened now. "Where did you hear that name?"

"I... it cropped up in my research. Was he not the owner at some point?"

Malahide laughed out loud at that statement. "The owner? The owner...? Oh, my dear Dr Lane, I think you need to look again at your so-called 'research.'"

"I'm... I don't understand."

"Then allow me to explain." This time he laced his fingers and leaned forward, onto the desk. "The Lemarchand name is one associated with madness in this region: it is in the blood. Many years ago one of their clan did have an association with a nobleman of these lands, which is where the confusion might have arisen, but never once did any of them *own* this place. They did not have the means."

I thought about the receipt now, the pillar – had it been falsified by someone selling the piece to the gallery? Perhaps by Malahide himself? But to what end? For what purpose? Why not just sell the thing himself under his own name? Unless he didn't want anyone to know. These were things I could not quiz him about, as I was not supposed to know.

"They are a poor family, have been for long, long time. Nevertheless, one does what one can to help."

To help? I grasped his meaning, then, connecting what he said about the madness to the Institute. "You have members of the Lemarchand family here?" I almost blurted out.

"*One* member," Malahide told me. "His wife and children did not know what else to do with him, other than to seek my advice. He is... *was* quite a severe case. Violent even. Fortunately he is much more sedate these days."

Sedate, I thought, or *sedated*?

"I've obviously gotten hold of the wrong end of the stick," I said to Malahide.

"Indeed," replied the man, looking at me again over the rims of his spectacles. He smiled suddenly and took out his pocket watch. "My," he observed, "time really does fly when you're... I expect you'd like that tour now?"

"If... if that's all right?"

"Certainly." Malahide went to the door and called out for an orderly. I was thankful when it was Henri who responded again; I like to think maybe he was even loitering nearby, aware his duties were not concluded. "Well, Doctor, it was nice to make your acquaintance. Do let me know if there is anything else I might do for you while you are on these shores." He held out his hand as I rose from my seat; the grip was definitely firmer this time.

"You're not coming with us?"

"You have your paper, Doctor; I have my reports." With that he flashed me another smile, before seeing me out and leaving me in Henri's hands. "Do let Henri know if you want to see anything in particular. Nothing is out of bounds."

I spent a much more agreeable hour or so being escorted round by the orderly, who took me to a selection of some of the rooms, including along those ground floor levels, which were not unlike soldiers' billets in their make-up: sparse, but comfortable-looking at least. Some of the residents were at home, reading or – in the case of one grey-haired man – just staring out of the window at the view, which I had to concede was idyllic. Some of the more severe cases, Henri told me, were being treated in the hospital wing, where I saw several women in nurses' uniforms attending to those in bed. It was similar to many other hospitals I had been in. If this place – and Malahide himself – was hiding anything, then they were doing an exceedingly good job of it.

As we toured around, using the stairs at my insistence, I engaged Henri in conversation, discovering that he was born in Leon and had left home as soon as he was able, to see the world. "Being a ship's cook seemed like the most sensible option," he told me. He was not old, in his late twenties I would hazard, but had already seen more of the globe than many men – including myself. "However, there comes a time, does there not, Dr Lane, when a man must return to his homeland and settle down?"

"And this was the job you chose then?" I asked him.

He shrugged. "It is rewarding work for an honest day's pay. What more can you ask?"

When I felt our time was drawing to a close, Henri asked if there was anything else I wanted to see, recalling Malahide's instructions. "Actually..." I said, "Dr Malahide mentioned a patient who might be of some interest. By the name of Lemarchand?"

Henri considered this for a moment or two, perhaps weighing up whether 'anything' might extend to 'anyone.' "*Oui*," he said eventually. "Monsieur Lemarchand will be in what we call the 'dayroom.'"

"Then," I said, beaming. "I think I should very much like to speak with him, Henri. And directly, if it is all the same with you."

CHAPTER TEN
Games, Puzzles & Toys

THE 'DAYROOM,' WHICH was on the ground floor, was a wide open space that – I imagined – must have served as some kind of ballroom in the past. A place where the previous owner held his parties over a century ago, perhaps? Now it was full of tables and chairs, with patients dressed in white smocks rather like the orderlies' uniforms (aside from the colour) scattered about amongst them. Some were playing cards (one was even building a house of cards, and failing), some occupied by board games such as draughts and Snakes & Ladders, and some working out puzzles. One patient not too far away was tracing his finger around an intricate metal maze, attempting to find his way to the centre, his tongue poking out of the corner of his mouth. Another, a young blonde woman who might have been Claire Thorndyke a few years from now, was slotting together pieces of wood to form some sort of shape. All seemed occupied, and happy enough in their tasks – with a male orderly posted in each corner of the room, and one halfway up each side.

Henri took me through the maze of tables, this way and that – stopping briefly to pick up a dice that one of the patients had accidentally thrown onto the floor and deliver it back to the man – then he pointed to a fellow sitting at a table on the far side. "There is M Lemarchand," he informed me.

I took in the man from a distance, also dressed in white, his closely cropped hair and large, brown eyes. They were fixed at a point under the table, where he was staring vacantly, although as I drew closer, I could see that his gaze was concentrated on something in front of him. He was folding paper, over and over, creating shapes. On the floor around him were the efforts of his labours thus far today, mainly birds fashioned out of the paper he'd been given, the remaining sheets of which I could see were arranged haphazardly on the table. The man finished his latest toy and brought it up where he could admire it. He pulled on an end of the paper, making the wings flap – up and down, up and down.

(And part of my mind flashed back to what Mrs Spencer had said, what she'd told us about the aftermath of the vagabond's visit – the sound of flapping wings.)

Lemarchand then tossed the bird into the air, as if expecting it to magically take flight – and for a moment or two it looked like it was going to do exactly that, hanging in mid-air, catching whatever breeze it could find in the room. Perhaps it would even escape, fly out through the top of an open window and into the sky where it would soar through the clouds like a real bird.

Then it dropped like a stone to join its kin on the ground, upturned and lifeless. The man grunted and snatched up another piece of paper.

"Origami," Henri said. "I saw such paper-folding when I was in the Orient. I learnt a little, and showed it to Simon." It was the first time anyone had used Lemarchand's first name, and it seemed oddly fitting. "But he can now do things with the paper that I can only dream of." I could hear the admiration in his voice; could sense that he really cared about this man. "One of his ancestors used to be a toymaker, I think. Indeed, I was told that Simon himself used to make trinkets out of wood and metal for his own children. It must have been in his blood."

Along with the madness Malahide had spoken of, I reflected.

"We cannot allow him his tools now. It is too dangerous."

"Dr Malahide said that he was doing much better, though?" I said. "That he was no longer violent. No longer a threat."

"Not a danger to others, Dr Lane," Henri replied seriously. "To himself. The medication he is on calms him, but the risk cannot be taken."

"I see. Do you mind if I speak with him?"

Henri shrugged. "Go ahead, he speaks good English." But I noticed the orderly kept close by as I approached. "Hello," I ventured, halting by the side of Lemarchand's table. He did not even look up at me, but continued with his labours, folding the new piece of paper over and over. "Simon, isn't it? Would you mind if I talked to you for a little while?"

When I got no reply to this either, I pulled out the spare wooden chair round the side of the table and sat down. "That's really very clever, you know. I wish I could do something like that, but I'm hopeless at crafts. I *can* write, though." I took out my notebook and my pencil to illustrate this, and there was a twitch of movement, the slight raising of an eyebrow. "Simon, I know this is difficult for you, but I'd like to ask a few questions; about yourself, about this place. Is that all right?"

Another twitch, almost imperceptible. He suddenly stopped folding the paper, placing the half-finished creation on the table between us – and affording me a glimpse of his arms, the sleeves riding up as he did so. The man's flesh was a mass of scars – some of them quite recent, in spite of what Malahide had told me – which reminded me more of Holmes' self-inflicted wounds. I couldn't help letting out a gasp, and looked over my shoulder to see if my guide had spotted them, too. Henri was now deep in conversation with a colleague, however, so I had no way of knowing whether the information was new to him or not.

Turning back to Lemarchand, I asked, "Are they treating you well here, Simon? You can tell me if they are not. I'm a friend."

He raised his head, staring straight at me for the first time and giving me a look that said he didn't have any friends in the world. Then his eyes flicked downwards; not once, but twice.

"Dr Malahide –" Another twitch, at the corner of his mouth. "He tells me that your particular affliction runs in your family. That they have an association with this place, with the previous occupant?" Lemarchand's lips parted, and I could see that his teeth were gritted. I risked another question. "Do you know anything about a pillar, Simon? It was sold by someone here, to a gallery in London a short while ago. The receipt says it was sold by you."

He continued to gape, and I could see in his eyes that he was trying to fight the medication he was on. Laudanum? I wondered. I was familiar with its relaxing effects – but also sadly with its addictive nature. I continued, hoping to give him the extra push he needed.

"There was a hole in the pillar when we found it – in a place where it looked like a ritual had occurred. A ritual involving a sacrifice, Simon. A human sacrifice. Do you know anything about that kind of thing?"

His lips drew back further, teeth more prominent.

"The hole in the pillar looked square, looked –"

"*Box!*" Lemarchand managed through those gritted teeth. "The... the L-Lament... Con... Configuration."

"I don't understand," I told him, but nevertheless wrote down the words.

"A... a puzzle," he said, as if that explained everything. "And... and a gate... gateway. S-stolen..."

I continued to scribble down Simon's words, asking him for more details as I did so, as much as he could impart. "It was stolen from you? The pillar, the box?"

"No... not from me... G-great... grandfather..." The effort must have been tremendous, the veins standing proud on his neck and his temples. "Tricked... H-he muh-muh-made the b-box... Made it easy for... for them. To... to control."

"For whom, Simon? Who's behind all this? Malahide? Is he working for someone?"

"The Order," he said plainly, and I started to speak but Simon hadn't finished. "O-Order of the Gash!"

An order? Some kind of religious sect? Though clearly they had their fingers in other pies as well. And their ultimate aim? Well, Lemarchand had said it himself: control.

"We... we are *all* j-just... toys..." he hissed, but when I shook my head in confusion he added, looking downwards. "Be-be-below... Kept... kept below... Beneath!"

I was furiously scribbling away when he reached out with his right hand and grabbed my arm, pulling me in close. "H-help," he pleaded. "Help free... Please! Freedom..." Before I could do a thing, he snatched the pencil I'd been making notes with – which I'd only just been using to get his last words to me down; which was still sharp from my time in Malahide's office – and he brandished it like a weapon at me. Now, I've been threatened many times, and by some of the best in the business of intimidation; I've known when my life was in jeopardy. And at that moment I felt Lemarchand meant me no harm.

I realised he would rise from the table, his aim to use that pencil on himself, raising it to jam the thing into his own jugular – to escape, to taste the freedom denied to his origami birds.

But it was not to be. Orderlies were upon him, Henri grabbing his wrist and pulling the pencil downwards again – but also looking over at me and frowning. Just how much of all that had the young man heard? I saw Lemarchand's eyes, wild now, gaping past me to the doorway. I traced his gaze and saw Malahide standing there, looking coolly across at the scene. Other patients were getting agitated now, whipped up by the excitement – and more orderlies and nurses were entering, some armed with syringes, Malahide issuing instructions. Gerard was there too, wading in and gleefully restraining people who had been peaceful only a few moments earlier.

Before too long, it was Simon's turn – one of the nurses injecting him in his upper arm, through his clothes. Then his eyelids grew heavy and he was a dead weight in the arms of Henri and the other man.

Malahide wandered over, through the chaos, with his hands behind his back – tutting. "Oh dear, oh dear. What a fuss! And he has been so well behaved for so long. Pity." He turned to me as I was getting out of my seat. "I am so sorry, Dr Lane. I do hope he did not hurt you in any way?"

Regaining my composure, I shook my head. "No, no. Your... your staff were most efficient."

"As they are trained to be," Malahide responded with a curt nod. "I wonder if I may ask a favour of you."

"Of course, Doctor."

He reached over and took my notebook from me, just as Simon had relieved me of the pencil. Malahide opened it up, flipping through the last few pages – which he tore out. "I wonder if I could prevail upon you, when the time comes to write your paper, not to mention this little... incident. I'm afraid it might put the Institute in a bad light."

The doctor handed my notebook back to me, the jottings I'd made during our time in the office still intact. Then Malahide ripped up the other pages and tossed them onto the floor, where the birds with clipped wings lay in droves. "The ramblings of a lunatic," he said with a hollow laugh. "Whoever would believe them anyway?"

"Quite so," I agreed, placing the notebook back in my pocket and smoothing down my jacket. "I will respect your wishes, obviously. After all, you have been gracious with your time and with your hospitality."

Malahide seemed content with that, or at least acted as if he was. Then he apologised once again, and said that he would arrange for Gerard to run me home early – the staff of the Institute apparently had access to a number of Hansoms

– whereby I could notify my original driver that his services would not be required. My visit, it seemed, was being cut short.

As the doctor walked me out of the room, with a view to walking me out of his facility as quickly as possible, I looked over my shoulder one last time – at Henri, and at the unconscious Simon.

And his words – his entreaty – echoed my head: *H-help... Help free...*

Please!

CHAPTER ELEVEN
Locks & Keys

FORTUNATELY, MY MEMORY is not so bad that I could not remember the key details of my admittedly brief conversation with Simon Lemarchand, and these I sent in a telegram to Holmes immediately upon my arrival back at the Hôtel Meurice (and after letting their driver know that he would not have to return to the Institute, for which he appeared extremely grateful). I felt that the rest of it, what I'd gleaned from Malahide and the tour, could be summed up in one. two words: *something's amiss*.

The business with Lemarchand's ancestor, the 'stolen' pillar, the box he had called the 'Lament Configuration,' the Order of the Gash – it all went into a short report that he could peruse before returning to me with his thoughts. For my money, we were dealing with another organisation, like as not originating on foreign soil, that was out to wrest control of the city (whether its current caretakers deserved it or not, after what I had witnessed, was another matter – it was always better the Devil you knew). It was an organisation that had the capacity to overshadow that awful 'House' Holmes once scuppered; that might have a reach and ambition beyond that of even

Moriarty and his empire. It was a serious business indeed, and one which – to my mind – demanded urgent attention.

I did not know yet how Cotton fitted into things, but Spencer was a soldier, Monroe had the means to blackmail half the government – maybe even members of the aristocracy and Royal Family – and Thorndyke, his lackey, was a policeman. Already it was looking quite grim. But I did not want to make a move without consulting Holmes, for I did not know how his own investigations were proceeding.

Try as I might, I found it hard to settle that evening – even after partaking of a few glasses of the drink I always turn to when particularly rattled, whisky and soda (in this instance, a particularly fine twenty-year-old single malt the manager recommended). I was not hungry, nor could I sleep very well, and when I did close my eyes all I could see was Lemarchand's face, those cuts on his arms (and elsewhere?). It was pure torture.

In the end it took almost two full days of waiting to hear back from Holmes – and even then it was a simple instruction to remain where I was and do nothing until I heard from him again. No explanation for this, no update on what was happening to him at all! Clearly I was the only one who thought time was of the essence. For Lemarchand especially, I feared that it might be running out... if it hadn't already.

I could count on the fingers of one hand the times I had gone against Holmes' wishes, and in every single instance afterwards I wished that I had not. Nevertheless, if that man died, his blood – the legacy of his entire bloodline – would be on my hands. I felt the urgent need to act, and so act I did that very night.

Amongst the clothing that I'd packed, I'd squirreled away some darker-coloured items: trousers, a sweater and a pair of gloves. Not the dress of a gentleman at all, more that of a thief, but where I was going I did not wish to be spotted. I had also packed my trusty pistol. (I was favouring the Webley Bulldog at the time – quite popular with the police and private citizens alike – although in the past I had also used an Enfield and Webley Mk I, as well as my original service pistol, an Adams Mk III .450 caliber... I know how critics of my work and the stories do so love to argue over details such as these; a shame, then, that this document will be going up in flames eventually.) If I could, I would have gone to that Institute with an army and all the guns we could lay our hands on, rifles and pistols. Every time someone came into the lobby of the hotel, I expected it to be Holmes – showing up to help – or in disguise as someone else? But no; there was only me, and I had to do something.

How I would get inside without being seen, let alone free the poor wretch who had spoken to me, was anyone's guess. With the aid of Henri, perhaps? He had seemed like a good man... although I hadn't known him long, and had no idea if I could rely on him. I contemplated going to the authorities, but what would I say? Malahide had been right when he said nobody would listen to the ramblings of a lunatic, much less care what was happening to him inside there. I had no proof anyway, only my own notion that something didn't sit right in that place and a few mumbled utterings that didn't make sense to me, let alone anyone else. Not even officers who knew me would act on so little. I could perhaps impose upon our friend Inspector Abberline, with whom Holmes had worked closely on the Ripper case the previous decade – and, along with his assistant Thomas Lloyd, had gained a reputation for unusual cases since, such as the Gods of Rome affair, or the business with the Just King... But it would have taken too long to bring him here.

It was decided, I had no choice but to go on my own. Fortune favours the bold and all that. Although, looking back, all things considered, it occurs to me that on this occasion perhaps I did more resemble that bumbling idiot the movies would later present me as.

I secured the services of a cab driver on the street, one who would be a little less squeamish about our destination – especially if the price was right. The only problem was his lack of English, but then my money spoke for me on this occasion. He dropped me on the outskirts of the estate, so I could make my way on foot – and seemed to understand when I pointed at the ground and said, "Wait. You wait, *s'il vous plaît*." The man nodded and held out his hand for more money, which I reluctantly parted with.

No sooner had I done so, than he grinned and started up the horses again – driving off into the night. I was about to shout after him, but thought better of it given the circumstances. So I stood there, contemplating what to do. Even if I began the long walk back again now, it would take me forever – and I wasn't even sure of the direction. I'd come this far, so the best bet seemed to me to carry on with the mission. If nothing else, I knew there were Hansoms at the Institute – I could always 'borrow' one.

Thankfully there was some light from the half moon above, and before too long I spotted the Institute, which looked even more imposing and run-down at night-time. In fact it appeared just as deserted as that gallery back in London; I hoped I hadn't left it too late and – as incredible as it might seem – they'd moved the whole operation somewhere else, as they had then.

The only light I could discern emanated from the back of the large house, spilling out on to the gardens beyond – suggesting that the curtains were not yet drawn – so I crept around the side and pressed myself up against the wall, risking a quick peek through the window.

It was a room I hadn't seen before, larger than the patients' wards, but much smaller than the ballroom. Inside were a handful of orderlies I did not recognise, though what they were doing in there was anyone's guess – there certainly weren't any patients around that I could spy. But there *was* something in the centre of the room; I shifted my position slightly, standing on my toes to get a better view, and then I saw it.

The box.

Not a box like the one that had once nestled in the pillar back at the Vulcania, the puzzle box, the Lament Configuration. No, this was much larger, more like a crate. Another statue that didn't belong to the man who ran this place, something else for him to sell on? Whatever the case, the orderlies appeared to be guarding it – never taking their eyes off it. Just what on Earth was going on?

I had to wait a little while to find out, when Malahide appeared in the room. I didn't even see him enter, but then my angle didn't afford me a very good view of the door. I was close enough to the glass to hear him telling the orderlies to leave, however, and I heard the distinctive click of a lock being turned. Whatever he was up to, he needed complete privacy to do it.

Glancing about him, though thankfully not in my direction, Malahide bent and patted the box. When he rose again, he had a blade in his hand that he used to lever open the top. The sides fell away, revealing what was inside.

It was a person. Curled up into a ball, hugging itself, arms clasped around its body. There couldn't have been enough room in that crate to even move – and I had thought it confining in that damned lift!

Callously, Malahide kicked the shape.

"Get up!" he shouted at the thing (in English, I noted... I was beginning to wonder if Malahide was a Frenchman at all). Then, sick of waiting, he hauled the figure to its feet. It was only then that I saw why it was hugging itself: it was wearing a strait-jacket. And it was only now that I recognised the man: none other than Simon Lemarchand: a toy released from its chest.

"I hope you have had sufficient time to think, in there; to repent," Malahide said to him. Good Lord, I thought to myself, had the man been in that contraption all this time? Since I was forced to leave? Was this one of Malahide's 'treatments'? To correct Lemarchand, punish him for his behaviour with the pencil?

"I know what it is you want, Simon," the doctor continued. "What you crave above all else." Now he had his arm around the man's shoulders, leading him out of the detritus of the crate as if he was that fellow's best friend. Lemarchand's legs were unsteady, barely able to hold him upright, let alone carry him along. "It was simply not the right time the other day, nor the right place – and what a waste that would have been! But tonight... tonight, Simon, I have decided to grant you your ultimate wish. Your freedom."

Malahide began to cut the straps on the strait-jacket. Lemarchand gawped at him, and I thought for one moment the doctor might be doing just that: setting the man free. "We have already achieved so much together, you and I," he said to Simon. "You have given me the means by which I have been allowed to communicate with my master. Your blood, the key!" Underneath, Simon was naked from the waist up and I could see the extent to which those scars covered his body, some old, some new: a repeated, vicious rending of his skin. I fancied here and there I even spotted words, as if he had been written upon; a human book of blood. But I knew that could not be – such a thing was beyond contemplation, beyond imagination. "Now... now..." Malahide stepped back, dropping the strait-jacket to the floor – and he no longer had the blade.

Lemarchand did.

At first I thought he'd snatched it from the doctor, just as he had the pencil from me – and I was about to cheer him on – but he was in a much weaker state than he had been a couple of days ago. It was only as Simon held up the blade, watching the light as it reflected off the metal, that I understood what he was about to do.

"Now," Malahide repeated, "tonight, we will turn that key."

I don't know how I didn't see what was coming next; after all, hadn't Henri told me that the wounds on Simon's arms were self-inflicted? Hadn't I witnessed him attempting to do this very thing myself? To *set himself free*?

Before I could do or say anything – perhaps shout through the glass – Simon had run the blade across his throat. The skin opened up and his head fell back, allowing a geyser of redness to burst forth.

Malahide had stepped back again, but was still splattered by some of it, ruining his fine suit. Even he had the decency to pull a face at what he was seeing, what he'd facilitated; as Simon crumpled to the floor like one of his paper birds, swimming – or drowning – in his own blood... so much blood. A pool of it, gathering around him.

Still I thought I might be able to save the poor fellow, climb in through the window and stem the bleeding at his throat somehow. But it was already too late; if nothing else, what happened next convinced me of that.

For now someone – some*thing* – did truly appear out of nowhere. Arms shooting up out of the crimson on either side of Lemarchand, enveloping him more closely than any strait-jacket. The arms themselves were strange: not properly formed, like something I might have seen on a dissection table at medical school. There was no skin on those arms, and they glistened with moistness and slime – the brachioradialis, pronators, supinators, two fascial compartments... I reeled them all off in my head, through sheer habit as I'd learned the names of them parrot-fashion for exams.

Then legs in a similar condition likewise emerged from that thick puddle, and I did the same: quadriceps femoris, the central rectus femoris, the three vasti... I mouthed the names of the parts as I saw them; it was the only thing stopping me from going insane.

There could be no possible way a man might have hidden

under Lemarchand, and besides it had been bare flooring – just like the rest of the Institute. But now there were definitely two figures, one beneath the other.

Be-be-below... Kept... kept below... Beneath... I recalled Simon's words to me. Had he been talking about this... this monstrosity? This *Hellish* creature that even now looked like it was devouring him alive? For he was alive, just, and if he had been able to, I think he would have screamed – as much at being deceived, being tricked (as his great-grandfather had been), as what was being done to him. He'd wanted his freedom, but at what cost? He wasn't just losing his life that I could see, he was losing his very soul: his body deflating, absorbed by the newcomer, the wet noises of the feast on the verge of making me gag.

In all my years, I had never seen the likes of this – and I had witnessed some pretty horrendous things, both abroad and at home, serving as a colleague to my best friend. But nothing, absolutely nothing could have prepared me for...

Even now, thinking about it, writing about it, I find my hand is shaking – more than it usually does. I must persevere, however, for I have come this far.

Not even Stoker could have made this vampire appear romantic. It was vile in the extreme. I wanted to look away, but could not; I was rooted to the spot, my own body betraying me. But then, I think a part of me actually *wanted* to see this. Wanted to know – not only what was happening, but why.

Soon there was nothing left on the floor but the skinless man. Not even the blood Simon had spilled, for this beast had somehow sucked it all up to replenish itself. The red figure stood, slowly, taking his first breath and grimacing as if it hurt. I'm not ashamed to say I was glad of that. I recalled that I had once, in my early years, been shown a reproduction of Vesalius' sixteenth century book *De Humani Corporis Fabrica*, a revolutionary Renaissance study of the human body. In it were illustrations of skeletons, stomachs, brains – but also figures shorn of their outer layers in various poses. I'd never forgotten those pictures, and I swear it was as if they had come to life right in front of my very eyes.

Only now was I able to blink, hoping that I was simply hallucinating – my mind showing me memories as if they were real. The Institute's influence? Or the doctor's? Had I, too, been hypnotised somehow when I was last here? Did the vagabond's talents extend to Malahide as well? Or maybe I'd been poisoned by some Egyptian concoction? In any event, the scene was still playing out in front of me.

I still could not move, however, and could do nothing but stare as Malahide, looking as scared as I felt, said – only then switching to perfect French – "*Bienvenue, seigneur.*" Then the doctor bowed, as if this newcomer was some sort of nobility.

The aristocrat? It *couldn't* be... Even if he was still alive, that would have made him a century and a half or more old. Although not the strangest thing, I reminded myself, considering what I had just witnessed.

"Aaah," said the man, looking down at himself, holding out first one arm and then the other; turning them over and admiring how he had knitted himself together. Was this Malahide's master, then? The one he'd spoken about? Perhaps the principal of the Order as well? Had all this – the deaths in London, the gallery, the pillar – been about trying to resurrect a dead French nobleman who practised Satanic worship?

They spoke to each other quickly then in French, only a little of which I could remember and get translated once I had a chance to write it down. Something about Malahide being right about the location, the spot where the aristocrat had died. About him having forgotten what it was like to be alive, that he was hungry... And the mention of a name:

Sherlock Holmes.

That was it, enough to snap me out of my reverie. Monster

or no monster, demon or not, I had my pistol and I was more than prepared to use it. I drew the Webley, took aim, and fired through the window three times. I'm pleased to report that even at such an awkward angle, and with a barrier of glass between myself and the skinless man, two of my bullets hit their mark, one striking him in the back, between the shoulder-blades and the other embedding itself in his skull.

"*No!*" Malahide cried out, as the bloodied mess of a thing collapsed – not just to the ground, but inwards, losing coherence; losing integrity like a house of cards collapsing. I only hoped the whole Order would do the same now its leader was out of the way. In seconds, he was just a disgusting mess on the floor. The doctor's angry gaze found me at the window and he barked, "*Imbecile! What have you done?*"

Only what I had to, I told myself. But it was time to get out of there now; Simon was long past saving, not that he'd ever wanted the kind of freedom I could offer. I pulled away from the window, only to see lights going on all over the Institute. And those orderlies who had been guarding the box, now approaching me outside. Only a handful at first, but more were quickly joining them – I daresay they were used to reacting quickly; perhaps even had drills? The long-haired Gerard was amongst them, I noticed. "Stay back," I warned, waving the gun first in one direction, then the other. "I still have some bullets left."

They'd approach, then stop when the gun was aimed at them – all the time blocking off my escape. Then one of the men rushed me and I fired, hitting him in the arm; I am not a cold-blooded killer, after all, and these fellows had not really done me any harm (for all I knew they had no idea what their employer was about). I barely had a chance to turn when I felt other men behind me, grabbing my gun arm and forcing it up in the air where the rest of the rounds were fired. I continued pulling the trigger of my revolver, even though it was empty, as I was wrestled to the ground. There were just too many of them to fight, and in the end I ceased my struggling. These were people who were more than used to – and capable of – dealing with violent patients. I was held fast.

"*Amène-le à moi!*" ordered Malahide from the shattered window. I was dragged round to the front door where he was waiting, and drew back his hand; I tensed, expecting him to strike me across the face. But he paused, blew out a long breath, then let his hand fall to his side. One of the orderlies gave him my empty weapon, which he looked at as if someone had just handed him a live snake. "Doctor... Doctor... Whatever are we to do with you?"

"You could let me go," I said wearily.

"I think not," came the reply. "You are clearly a very dangerous man – and in urgent need of our help."

"What are you going to do, bundle me into the box?" I said. "Slit my throat?"

Malahide laughed. "Of course not, Dr Lane. Or perhaps you would prefer 'Watson'?" I tried to hide my shock at that, but didn't do a very good job, judging from the look of satisfaction on the man's face. "Oh, yes, I know *exactly* who you are. An impostor as well as an intruder."

(He could talk – as I later found out, Malahide was not his real name either, though he *was* a Frenchman, through and through.)

I struggled, looking around; thinking that at least some of these people must be legitimate, otherwise Malahide would just act openly against me. "Look, can't you see what's happening here? The man is evil, he is in league with demons – see, he even has blood on him!"

"You were firing your gun at me!" Malahide retorted. "*Of course* there is blood! One of your bullets managed to graze me." He did not offer to show the orderlies his wound, and anyway there was too much crimson on his front for that to be the truth. Nevertheless, they seemed to accept his account.

Some probably didn't even require an explanation, those who were in Malahide's confidence – and I was definitely counting Gerard among their number.

I resisted again, craning my neck to see behind the doctor.

"What are you – ? Oh," said the man, shaking his head. "I think maybe you are looking for your little friend Henri. I am sorry to say that he is no longer with us. We had to part ways after you left; he had become a... disruptive influence on Monsieur Lemarchand." He didn't come right out and say that they'd killed him, but the implication was there. Henri had heard too much that day to remain alive.

"Ah... now, ask him about Simon. Get him to *show* you Simon."

"Doctor, look at the hour. Simon will be in bed, asleep, as all our patients are – or *were,* until you began with your antics."

"You can't, because he's dead. You used him to summon the skinless man and –"

"Listen to yourself! Demons, skinless men! I think it is time we settled you in. Nurse!" Malahide called back over his shoulder and a woman with dark hair came trotting up to him. "Bring me something to help soothe the troubled fellow." She nodded and returned moments later with a syringe.

"Get away from me with that or I'll –" But I could do nothing and I knew it. Malahide administered the drug – I still do not know what it was to this day – and I began to immediately feel its effects. Everything suddenly had a blurry edge to it, and it was hard to focus. I had never understood Holmes' fascination with narcotics, but if anything was to put me off them, it was that experience at the Institute. When Malahide spoke again, his words were deep and echoing.

"There, now, that's better. Let's get him inside, shall we?" As I was carried in, I noticed Malahide whispering to Gerard. Then, once those huge front doors were closed again, Malahide told members of his staff to go and see that the patients hadn't been disturbed too much. This left only himself, Gerard and one of the other orderlies with me: a man who had a definite air of the military about him. The doctor's employees took one of my arms apiece and slung them over their shoulders, dragging me as Holmes and I had tried to carry the barman back at the Vulcania.

They took me down the corridor, which telescoped out ahead of me, courtesy of the doctor's drugs. "Whe... whar..." I was trying to ask where they were taking me, but I wasn't even sure my mouth was opening and closing, let alone forming the words and saying them out loud. It wouldn't have mattered anyway, because they were taking no notice of me. We paused at the lift Henri had introduced me to when I first arrived.

I tried to move, to break free of the men – but it was useless. Malahide dismissed the extra orderly and only he and Gerard accompanied me inside the cramped box, where he reached into his pocket and produced a key, sliding this into place in a hole beneath the control mechanism. Instead of clanking upwards, the lift began to descend. My stomach lurched and I felt sure I was going to throw up.

When the cage shuddered to a halt, the doors opened again and Malahide stepped out, with Gerard hauling me from the box behind him. I could hear the noise almost as soon as I was out: the screams, the cries, the whimpers. The sound of excruciating pain and loss of all hope.

The only light down here came from flaming torches on the walls, but even through my drug haze I knew exactly where we were.

This was a dungeon.

And yes, as I was taken down this corridor I saw barred cells on either sides, the stone flooring covered with straw. Some of the people imprisoned here were chained to walls – and not in the way those paying customers were back at the Vulcania, either. They were at impossible angles, some stretched, some hanging forward so that their shoulders jutted out behind them. None of them looked like they'd eaten in weeks.

A few were free to roam about their cells, though some were running into the walls. I saw some wearing the same kind of strait-jacket Lemarchand had on – and others with their hands free, to claw at themselves. One, in particular, upon our approach, ran to the bars and grasped them tightly. He was trying to speak, but only mumbles were emerging. It was then that I saw the stitching running around his bald head, where someone – presumably Malahide – had opened up his scalp and delved around inside, turning him into something akin to the creature Mary Shelley wrote about.

Yet more were strapped to trolleys with thick restraints – as I was carried past, one unfortunate's head lolled sideways to gape vacantly at me, his mouth foaming, a hole in the centre of his forehead which looked as if it had been drilled. And one was strapped to a chair, with cables running from it – which, every couple of seconds, delivered jolts of electricity that caused him to rise up in the seat, then slump back down. How long that had been going on for, I had no way of knowing.

We... we are all j-just... toys... Be-be-below... Kept...kept below... Beneath...

Help free... Please! Freedom...

This was what Simon had been talking about, these people and the hideous experiments going on here that no-one knew about. These poor, tortured souls. The doctor had been right about one thing, this wasn't the Spanish Inquisition – this was much, much worse.

"Come on," Malahide called back to Gerard, who hefted me and picked up his pace. "Almost there."

I don't know whether it was the drugs or not, but when I turned my head I thought I saw another figure in the nearest cell on my right. He was slumped against the far wall, and looked in a similar state to the aristocrat – skin removed, but much less mobile. The figure had used its finger to write something on the wall in its own blood, which reminded me of the lettering I had seen in crimson during my first ever investigation with Holmes. The message was:

Help me. I am in Hell.

Then I was dragged past and I had no way of knowing whether the whole ordeal had happened. But I did not doubt at the time that this was indeed Hell...

If only I had known it was merely a precursor.

"In the Chamber with him for now, I think," Malahide told his underling, and I was taken to a room at the end of the corridor, full of equipment and instruments. Some of it looked old, some of it new – some medical in nature, some designed for doing the worst kind of damage to the human body in order to extract information. Spikes, chains, electrodes: this place had them all.

I was relieved of my outer clothing, left in my undergarments, and then shackled to the wall. Malahide lifted my drooping chin and said, "I look forward to working with you, Dr Watson. Or should that be working *on* you?" He laughed.

I growled back, managing to spit a couple of words out, "The aristocrat!"

Malahide cocked his head; he understood my meaning. All this was worth it, if it meant I had cut the head off the snake. "Oh, my dear Doctor – he is not dead, if that's what you believe. Yes, you have delayed things, I admit. But I shall continue with my labours. I will use the blood to bring him back again."

My brow furrowed at that, for I had thought it was only Lemarchand's blood that could do such a thing – and he was gone.

"Perhaps even your blood, when I am done with you. It matters little whose it is." He let my chin drop and I had neither the strength nor the inclination to raise it. "There again, maybe when I am finished I will simply lock you up down here to rot and throw away the key? In any event, you will not be around to witness what we have in store for your friend, the great detective Mr Sherlock Holmes."

Malahide laughed again, much more gruffly, and this time Gerard joined in. Then I heard the door to the Chamber slam shut.

It might have been then that the torches went out; or I may have lost my fight to hang on to consciousness. Either way, and with no moon to guide me, I was now, finally, pitched into total darkness.

PART TWO

Sherlock Holmes

CHAPTER TWELVE
The Falls

SHERLOCK HOLMES WAS comforted by the knowledge that his friend, Dr Watson, was safe.

Far away from London, engaged in a fact-finding mission, yes, but safe. Holmes had made sure he would be comfortable, in one of the finest hotels in Paris, and ensured that – even though Watson was visiting the institution connected with the case – people knew where he was. There was no possible way he could come to harm over in France, if he did as Holmes had instructed; which was more than could be said if the man remained by Holmes' side, he felt sure.

It was simply too dangerous for Watson to stay. Already he had been placed in far too much peril; had more knowledge of this new game than was good for him, which was why Holmes had to steer him towards the gallery, then the Institute. He had already been through the papers they'd managed to salvage from the Vulcania, of course, had already found the receipts and paid a visit to the gallery alone (ahead of Mrs Thorndyke's mention of the place, thankfully). It was as he was sifting through the information in that back room the first time that Holmes struck upon the idea of directing Watson to France. He would need to follow up the lead at some point anyway, and his companion was more than capable of doing just that – it would have been suspicious if Holmes had simply created a false trail for him to follow.

While Holmes remained, and faced what was to come. The true trial, the real danger. Just one more lie to keep Watson out of harm's way, he told himself. Just one more deception...

It had begun the moment he held his tongue about the letter. Even as the boy had handed it over, and they'd read it, Holmes had known there was no sick Englishwoman waiting for Watson back at the *Englischer Hof* in Meiringen. Yet he'd allowed his friend to trail off to see to the imaginary lady, girding himself to meet for one final time with his great nemesis, Professor Moriarty. To protect Watson, to keep him out of harm's way. It was the only reason he'd asked his friend to accompany him in the first place to Strasburg, since to leave him and go alone would have meant also leaving him to the tender mercies of the Professor's accomplices.

The note Holmes had written himself had been the hardest thing he had ever set down. He acknowledged that his actions would bring great pain to his friends, especially to Watson – but the alternative was unthinkable. His sacrifice was tolerable, if it meant that those friends would remain untouched. If there had been any other way... But there hadn't, and as he signed off *Very sincerely yours* his thoughts had remained with the best, perhaps the only true friend he'd ever had.

And then: the fight.

Moriarty's anticipation of his every move, even the baritsu techniques Holmes was using. He'd seen no possible way of ridding the world of the monster without seeing his task through to the bitter end; that of all the things he had done in his life, this one action would make the greatest difference. So, Holmes had grabbed hold of Moriarty's collar, stepped back, let gravity take its course, and –

The fall.

Holmes and Moriarty hanging on to each other, even with death rushing to meet them. Then suddenly, he was alone – his rival falling away through the gushing, almost glowing water. Alone, as one expected to be when meeting the Grim Reaper. Except –

He had survived; had woken up on the rocks a little way from the base of the falls, drenched but otherwise intact. Holmes had staggered to his feet, almost slipping and thinking to himself what an irony it would be to break one's neck now, after falling so far.

Later, he'd read Watson's account of this adventure: 'The Final Solution.' Read his description of the Falls as an abyss, a dark chasm leading to a boiling pit. The memories had flooded back, of that terrible, terrible place; of realising how very little his life and his struggles had actually meant in the greater scheme of things.

Yet he'd at least been comforted by the fact that his impending doom would afford him a glimpse of something beyond all this – then surely everything would make sense. He, Sherlock Holmes, would have finally solved the last, greatest mystery.

For a short while, at least, he did think that perhaps he'd been delivered into some kind of Heaven – a Valhalla, as the Vikings called it – such was the scene that greeted him when he shook himself off and stumbled away from what should have been his watery grave. Was death just like life, only richer? A bolstering of the senses, even more than *his* were already? Everything was brighter, sharper; smells and sounds enriching his nose and ears.

Was death merely a continuation of the story you were telling when you were snatched from the world? A hallucination, a spiritual experience? He even entertained the notion – momentarily – that he might be a ghost, that only his spirit had survived the dreadful business and his body was at the bottom of that abyss, battered, bloodied and beyond any hope of rescue, along with Moriarty's.

How could he be alive?

He *shouldn't* be. By the time he had finally made his way back up to where he knew Watson would return and find the letter, seeing him there eventually and witnessing his grief, Holmes had already decided not to alert him: even before a fresh encounter with Moriarty's henchman persuaded him of the danger that still attended his companion. He had decided that he needed time to unravel what had happened, why he was still walking around and breathing the sweet, sweet air when the professor was not.

They had both fallen. But only one of them now remained.

That is what had been the fundamental driving force for his actions, to travel, to try to uncover the meaning of it all. For what purpose he might have been spared. Part of what Watson believed was true, that he had been learning how to control his body, testing the limits of it; though he suspected his friend thought he was pursuing suicide by degrees. But he was not trying to end his existence, merely investigating the boundaries of his life – to try and provoke whoever, or whatever, had saved him into revealing itself.

He had never done anything as reckless as putting a loaded gun to his head and pulling the trigger, but he had played a deadly game of chance in Russia with men who bet on the results. He had survived many, many rounds when others had not. They'd died in front of him, their brains splattered all over the table and the walls.

He had not lain on the tracks in front of trains, to be run over, for that might put others' lives at risk, and those were not his to gamble with. But he had engaged in a deadly form of harness racing in America – another underground activity the authorities tended to frown upon. Being pulled along by a horse at tremendous speeds around a track with other competitors, some of whom were armed, it was more like the ancient chariot races of old than any kind of civilised sport. Holmes had been thrown clear from his ride on many occasions, but walked away with only minor injuries every single time.

He graduated from bare-knuckle street fighting – which had allowed him to refine and build on his initial baritsu training – to sparring in the fighting pits; emulating the gladiators in their use of nets, swords and spears. Here he would also face ferocious animals and best them, though often not without the scars to prove it.

All the while painfully aware that he was becoming addicted to the thrill, to the rush of excitement, as his other addictions also grew in scale. Moving on from trying every kind of drug he could lay his hands on, to dosing himself with poisons and toxins – increasing the amounts every time. It was true, some of them had made him incredibly ill, had caused him to see things that could not possibly have been there. Yet they also facilitated his efforts to touch the darkness that he had seen during his time with medicine men around the world, in sweat lodges and freezing cold lakes. Increasing his sense that something was on its way, something he had been spared to face.

Something he would need to be prepared for.

Hence what Watson would call his 'self-harm,' he saw as anything but. It was only strengthening him. In the East he had allowed practitioners to cover his body in pins; in Polynesia, he had spent time with a tribe who walked across hot coals and swallowed fire, so as to experience such things himself (taking their exercises to extremes, it had to be said). He had practised the *Okipa* ceremony more times than he cared to recall, allowing his body to be pierced and suspended by hooks and chains, something he continued to do privately upon his return to London.

Unmaking himself, so he could piece himself back together differently.

He hadn't been able to share any of this with Watson, of course. He simply wouldn't have understood. Not the fall, nor what came afterwards: his penchant for standing on the edge of great heights, for instance, and looking down; wondering if he would survive should he step off, but at the last moment pulling back. Submerging himself in water to bring back more memories, trying to recall what had sparked all this; to remember what it was like to *drown*...

So, he had deceived his friend once more, made up a story about defeating Moriarty, sending him spiralling into the waters on his own – a story his friend wrote up practically word for word. A romanticism he hoped Watson might appreciate if he were ever to discover the truth of the situation.

Nor could he disclose *why* he'd returned to London, when his quest was only just beginning. It was true that he'd heard of Moran's exploits and saw a chance to relieve the world of the last of Moriarty's accomplices, thereby making it safe for himself to return – and for Watson, who had not even realised how much danger he'd placed himself in by taking up the case. But there were more weighty matters at stake than the capture of one sniper. The evil had he felt approaching, massing, was about to target his city. He'd heard rumours of a group, a sect, who would offer riches and delights beyond imagination, make people 'vanish' if they stood in their way. More than a criminal organisation: fanatics, dedicated to the virtues of pain. And their leader? Someone known only in whispers as 'the Engineer.' It was this, more than anything, that provoked Holmes to come back – otherwise he might have stayed 'dead.' This, he felt, he remained certain – more certain than anything in his life – was the reason.

This was his purpose, something that would make his existence worthwhile.

Being back, however, he could not hope to mask his presence from Watson – so he had chosen to reveal himself to the doctor, quite literally by peeling off his disguise in front of him. Ever the performer, always the theatrics. By returning to his old line of work, he could also keep an eye on his friend, manoeuvre him away from the terrible conflict when it presented itself. They had taken on cases in the meantime, mere distractions for Holmes – some mind-numbingly so – and he had attempted to continue his own training, conscious that Watson was watching him closely in turn. The doctor had even tried to follow him on a number of occasions, employed the services of others to track his movements. Yet still Holmes had kept Watson mostly in the dark as to what preoccupied him; distanced the man, in fact, believing it would make it easier when the threat reared its ugly head. Easier for Watson to accept Holmes' actual death – for he was aware that at some point he would have to make the sacrifice he'd prepared for at Reichenbach. That battling this new menace might mean the end of him.

That the endgame was almost upon him.

Imagine his excitement when Laurence Cotton contacted him (*My brother has vanished...* Those exact words in the telegram!), and he realised this was the start of it – after nearly two years! The infiltration had begun, and he saw more signs of it with the Spencer, Monroe and Thorndyke disappearances. It was no coincidence that this was happening, that the fate he'd tempted for so long was now tapping him on the shoulder. It was almost time for his curtain call. The pieces were falling into place, being arranged just so. More information, more clues – and he was easily able to uncover the name of the sect: the Order of the Gash. That, and their weapon of choice: some sort of mysterious box. Innocuous as it appeared, it was apparently lethal – though information about it was vague in the extreme. As his obsession grew with these cases, so too did his desire to ready himself. To be prepared. Poison was not enough now, and so he exposed himself to infection as well. He had to be able to face whatever was coming.

And he had to get Watson away from its focus, before it erupted outwards like the fire at the Vulcania. Needed to send him on a fact-finding mission, even though Holmes knew some of the facts already. The information Watson had gathered about Lemarchand was interesting, and filled in some of the blanks – when there was time he would look into the relationship between this aristocrat and Lemarchand's great-grandfather, the origins of the box; or as Watson had called it, the Lament Configuration. The name was apt: certainly, its victims and those left behind had cause to lament.

He had finally shared some of this with Mycroft, when he went to see him after the blaze. If Watson had felt slighted because he was the one Holmes turned to during the 'hiatus,' then the conversation they'd had that day would have made the man livid.

"You are aware, of course, that the business with Monroe is only the tip of the iceberg, brother?"

Mycroft had shifted about in his seat uncomfortably, the leather making terrible squeaking noises. "I had suspected as much," said the large fellow, with a sigh.

"Then you are also aware it is connected to a new 'power' at large in London."

Mycroft didn't answer that one either way, he just asked, "What do you know of it?"

"That it is unlike anything we have ever encountered before. That it is like a virus which spreads, but needs to be stopped. That I will be the one who has to do it. And that it is something I have to see through to the end... alone."

"I understand. How does the good doctor feel about that, pray tell?" He studied Holmes' face. "Ah, you haven't told him – at least not everything. You wish to keep him out of this affair as well."

"To keep him out of it. And keep *you* out of it."

Mycroft nodded sombrely. "For very different reasons, I'll warrant. Little brother, I'm sure I don't need to inform you of the consequences should you fail in your task."

"You do not."

"Then all I can do is wish you luck, and say that you know where I am if you need me."

It was Holmes' turn to nod. "Where you always are, Mycroft."

They'd parted ways, then, and Holmes had spent the next day – after paving the way at the gallery – in a chemically-induced haze (something of his own making), in one of his secret rooms. It was not, for once, intended to prepare him for things to come, but to distract his mind from them.

Now, however, with his friend safely out of the picture, the finale could begin. And it was no coincidence that less than twenty-four hours after he had bid his companion farewell – knowing but not revealing this would, more than likely, be the last time they ever saw each other – he received a telegram asking for a meeting.

It was not from the Order itself, but Holmes knew that in answering it, he would draw closer to his prey. Just as Thorndyke had been lured to his end by the boy – something also on Holmes' agenda; he hadn't lied to Watson about that – he himself would answer one final entreaty to look for a missing person.

A missing reporter by the name of Kline.

CHAPTER THIRTEEN
The Devil's Tavern

THE REQUEST FOR a rendezvous came from Kline's investigative writing partner, J. Summersby. It was not asking for an audience at Baker Street, but to meet with Holmes at a public place. A public house, in fact, called the Prospect of Whitby, which Holmes was well-acquainted with – as he was with all the establishments in London and their history. This was something he commented upon when, having entered the shadowy inn – on the banks of the Thames, in Wapping – he spied Summersby sitting at a table in the far corner.

Holmes purchased a pint of ale to blend in, and joined the reporter.

"Interesting choice of venue," he offered. "Formerly known as the Devil's Tavern, due to its associations with thieves and murderers. It survived the Great Fire of London, only to burn early this century – when it was rebuilt and renamed."

Summersby, wearing a cloth cap and jacket that appeared to be made from the same material, looked up. "You're not so bad at surviving fires yourself, Mr Holmes – not if the rumours are true."

"I don't have the faintest idea what you mean," Holmes

replied and offered the reporter a thin smile. "Any other journalist might have asked to see me at the Old Bell, Fleet Street – but then I doubt very much you frequent the place. There is more than a chance, if you did, that your true identity would be revealed, *Miss* Summersby."

The woman sitting opposite him, who on a cursory glance might well have passed for a man, scowled. "I have never done anything to hide that from anyone," she informed him unfalteringly.

"I must have missed your current attire in the society papers," Holmes immediately rejoined, "incidentally the more usual breeding ground for female reporters."

"At present," spat the woman. "But it will not always be that way."

"Indeed," Holmes concurred. "I have heard of several members of the fair sex – especially in America – reporting on topics that are more usually reserved for the male members of staff. Sports, for example... Forgive me, I did not mean any disrespect. Quite the contrary, Dr Watson and I have become quite enamoured with your work."

She nodded. "As we have always been with yours. In fact, I have studied your methods closely, via Dr Watson's tales. Will he not be joining us?"

"He is occupied with other matters, not entirely unrelated. It is a pity, for he would have liked to have met you, I think. All of you being writers – though obviously yours and Miss Kline's area of expertise leans towards the more factual."

Summersby's brow furrowed. "How did you –"

"Your writing style," said Holmes, waving a hand. "In your missive to me, the hand of a woman is easily detected by the expert eye. And in your accounts, which I am assuming are submitted by post or delivered by a third party? The empathy you both have for your subjects, for example; something that is sadly lacking in that of your male colleagues' work, Josephine."

The woman looked even more perplexed at the mention of her first name, so Holmes continued. "I'm sure you are not unfamiliar with deduction yourself, given your occupation and what you have just told me. Your chosen seat, for example, giving you a full view of the tavern. Quickly, the man off to your right: his business."

Without even hesitating, Summersby replied, "He's in the market for stolen goods, and the man opposite is selling. There, see, he has a sample – a brooch in his palm, though he is doing his best to conceal it. He is dressed in muted clothing, is probably the burglar himself, hoping to pass off the items as quickly as possible – judging from the way he keeps looking around him, looking to the door. The police can't be far behind."

Holmes clapped his hands together, beaming like a proud parent – or teacher. "Bravo! You see, it is instinct – in your nature, Josephine. You take in details, the same as I, and you register their significance. But I would not worry if I were him, the police probably haven't even realised there has been a crime committed yet.

"Now, then. To work. I am assuming you have contacted me about Miss Amelia Kline, a surname she changed from the usual spelling to conceal her German heritage. It is one thing to try and sell your stories when you are a woman, quite another to be of German descent as well. You were both following the case of the detective, Inspector Thorndyke. We met with his wife a few days ago; charming woman."

Summersby agreed. "One of our sources informed us that they'd last seen Thorndyke heading to Limehouse, in the East End."

"London's Chinatown," mused Holmes, rubbing his chin. "I know it well."

"We tossed a coin to decide who would go after him and make enquiries, undercover, naturally –"

"And you lost. Or won, in hindsight," said Holmes.

"She was supposed to leave a message to let me know she was all right, and what progress she was making... but I have received no such communication, Mr Holmes. I thought about venturing in there myself, alone; I could not call upon any of my colleagues, for obvious reasons."

"It would be a sign of weakness," Holmes concluded. "Not to mention giving away your secret."

Summersby pursed her lips, then reluctantly nodded. "But I thought perhaps, as you are also engaged in searching for Thorndyke – unless I am mistaken – then you might be able to help. That perhaps we might explore the area together?"

"Your concern for Miss Kline; would I be right in thinking it extends beyond that of a mere friend?" Holmes sat back and waited for his answer.

"We... we are as close as any two people might be, Mr Holmes, if that's what you mean. I would have thought you, of anyone, would be able to appreciate that."

Holmes said nothing in return.

"We work together and –"

"Not many writers work *so* well together," Holmes observed, flatly. "Let alone write as if they were one. It is a rare thing." He said no more on the subject than that; for there *was* nothing more to say. "I feel it only fair to inform you that I believe Inspector Thorndyke not only to be missing, but deceased. That I believe the same fate befell Mr Monroe before him." He did not mention the others, for Holmes did not know how much the reporter had found out.

Summersby opened her mouth, then closed it again, clenching her jaw. It looked like she was trying not to cry. Then she said, "Miss Kline is not dead. I would... I would know it."

"It is a belief you share with Mrs Thorndyke," Holmes informed her, but did not belabour the point. Summersby was used to confronting the harsh realities that life had to offer, used to dealing with facts – unlike a lot of her contemporaries, who seemed to think it was acceptable to write stories even more fictionalised than Watson's accounts of his exploits. Holmes was not going to lie to the woman. He was aware of the irony; he *had* lied to Watson on many occasions, especially recently.

Summersby's eyes narrowed. "She is not dead," the woman repeated and Holmes gave a curt nod. If nothing else, she was living proof of the existence of faith in lieu of evidence. Perhaps *he* should be taking a leaf out of *her* book?

"I once knew a reporter, a long time ago," said Holmes, "who went undercover to experience what life was like for the dispossessed. But, because he was not like the others – even with his make-up, his grotesque but false twisted lip – he drew attention to himself. It earnt the man money from passers-by, enchanted that he could recite poetry and famous quotes from books… More money, actually, than he was able to earn in your profession, as incredible as that might seem."

"I am familiar with the story, Mr Holmes. The wife reported that she thought him dead, but he was discovered alive, if I remember rightly?"

"That is quite so," Holmes replied. "The point I was making was that he drew attention to himself, *and* it was a novelty. If Miss Kline was to do the same during her covert mission, I am not sure the end results would be quite so favourable."

Summersby fell silent, as if digesting the information, then asked, "Will you help me or not, Mr Holmes?"

"I will indeed, Miss Summersby. I will venture to Limehouse first thing in the morning and –"

"The morning?" Summersby snapped, then looked about to make sure *she* hadn't drawn any undue attention. More softly: "What is wrong with right now? We should –"

Holmes held up a finger. "I am expecting a telegram from my companion, Dr Watson, who is playing his own part in these proceedings, as I have said, albeit from some considerable distance away. Therefore, in the morning, I shall set off and begin my search for Miss Kline. Alone." Miss Summersby opened her mouth to speak, but Holmes cut her off again. "It is a stipulation of securing my services, I'm afraid."

Summersby nodded, and Holmes wished then he would be able to bring her back better news. But, as with the other connected cases, he already knew that the fate of Miss Kline would not have been a pleasant one. It was the same fate he was expecting himself, in the end, when he caught up with the Order – with this Engineer.

A fate, though he used the phrase sparingly if at all, worse than death itself.

CHAPTER FOURTEEN
Chasing the Dragon

SHERLOCK HOLMES DRESSED appropriately for an undercover assignment on the streets of Limehouse; in ragged clothing, as dishevelled as possible.

It did not matter that he was heading out early in the morning to begin his search, for the people who sought out the secrets of this place did so at all hours of the day – many did not even realise what hour of day it was, once they had tasted the 'delights' it had to offer. Holmes would be doing so himself soon enough, to build trust and to follow whatever leads there might be.

All of which would take time, he realised. He had some contacts already in the area, and called upon those to begin with, asking if any of them had seen a 'slight gentleman, boyish-looking, who seemed out of place.' The trail led him to one opium den after another, where he partook of the drug – having already built up a resistance to it. Holmes was beyond such petty triflings, was now used to much stronger fare than he could find inside those pipes, laying beside others in basements or crowded lodgings, wrapped in blankets and staring out into space.

Holmes observed the comings and goings of those who traded in such pleasures; caught whispers, half-heard rumours and tall tales. It was clear to him when he overheard mention of the Order that he was in the right place. Perhaps it was their plan to ensure that the whole of London was addicted to these substances? Maybe that was their primary form of control?

It was on the second day – and after finally answering Watson's telegram, expressly forbidding him to take any action – that he grew nearer to his enemy. He had heard talk of a tea shop owned by someone called Kircher. A place where one might go to speak to a representative of a new faction that was making waves in the area – indeed, across London.

A recruitment office, by any other name.

Once there, Holmes made discreet enquiries – and was offered food and drink while he waited for his answers. It was clearly laced with something; an ingredient not even he was familiar with, but he was confident that his body could endure.

He was wrong. It began working on him almost immediately, dulling his senses, leaving him incapable of defending himself when he was dragged roughly from that place and deposited in the back of a cart. He did not know whether they had seen through his ruse, or they were just being cautious, but in the end it did not make much difference. He slipped in and out of consciousness, and when he woke for the final time, he was being manhandled through a dark passage. No, more of a tunnel; underground. For there, ahead of them, was an abandoned rail carriage, dimly lit. Was this where the Order ran things from? Holmes wondered. But there seemed to be only one solitary figure inside, sitting with a blanket wrapped around itself.

Holmes was shoved through the door and deposited unceremoniously on the floor in front of the figure, who rose now, still clutching the blanket. Blinking, Holmes looked up and stared into the cool blue eyes of a bearded man dressed in rags. It had to be the vagabond Mrs Spencer had described: able to hide in plain sight amongst the lost and forgotten, the perfect place to enlist more like him.

"Welcome," said the man, taking a step towards Holmes.

"Wh-where..."

"Where are you? I hardly think that important, do you? You are where you *need* to be. Where you always wanted to be, Mr Sherlock Holmes."

So they knew who he was, in spite of his efforts. He did not ask who this man was, because he already had a clue to this part of the puzzle and thought he would return the favour.

"And you... you are the Engineer," stated Holmes.

The man grinned through his filthy matted beard, revealing rotten teeth. Then he patted his chest with a gloved hand and shook his head. "You flatter me."

Not the Engineer. Then who? Kircher? Holmes attempted to stand, but only got as far as one knee.

"I," said the man, "am merely a guardian."

Was that what they called the officers in this Order of the Gash? Holmes wondered. A title for the higher-ranking soldiers? "You... you are the one who cleans up," Holmes managed. "Afterwards."

The man cocked his head. "In a manner of speaking. I also broker deals."

Definitely high up in the organisation. A second-in-command, then?

"I can see you want to ask me. So ask," said the man, now only a few feet away from Holmes.

"Inspector Thorndyke...?"

The derelict shook his head.

"Miss Kline...?"

Another shake of the head. "They made their own bargains, Mr Holmes. Just as you will make yours."

Holmes looked up at the man and sneered. "The boy?"

The bearded fellow paused; then he retreated to the dark

recesses of the carriage. But he returned, bringing a child with dark, tousled hair. The vagabond was holding his hand, ushering him forwards. The child stared at Holmes, terrified. "All links in the chain," said the man, "and at the other end –"

"A hook," Holmes finished for him. Like a fish on a line, his investigation had led him inexorably to this place. "Let... let him go," Holmes demanded.

"That was always our intention," said the man, spittle flecking his beard. "We are just waiting for... Ah, here she is."

There was the sound of a scuffle behind him, and Holmes looked over his shoulder to see Josephine Summersby being jostled into the carriage. Perhaps she'd been following him, in which case Holmes applauded both her obstinacy and her stealth – nevertheless, she'd still been caught. What was the Order going to do to her? That was the question. One which was answered fairly swiftly.

The tramp let the orphan boy go, shoving him in the direction of Miss Summersby. "There is no room here for innocents," he said.

The lad ran past Holmes and into the waiting arms of the reporter. She gathered him up, looking over to Holmes questioningly – wanting to know what had happened to her partner. "That is the bargain: we have taken something from you, and give you something in return." It was all she needed to know for the tears to break free. Holmes thought for a moment she was going to abandon the frightened boy and fly at the men on either side of her, but instead she shook her head in resignation. The risk to the child would be too great. It would have been hopeless anyway.

"You bastards!" she shouted instead.

"Take the boy and leave us," the bearded man said, bluntly. She didn't really have a choice, because again Miss Summersby was being 'escorted' out by the men in this guardian's employ. "I have business to conclude with Mr Holmes."

Holmes realised that even if the reporter did know the whereabouts of this place, even if she returned with all of Scotland Yard in tow, there would be nothing more here than there was in the deserted gallery. Not even receipts as evidence. The vagabond had been right when he said that their location was not important.

But what happened next was.

The bearded man crouched, so that he was on a level with Holmes – commanding his attention. The detective sniffed the air, but could smell nothing of the vanilla that had surrounded the deaths, from Cotton to Monroe. No, this man simply smelt of decay, and at these close quarters Holmes couldn't help but notice living things in the fellow's beard.

"This has all happened before, many times," said the man absently. "And it will do so again... I know what it is you really hunger for."

Holmes had a feeling he knew that about most men.

"It is not pleasures of the flesh, like so many, but... knowledge. Matters of life and death, and everything in between." The man fumbled about inside his pockets, and when he brought his hand out he was holding something.

Holmes' first glimpse of the Lament Configuration was nothing short of magical. A revelation. Like the man's speech, the eloquent beauty of it was at odds with everything about the vagrant. Though the light was poor in this place, the gold shone brightly from every surface of the lacquered box. And the vagabond seemed to know exactly which way to tilt and turn it to entice.

Memories raced through Holmes' mind as the light flashed across his eyes. Memories of childhood rivalry with Mycroft, of a desire to discover how things worked: mechanical devices like wind-up toys; cause and effect; the world around him, but also the people in it. Now the Falls, the massive body of water rushing up to meet him as he tumbled down with Moriarty; as the man fell away from his grasp and Holmes thought he saw something... Then nothing: only blackness. He wasn't sure, but he thought he let out a yell at this point.

The vagabond patted the box with his other hand, running filthy nails over the surface. Drawing attention to the details: the tiny shapes in black etched into the gold; one side with a wheel in its centre, another with a square – both with matching twins on the opposite sides to them; two more with smaller circles in the centre, the patterns spreading out almost into leaf-like shapes. It captivated Holmes – and he didn't think he'd ever wanted anything so badly in his whole life.

"Inside, you will find the answers you seek," promised the man.

Holmes squeezed his eyes shut, snapping out of the trance. In a way, Watson had been right. This thing, and its owner – if indeed it had an owner – could beguile even the strongest of minds. The *did* use mesmerism as part of their sideshow act. "Like Cotton and Spencer found their answers? Like Monroe, Thorndyke and Kline? And how many others?" This box brought death, not answers – though some theologians would argue they were one and the same. A murder weapon and yet not.

"Each one is taken on its own merits," the guardian replied. "Yours... is a special case, Mr Holmes."

The detective surprised himself then by reaching out to snatch at the box. He did not really know why, perhaps simply to get it away from here – to ensure that this weapon (for what else could it be?) was never again used to harm anyone. The Lament Configuration was pulled away from him, though, and he knew his motivation had nothing to do with any of that. He simply *wanted* it; wanted to feel it, to solve it – to uncover its mysteries, whatever the repercussions.

Again, he surprised himself by whispering, "*Please...*" Weak in more than just physicality.

"What is it worth to you?" asked the man with piercing blue eyes.

Holmes still had some money on him that he hadn't yet spent on intoxicants, which he began dragging out of his pockets and spilling onto the floor.

The vagabond laughed.

"I have more," Holmes told him. "If you just let me –"

"No need. This," said the man, bending to pick up the money, "is exactly the amount I had in mind. Take the box, it is yours." He handed Holmes Lemarchand's puzzle – sending a crackle of electricity through his entire body and sobering him up a little. For long moments Holmes just held the thing, staring at it. Then he looked up and realised that the vagabond was gone, leaving a parting line that echoed around the empty carriage. "It always has been."

Holmes staggered to his feet, attempting to trace where the voice was coming from. There were no men behind him, so he lurched to the door and out through it. He glimpsed a shadow moving *through* the shadows, exiting by means of another door. Holmes followed, finding a set of steps that he began up. "Wait!" he shouted after the vagabond, knowing how foolish he had been to let his quarry go like that; so focussed on the box was he.

Rising, rising, thinking he would never reach the top – and then he did; falling out through a door and into the fading evening light.

Into a deserted alleyway. Holmes stumbled, striking the opposite wall and almost losing his grasp on the box. "Wait!" he called out again. Then he saw the vagabond, heading towards the mouth of the street – blanket behind him still flapping like a cape – and, as best he could, Holmes gave chase.

The man did not appear to be in a hurry, and the detective – carrying his precious charge in both hands so that he would not drop it – was beginning to catch up. So close, so close.

Soon he was only inches away from him, near enough in fact for Holmes to take one hand off the box and reach out with it.

There were more questions, things the box could not answer for him: like who was the Engineer? What did the Order have in mind for his city – for the world?

Holmes' fingers brushed against the blanket, almost upon the man... when suddenly he was a man no more. The cape spread wide, so that it more accurately resembled a pair of wings. In the blink of an eye, they had *become* wings; huge and leathery, with spines running the length of them between flaps. Holmes stopped in his tracks, falling backwards to the ground. He could do nothing as the vagabond that had been standing before him a few moments ago turned, and looked at him with the head of some kind of mythical beast. A dragon, just like those he'd seen painted on so many signs in this part of London – except there was not a scrap of flesh on the thing. Flapping and flapping, rising into the sky...

The detective lay there and observed its passage into the darkening sky, into the clouds; understanding that what he had just witnessed could not be real. That it was a combination of whatever had been put in his food and drink, and the vagabond's skilful hypnotism – yet quivering nonetheless.

In any event, the keeper of the box had struck a bargain with him. Holmes looked down at what he was still holding so close to his body. The shiny box that was now his and his alone.

A deal had indeed been brokered, and Holmes knew that he had another piece of the puzzle. That he had a new task now, a new search for secrets.

And his work had only just begun.

CHAPTER FIFTEEN
The Box. You Have Opened It...

HOLMES DID NOT take the Lament Configuration away with him immediately to begin his labours.

For one thing, he had to be certain that the effects of the drugs he'd been exposed to had worn off; no more dragons taking to the skies! (Although what was it Mrs Spencer had said? About the flapping of wings?). For another, he realised, as with any worthy undertaking, that preparation was all. The detective had already seen to his affairs – some time ago, actually; indeed, little had needed altering since he had disappeared the first time around. That was not the issue. He needed somewhere private to conduct his business, somewhere he absolutely would not be disturbed. That was clearly not Baker Street – for, apart from Mrs Hudson's attentions, he was bound to have been contacted by Miss Summersby and probably also Watson, angry that he had not received further instructions... and was not likely to. Holmes hoped that, in the absence of a missive, Watson would return home in due course – by which time this episode would have reached a conclusion one way or another.

Should he construct some sort of shrine, as Monroe had? It hardly seemed necessary given that he had been sought out by the Order for attention. Moreover, Holmes was not about to murder someone in a bizarre ritual just to aid in the solving of a puzzle. He still had no idea what would happen should he be successful, but he still felt sure it was connected with his amazing survival at the Falls. More certain than ever now, in fact, after the vagabond had forced him to relive those moments with Moriarty. He had seen these kinds of boxes before. Though obviously inspired by Chinese tradition, this one seemed unique: the Frenchman's touch, probably. What lay inside such devices usually were messages, codes. A door, as Lemarchand's ancestor had called it in his conversation with Watson – figuratively of course. Answers, definitely.

Death?

Well, there was only one way to know for certain, and he had drawn out the preamble long enough.

No elaborate shrine then, so perhaps the candles – following Francis Cotton's lead, as unsettling as that thought might be. It hadn't taken any of those men long to complete their objective, so he did not anticipate it would be a lengthy process for him either. Certainly not as long as it did eventually take him in the end, sitting in that room he had paid a lot of money for – drawn from a private account only he knew about and had access to (not even Mycroft was aware of its existence).

At no point in his history of drug and poison-taking, of sweat lodges and tests of endurance, did he lose track of time in the same way that he had when he was trying to solve the Lament Configuration: cross-legged and determined. He did not partake of food or drink; did not talk to another soul while he was concentrating all his efforts on the box. The only evidence of the passage of time was the thick candles slowly burning down.

Yet it did not want to yield to him. As hard as he might try to crack the thing open, it appeared at certain points impenetrable, which frustrated him no end. Holmes had always prided himself on being able to see solutions to problems that others could not, but here was a puzzle that had been deciphered by a philanderer, a military man, a young hedonistic club owner (and murderer, let us not forget), a corrupt policeman and a reporter. All had died for their trouble, but far from deterring him this was just another spur. He had to discover the reason why, and how they could simply have vanished like that from locked rooms and in front of watchful eyes.

It did not matter that there was no audience to see the trick this time, *he* would know. He would have the *satisfaction* of knowing. And although he couldn't help thinking about those who had been left behind, that they would never have an inkling about what had happened – and that included Watson – it would not stop him from getting to the truth.

From finding out who the Order really were.

Who the Engineer really was.

So he continued. Drenched in sweat from his duel, watching the box slip through his fingers more than once – almost dropping it (though much later he was tempted to try to just smash open the thing to get to its marrow... what stopped him was the knowledge that very often puzzle boxes like these had mechanisms that would destroy what was inside if triggered by, say, a forced entry – besides, he was Sherlock Holmes! He shouldn't *need* to break into it!).

On and on, turning the box over in his fingers, even though a little voice in his head was screaming at him to put it down and step away. The longing he had felt to touch its surfaces gave way eventually to a sort of hatred that they would not co-operate with his explorations; the other side of love... not that Holmes was overly-familiar with these sorts of emotions. This was probably the closest he would ever come to being seduced by a wayward mistress – for, regardless of what others might think of his 'relationship' with Irene Adler, there had been nothing sexual about it at all. He would never have even entertained the notion... But here and now, this box, it was as tantalising a prospect as had ever entered his sphere of influence.

Holmes twisted the thing, desperate for something to give – but nothing ever did. It was so infuriating, he thought at one point he might be going mad. He swore – something he was not prone to do – and it sounded incredibly odd inside that confined space, being thrown back at him with his own voice. He was beginning to think there actually was no way inside and all this had been for nothing. It wasn't the box that was the key, but the man who had called himself its protector – someone who could apparently move freely through walls, fly through closed windows without making a sound and kill indiscriminately.

But surely, if he had wanted Holmes dead, wouldn't the vagabond have murdered him back there in that alleyway, when he had the chance? There was nothing to stop him – indeed, Holmes was not in a fit state himself to prevent it. Where was the sport in that, though? Perhaps the real sport was this game of cat and mouse he'd allowed himself to be a part of, and the final insult: that there *was* no way inside the box! He refused to believe that and carried on; continued until his fingers and thumbs were sore with the rubbing. He would have carried on until they bled, he felt sure, yet in the end that was not called for and the chink in the armour of the thing had presented itself at last. Just as he was considering giving up.

The click was just as loud as his curses had been. And it was only now that some part of his mind was vaguely aware of a bell tolling somewhere. Was it Sunday already? Had he been at this for so long? He brushed aside the thoughts and continued on with the box, now that he had been given a sign.

Now that he had taken this first step.

He concentrated on the ornate device, eyes straining, fingers working faster than ever, gambling over the exterior in an attempt to make that chink wider. There was another click, louder even than the first, and the tolling of the bell came closer

– not that Holmes registered this fact. He was too consumed with finishing this, now that he had made such progress so quickly. Then –

Nothing.

If he had been expecting it to be easy from this point on then – as he had been from the beginning – Holmes would find himself very much mistaken. No more clicking, no mechanical whirring like he used to hear in those toys as a child. After waiting a moment or two, all the time he was willing to spare, he shook the box – immediately regretting it; hoping he hadn't halted the process that had obviously commenced inside. To have come so far, only to have it snatched away – and know that it was your fault, as well – would be pure torture indeed.

He was shocked, therefore, when the box tingled – and then moved. So shocked he almost dropped the thing. It appeared that the tipping point had been reached and the box was taking over, doing the rest of the work for him. A corner rose at the top, clanking round so that it was now at a peculiar angle, the edges of it so sharp that if he hadn't withdrawn his fingers quickly, they would have been shredded.

One of the golden wheels, the one he had spent so much time caressing with his thumb, tracing its circle over and over, was starting to spin of its own volition, slowly to begin with, then faster the closer it came to its zenith. More changes followed, so that the box no longer *was* a box; sides no longer what you could call square. Sections rising and falling in a way he would never have been able to calculate, let alone replicate. Each time they did, he was drawn in to the tantalising sights between the spaces, like a preview of events yet to unfold. Each one a glimpse into the object's heart, revealing something much older than the box itself. Something that had existed forever, looking, searching – just as he had been on his travels. For a way out, a way *through*.

Though Watson had not gone into vast amounts of detail

in his telegram to Holmes, some of the words the madman Lemarchand had uttered now stood out:

Great-grandfather. Tricked. Made the box. Made it easy for them. To control...

To control what?

But all thoughts about that vanished when he heard the music. A lyrical tinkling theme emanating from the Configuration, similar to the kind one might find in a jewellery box when opened – a ballerina rising to greet the owner and twirling for their amusement. No such dancer appeared here.

Instead, the movements of the Configuration itself speeded up: contradicting the slow music that was being played. Holmes frowned, peering into the box once more. Then came the wind, a sudden gust in a place that had no windows; he'd made sure of that for privacy's sake. It was so abrupt and so violent, it blew out all the candles. Yet he could still see...

Shafts of blue light had found their way in from somewhere, spearing the room like a magician stabbing swords into a cabinet.

The room was shaking, dislodging dust from the rafters and walls. Walls that were threatening to cave in and flatten him where he sat. The one behind Holmes shook the most forcefully. He could hear the brickwork parting, being rent asunder. But not until he heard the footsteps at his rear as well did he finally turn to see that gap in the wall, and what had issued forth from it.

His mind was racing now. How could this be? He had examined every inch of this place, this room. There were no secret compartments, as in Monroe's quarters. There was nothing on the other side of that wall, save for empty space, that looked down upon yet another quiet alleyway. It was the same as Cotton's attic room, nothing there. Except there was now... Beyond the hole that had been created was something else; some*where* else. Dusty corridors that looked a little like those behind Monroe's secret doorway, or in the underground tunnels he'd been taken to, but these shouldn't – *couldn't possibly* – exist.

All he was doing was delaying taking in the quartet of figures he'd only glanced at briefly thus far. Delaying because of their strangeness, their *hideousness* if he was being truthful with himself. Regardless of the light, there were parts of them that were still in shadow, and for that Holmes was grateful. The first that he clapped eyes on was made of rotting flesh. No, more than that: diseased. Every inch of the 'man' that could be seen – for he was only wearing what appeared to be a dark loincloth, like some sort of savage abroad – was made up of yellow pustules and skin that was being eaten away to reveal the creamy bone beneath. His balding scalp – which was populated by tufts of hair – was stretched tight over his skull, so tight that the eyes bulged from their sockets, weeping thick, gelatinous liquid. He had no nose to speak of, just two ragged holes where one should have been – from which mucus bubbled and spilled as he breathed. He was thin, like some sort of plague victim – though unlike anything Holmes had ever exposed himself to – and when he coughed, blood appeared at the corners of his mouth. He saw Holmes pulling a face at this, and the man grinned, revealing two rows of stumpy yellow teeth.

Next to him was a female, her skin as pale as corpse-flesh – all except for her mouth which was ruby red, and her eyes which were almost totally blue. At first glance it looked very much like her hair had been gathered up in the Victorian style, to a shock of curls on top of her head – running down the back in ringlets; but Holmes swiftly identified these as strips of that alabaster flesh, sheared from the top of her head and intermingled with razor-sharp metal coils. The necklace she was wearing was also made of metal, stitched into the skin and running down to a tight, black corset that was cinched in at the middle and laced up with what looked like pieces of red gut, the crimson tendrils poking out here and there. The bottom half of her attire was a flowing leather skirt – except there were ridged flaps running down the length of it that exposed the ruined skin of her legs, again woven into the material. She held something in her right hand, also coiled – until she let the majority of this fall, to reveal a long whip which snaked to the floor. Along its length were tiny fins of metal and it forked out into three ends, each of which had lethal-looked spikes attached – designed for raking the flesh – that incredibly moved of their own accord. This one, he could not help thinking as he gazed at her, would not have looked out of place at one of the Vulcania's private parties...

The third figure was larger, and well muscled – arms bared in the vest-like top he was wearing, which ran down to a pair of leather britches. There were slits in the vest, showing that the same kind of painful attention had been lavished upon his torso: sore-looking cuts, opened wider by metal stitches, skin peeled back to show the wet underside. In contrast to the other two his colouring was healthier, pinker, but with more than the usual dash of redness – blood being pumped around that huge body by thick, wormy veins. His hands were gloved, but between each finger a blade had been inserted, which gave them the appearance of very short claws. It was the thing's head that caused Holmes to inhale sharply, however, for it was simply a lump of bony flesh perched atop its neck. The creature had no features – no eyes, no nose or mouth – that he could discern, just something that looked like bent fingers and a thumb; it was almost as if the entire head had been squashed and then moulded to more closely resemble a fist. As if a potter had fashioned something monstrous out of the clay on his wheel.

As much as the corridor behind them defied the laws of physics, so did these visions defy the laws of nature. Nothing could have survived the butchery that had been done to them and lived. Yet here they were, lingering, waiting for the last of their number to step forward. This was their leader, no doubt about it. For he had a commanding air about him, almost gliding forward as if on a cushion of air – his feet not visible beneath the long frock-like vestments that he wore. There was nothing effeminate about this; far from it. If anything, they looked like a priest's cassock or a monk's habit. Dark clothing covered him up to his neck and down along his arms. Apart from a 'V' shaped hole at the front baring his scarified chest, jagged cuts running this way and that. His head was the same, slashed at in every direction, yet he proudly wore the instruments that had almost certainly caused his wounds. His face and shaved head had shards of glass embedded in them at regular intervals: at his cheeks, his chin, his forehead – above eyes that were devoid of any whites – and at his temples, then all over his crown... Actually, it looked like he was wearing those triangular pieces of glass *as* some kind of crown; as if he was some sort of king of blood. Larger pieces of glass hung from a belt that encircled his waist, attached by more of that red gut used in the female's corset.

The effect, on the whole, was repugnant – and yet Holmes could not tear his eyes from the scene. He had somehow shifted around to face them, though he did not remember doing so. His mouth was dry and he was having trouble swallowing, let alone speaking – otherwise he might have asked, as he did with the vagabond, who they were. But then he knew that already, did he not.

This was the real Order of the Gash. Or at least part of it. Holmes blinked a few times before rubbing his eyes. Like the dragon, this was just an illusion, surely? A tiny portion of that drug lodged somewhere, working harder than he ever had to solve Lemarchand's puzzle? Something conjured up from the depths of his mind, his subconscious (though he doubted that anything this outlandish could ever have originated from his brain)? Or a product of the lack of sleep, lack of food and water? No matter how much training he had endured, there was still a chance that –

"The box," said their leader, breaking into his thoughts and pointing to the Lament Configuration on the floor. "You have opened it. We were summoned." His voice was deep yet rasping, perhaps a consequence of the shards of glass protruding from his throat.

Holmes could do nothing but stare.

The leader looked from him to his companions, then back again. "Do you understand?"

The detective found himself nodding like a child.

"Then you know who we are." This came not from the leader, but the one who looked ravaged by the plague; his voice was thin and reedy. "What will happen next."

"The exquisite suffering that awaits you," the female added, licking her lips.

"An... answers," Holmes said at last, finding his voice. "I was told I'd find answers."

"And indeed you will," replied their leader. "In time. But first..." He reached for one of the shards at his belt, detaching it in one fluid movement. There was no handle to the thing, but he held it anyway, ignoring – or perhaps relishing – the pain of the jagged edges. It looked for all the world like he was holding a dagger.

Holmes was beginning to regret the fact he did not have a weapon himself. Watson was forever chastising him for forgetting to bring along a pistol when entering dangerous situations. But then, what kind of weapon could harm these beings? What could he do to them that hadn't already been done – and savoured?

Was he about to go through what Cotton and the rest had endured? If so, then how would he ever discover the truth? How could there possibly be answers beyond death?

He'd thought himself dead before, though, hadn't he? Yet he had survived. He would survive this as well, he told himself. Holding up his hand he said, "Wait! The Engineer. Is that you?"

He was directing his question at the figure who'd been despoiled by glass.

The leader looked about him at the others; it was almost as if they were in silent communion. When he turned back to Holmes, his lip was curled. "What do you know of him?"

"I... I was told he was in charge of the Order."

The creature smiled, revealing more of his teeth. Or rather the wedges of glass that his teeth had been replaced with, rammed into the gums with considerable force. "In charge?" The concept seemed amusing to him.

"If... if that isn't you, then I wish to speak to him."

"You are in no position to demand anything," said the female and cracked her whip. "Except perhaps an end to your torment – though it will never come."

"I want to know what your plans are for my city." Holmes was rising, his limbs stiff from being in one position for too long.

"Plans?" the leader said, bewildered.

"What you are going to do to the people, to the world."

"The same as we have always done, to those who call us," the diseased one of their number broke in. "We shall play."

Watson's telegram returned to haunt Holmes.

We are all just... toys.

In spite of his terror, and regardless of the fact he was alone, Holmes stood straight and stiff-backed. "Then I, sir," he said, with the same determination in his voice he'd mustered to bring these unfathomable individuals here in the first place, "will have to stop you."

At this, the leader laughed. "*You*... will stop *us*?"

Holmes nodded. "I see no other way."

"Enough of this," said the impatient female. "Let us begin."

But already Holmes was ducking sideways, out of reach of the leader and his dagger. The largest of their number blocked his way to the door, somehow moving faster than Holmes could ever have imagined. Yet, without hesitation, the detective struck him several blows that should have incapacitated anyone, no matter what their size. The muscled creature simply stood there, immobile, somehow regarding his tiny prey. Holmes might as well have been punching stone.

He backed off, all too aware of the blades at this one's knuckles and how a blow in return would probably cleave him in two. He'd taken perhaps three steps when something tore down his bare back, opening it up in three places. The ends of the female's whip, which continued even now to rake his flesh. He felt the pain – *of course* he did! – but seconds after the initial shock, he was blocking it out. He'd trained for this.

Holmes ducked and rolled out of the whip's reach. When he righted himself, he was aware of someone behind him – reaching around to grab him. He looked down to see diseased hands on his chest, and where they touched his skin that too was becoming infected. "Why do you fight it?" whispered the plague creature. "There are such sights waiting for you." Holmes wrestled out of his grip, clutching his chest. It felt like it was on fire, a rash spreading quickly across his flesh.

Then came the chains and the hooks. From out of nowhere they sprang, left and right. Holmes managed to avoid a couple of them, but one tore into his forearm, another bit into his thigh. Again, he blocked out the pain – from these and the infection that was worming its way towards his heart. But he was held fast, being held for one reason and one reason only.

Their leader floated towards him, the glass blade still in his hand. He'd had to wait while the others had their fun, but now it was his turn. He ran his tongue up the tip of the dagger, a final ritual before bringing it into play. Next he held it aloft and was just about to bring it down into Holmes, when a loud bang interrupted him.

All eyes in the room turned to look in the direction of the doorway. There, standing in the entrance, was Dr John Watson, pistol in hand – still aimed at the ceiling where he'd fired. It was only now, apparently, when everything was still, that Holmes' best friend in the world was able to take in the four figures properly – and his face soured. Nevertheless, the gun came down, levelled at them, and he said, "R-release him! Right now!"

Their leader sneered.

Then all Hell broke lose...

PART THREE

Dr John Watson & Sherlock Holmes

CHAPTER SIXTEEN
In Hell

I was in Hell.

That's what it felt like to me. Hanging there in that chamber, no awareness of the passage of time, waking occasionally then drifting off again in a drug-induced slumber. The dreams came to me again, of the battlefield, of Mary. I think I screamed, but who would hear me in such a Godforsaken place? Who would hear me above the noise of the other inmates?

I was beginning to think I had been forgotten about when Malahide finally visited me.

He said nothing, asked nothing. He merely set about his tortures. I thought I had experienced pain, thought I had seen it inflicted upon others, but this man was an expert. He knew just which nerve endings to concentrate on, just how far to push me before I blacked out. I did not give *him* the satisfaction of screaming once, though!

By the time he was finished with that first session, I realised, with dawning horror, that he was only just getting started. There would be more horrendous brutality to come, and by the time he was finished I would be no better off than those dregs of humanity out there. No better off than Lemarchand, begging for a blade so that he could end his own suffering – little realising that it was only just beginning. I thought about those events a lot during my time down there in the dark, but that just seemed like a dream as well.

Or a nightmare, to be more precise.

The vampire man who'd fed off Simon, standing there, steaming, with no skin. Not even Poe could have conceived of such a thing, with his imagination. Even now, penning these words, it seems a preposterous thing to ask anyone to accept. They would think that Malahide had been right to lock me up.

When he'd left, I drifted off again – not because of the drugs, for their effect had waned some time ago, but because of what I had endured at Malahide's hands. More dreams; faces flashing before my eyes: childhood friends, tutors at medical school I had not seen in an age... Mary, looking the same as she had the day I met her – so, so beautiful. And Holmes, always Holmes. It was the one thing I regretted most then, thinking I would never see him again: not having made more of an effort to get to the bottom of what was troubling him so; what was making him act in such a strange way.

Then suddenly there was someone else in the room with me. "H-Holmes?" I spluttered, only half awake. The figure was in shadow, walking towards me – then he lit one of the lamps nearby, giving me a good look at his face.

It was only at this point that I realised my mistake. "H... Henri?"

Either I looked confused, or he was just sickened by the state of my body, but he shook his head sadly and said, "Let me get you out of those chains, *monsieur*."

I was in no fit state to take much of it in at the time; in fact I thought, for a moment, that he was a ghost – and immediately as I did so, I heard Holmes' voice in my head telling me there was no such thing. Malahide had as good as told me this man was dead, yet here he was, dressed as an orderly, undoing my shackles, having to hold me up as I dropped forward into his arms. "I am only sorry I could not come sooner, but I had to choose my moment carefully," Henri told me, handing me my own pair of orderly pyjamas, which he then had to help me get into. "Are you able to walk?"

I nodded, but even as I was trying to take a step or two, I stumbled and had to lean on Henri. "Just give me a moment," I said. While he did, he told me more about what had happened. Malahide had him thrown out not long after my departure, leaving him beaten on some street corner in Paris.

"I am like you, I'm afraid, Dr Lane – I see too much," he said.

"Watson," I breathed. "My name is Dr Watson."

He went on to explain that once he had recovered sufficiently to return, he waited until the shift change and got in through one of the back doors, near the kitchens which he occasionally helped out in. "I may not have been here long, but I know my way around it... how you say, outside in?"

I couldn't help but chuckle at that.

"But how did you know about *this* place?" I asked.

"I've had my suspicions for a while. You see I also listen as well as watch. And I read..." He fished something out of his pocket, and I could just about see that they were the notes I had made when talking to Lemarchand back in the dayroom. Henri had patched them together and worked it all out – quite the little detective. "I had observed Gerard putting a key away on occasion when he was coming out of the lift. I knew it led somewhere else. So I... borrowed it from him." Henri laughed. "He did not care for the way I asked. But I had no idea *you* were down here."

"It's a very long story," I said, as we finally got going – Henri half-carrying me out into the corridor.

Hearing a sound, I looked up to see the lift doors at the far end opening. Inside were Malahide, the orderly who had looked like a military-type – probably the only other person who had access to this place – and Gerard, rubbing the back of his head. Henri had not done such a good a job of 'persuasion' as he thought, and the man had lost no time in alerting his boss. If only we had not dawdled to wait for me to get my bearings.

"Just what do you think you are doing?" Malahide said. "I thought I had made my position very clear, Henri. *Your* post here has been terminated, and so will you be in a moment."

"Get behind me, Doctor," said Henri, but I refused to let him shield me. As Gerard and the soldier orderly advanced, I raised my fists, though I felt as weak as a kitten.

Gerard went straight for my new friend, obviously wanting to settle the score. But he was not as fit as he thought, and Henri was easily able to sidestep the attack, swinging the man around and depositing him on the floor. The other orderly changed direction and lunged at Henri as well, punching him in the stomach and doubling him over. Gerard was rising and making to join in, but I tripped him up and he slid down the corridor towards Malahide, who was keeping well back, letting his troops do the work.

It was Henri's turn to be swung now, as the soldier orderly flung him around and into the wall. I went over to him as fast as I was able. "Are you all right?" He gave a resigned nod.

There was a lull in the fighting as the orderly helped Gerard up.

"Finish this!" ordered Malahide.

I was about to stand up, to try and protect Henri, when he gripped my arm. "*Non*," he said. "Wait."

"Wait... wait for what?"

He grinned. "You were not the only one I freed, Dr Watson." Then Henri banged on the nearest cell door, rousing the person inside. There was more banging and clattering as Malahide and his cronies looked about them. The inmates were coming to their dungeon doors and flinging them open, experiencing freedom for the first time in... well, for some of them it must have been years. I was a little concerned that they would not be able to tell who their true enemies were, that they might mistake us for jailers, but I did not have to worry. Even the ones who had been operated on, experimented upon, recognised the face of the man who had done all this to them.

At first the three men ahead of us didn't seem too bothered. The inmates were not that strong, they could handle them. But there were too many, and rage was fuelling their actions. They swarmed over Gerard and the other orderly, savaging them like animals. Malahide tried to run, but one of them leapt on his back, dragging him to the ground.

Only now was Henri getting to his feet, helping me up as well. "Keep to the sides," he told me, and we started walking gingerly. Once I stopped, began to move to try and help their prey – nobody deserved this, not even them – but Henri held me back and shook his head. At the end of the corridor, as we were about to get into the lift, I saw Malahide reaching up with one hand. "Help me!" he was screaming. "For God's sake – help!"

"He has chosen his side," Henri intoned, "and it is not with God." He pulled me into the lift and closed the doors, setting the thing in motion. Nothing was said as we reached the upper level; I don't suppose anything needed saying really. Before we got out, though, Henri turned to me and whispered, "Walk as if you work here, and no-one will notice. Do you think you can manage that, just for a little while?" I nodded. "We are going out of the front this time."

So that's exactly what we did. I have to say we didn't see that many members of staff on our way, and those we did were busy with their own duties. Once we were outside (and I was surprised to see daylight; even more surprised to learn later that I had only been held captive a day or so), Henri told me that he had a cab tethered not far away – something else he had 'borrowed'. "Why didn't you just go to the authorities?" I asked.

"They would not have believed me," he replied. "The 'good'

doctor has friends in high places. Besides, to the outside world this appears to be a respectable place. It is what you cannot see that is not."

"What's kept below," I said, recalling Lemarchand's words. "Beneath."

Henri nodded firmly.

"Well, they'll believe *me*," I assured him. "I have friends in high places, too. I'll explain on the way back."

Which I did, telling him all about myself and Sherlock Holmes, what I was doing there and what I had seen – or thought I had seen – the night of my capture. When I had finished, Henri remained quiet; I could see he was wrestling with it all. But he did not call me a madman, did not say I'd imagined it or that it was something Malahide had done to me, he just nodded again slowly.

When we returned to town, to the hotel – ignoring the strange looks we drew because of how we were dressed – I sent a telegram to someone we knew in the French government; another person Holmes had done a favour for, immediately prior to his tangle with Moriarty a few years ago. The Institute and those who ran it would now come under very close scrutiny, I felt sure. Once I had cleaned myself up a little, I treated Henri to the biggest slap-up dinner imaginable – including a steak he insisted they almost cremate – and took great delight in seeing him eat. My appetite was yet to return, sadly.

"I'll be leaving for England on the first available steam ship," I said to the man, who was now wearing one of my suits, the tie done up loosely at the collar because he wasn't used to wearing one. "Why don't you come with me, Henri?"

I thought he was going to choke on his mushrooms. Henri waved his hand until his last mouthful had gone down. "That is a very kind offer, Dr Watson – but I must decline. I think I need to be very far away from what is happening back in London with your friend. If it is not too late, that is."

I thought for a moment he was talking about Holmes, for I had told him about the conversation between the aristocrat and Malahide, the name that had been mentioned. Indeed, Holmes had still not been in contact with me, which was the first thing I checked when I got back to Paris. "*Non*, you do not understand me. My mother used to call it being 'touched by the darkness'. And once you *have* been..." He paused and looked at me. "I think that is what has happened here – I think we have all been touched by it, some more so than others. My only hope is to get as far away as I can."

"But where will you go?" I asked, hurrying past what he'd said – which had caused the hairs on my neck to bristle.

"I have always wanted to visit America," said Henri. "It is one of the places I have not yet seen."

"Very well, then I shall wish you well, Henri, and offer you my thanks once more. I owe you my life, and if there is ever anything I can do for you..."

He smiled and shook the hand I was offering. "Thank you, Dr Watson. And I hope all goes well with your case and Monsieur Holmes."

I remembered then that there was something I'd been meaning to ask him. "I never did catch your second name, Henri."

"It is D'Amour," he said, still smiling at me. "It means love."

"My, that's a very striking name," I told him and meant it; once heard it would never be forgotten.

We said our goodbyes not long after and I packed to head back home again, hoping against hope that I really wasn't too late.

THE TRAIN RIDES and trip across the Channel allowed me time to rest up a little. My body would recover from Malahide's attentions, and probably quite quickly, but my mind – that was another matter entirely.

When finally I arrived at Baker Street, however, I found no sign of Holmes, and Mrs Hudson was in a terrible state. "I just know something has happened to him, Doctor. I just know it!" That was exactly what Mrs Thorndyke had said, and I prayed that both these ladies were wrong. Upon searching the study, I found the telegram that Mr Summersby had sent pleading with my friend for his help – and I realised this was as good a place as any to start my search for him. I could visit the place mentioned in the telegram – The Prospect of Whitby – but I did not have a clue whether Summersby would return there, nor what he looked like even if he did. And in the meantime, what if Holmes should return to Baker Street?

So I sent an urgent telegram to the man via his newspaper and waited.

It took a further two telegrams to elicit any kind of response from Summersby, and when it did eventually come it was not in the form I had been expecting. Not a missive, nor a request to meet at the tavern or any other place; it was by way of a caller at our lodgings, a woman with auburn hair, clearly in a state of the utmost distress.

"I am sorry to inform you that we are not taking on any new clients at the moment, my good lady," I told her as Mrs Hudson showed her in.

"I am already a client of Mr Sherlock Holmes'. You have been trying to reach me, Dr Watson. I thought it best to come in disguise."

It seemed like a queer thing to say, but not when she explained that she actually *was* the reporter Summersby. As we sat and Mrs Hudson furnished us with a brandy apiece, for we both must have looked like we needed one, Miss Summersby – Josephine, as she insisted – informed me that she had indeed met with Sherlock and set him on a path she feared might have been his undoing; by sending him into Limehouse, where her colleague had disappeared looking for Inspector Thorndyke.

"I was so worried about Amelia, my writing partner Miss Kline, that I virtually begged for his help, Doctor."

I assured her that Holmes had been on this path for a while before she even contacted him. "I myself have returned from my travels with information about the organisation involved in all this, and I'm sorry to report the news is not good."

She hung her head, weeping. "I know, I know. You see, when he said he did not want me to come along, I followed his trail – just as he was following the Inspector's and Amelia's. I saw the men capture him, but then almost immediately someone behind me covered my mouth with a cloth and I fell into unconsciousness."

"What happened next?" I enquired eagerly, inching forward on my chair.

"I was roused with strong smelling salts, and saw that we were in a tunnel. One of the underground train tunnels, for I was shoved into a nearby carriage. Mr Holmes was already part-way through a conversation with the most dishevelled-looking man I have ever seen. I swear to you, Doctor, he looked like one of the homeless." My mind flashed back then to Mrs Spencer's description of the intruder in her garden and I knew Holmes had finally encountered the man; that *he* was at the end of Holmes' search. "He had the orphan with him, but he let the child go and gave him freely to me, saying that it was because they had taken something from me."

My brow creased and I rubbed my chin. "That something being your partner, I assume?"

Tears tracked down Miss Summersby's cheeks. "I took it to mean that, yes. But... but I am still hopeful, Doctor, in spite of it all. And in spite of everything Mr Holmes warned me about."

"But now he has Holmes."

She shrugged. "I did not see what happened after that, for I was drugged again and only woken by the boy shaking me and crying. We had been deposited by the river, not far from where I first met Mr Holmes."

"So you have no idea where you were taken?"

Miss Summersby shook her head. "None whatsoever."

"Where is the child now?"

"He is safe, with my parents – they have a small place in Brighton and I felt that the change of scenery and sea air would do the poor mite good." She sniffed, drying her red eyes. "I questioned him before we left, but he is virtually a mute. Either he did not see a great deal, or he is too traumatised by the whole affair to speak about it. Doctor, these are incredibly dangerous people – I understand that now."

"I see." There was not much more to talk about after that; it was clear what my next course of action should be – to venture into Chinatown myself and see what I could find out. Miss Summersby was obviously known to these people, so I would go alone, and report back my findings. Regrettably, I knew even as I closed our front door, after saying goodbye, that my undercover skills were not a patch on Holmes' – and he was much more familiar with such territory than I.

Nevertheless, I tried. My enquiries in Limehouse led nowhere, perhaps because I made people nervous, or maybe it was simply that questions about the Order – no matter how subtly they were broached – instilled terror in even the stoutest of hearts. I could understand that completely. After much searching, I considered descending into the underground tunnels and looking there, but where to start? I began to fear I would get nowhere with my investigation, especially without Holmes on hand to offer his unique assistance. Indeed, he had become the very focus of this case for me – to discover what had happened to him after he'd spoken to the vagabond.

Luckily, upon a brief return to Baker Street, Mrs Hudson told me that one of Holmes' urchin boys had left a sealed message for me, in exchange for Mrs Hudson parting with another shilling. It said there were rumours Holmes had paid for a new, private room in one of the houses not too far from Upper Swandam Lane, which meant that my old friend was still alive at least.

I grabbed my coat, and was about to leave, when something made me go back and fetch my pistol. I had, of course, lost my Webley Bulldog back at Malahide's Institute, but I am nothing if not prepared. I had a Tranter tucked away at the back of my wardrobe which would serve my purposes adequately enough. I tried to put its necessity down to the fact that the neighbourhood I was venturing into was far from pleasant, but I had been in much worse without my pistol and felt less ill at ease. No, something was about to happen – I felt as sure about that as Mrs Hudson did that something had befallen Holmes... or was about to.

After a few hours my enquiries had brought little result: it was the same as Limehouse, either people were too scared or my manner was off-putting. Then, I was approached by a man called Tanner, who said he might be able to help me for the right price. When I handed over the money, and he still wanted more, I'm afraid my temper went.

"Will this be sufficient?" I asked him, pushing him against a wall and bringing out the pistol. As a physician, I swore to do no harm – though I have broken that promise, on occasion, to save others or myself – but I had been through a lot in a short space of time and my patience was wearing thin. It transpired that a person matching Holmes' description had rented not only a private room, but an entire house from him for a considerable amount, on the understanding that it would remain a private transaction. The very fact that this miserable excuse for a human being had been trying to wheedle more money from me to do exactly the opposite, just made my blood boil all the more. Little wonder it had not remained a secret for very long. In the end, I got the address and told him to be on his way before I changed my mind.

The building itself looked like a good breeze might blow it over, but when I came to try the front door I discovered it was locked tight. I had more success with a window on the ground floor, smashing it with my elbow and reaching through to open it, being careful to avoid the smashed shards of glass on the ground, as I clambered in. After searching the lower portions of the building (with my gun leading the way), and finding nothing – the place had obviously been used at some point for various nefarious activities; storage for one, as I found a few empty crates scattered about similar to the one Simon had been imprisoned inside – I made my way to the bottom of a rickety staircase. Holmes had always taught me never to ascend to another level of a building until I knew nobody would be following me from below.

Only now, as I walked through the house once more, did I hear the bell tolling. A strange sound, as if from far away, but also coming from very nearby.

From upstairs, unless my ears were deceiving me.

It was as I placed a foot on the bottom step that the house began to shake, like a minor earthquake was occurring – not something that is usually associated with these isles; I had only heard of a handful up to that point, the last being in Carmarthen, Wales, a few years previously. It also felt very localised, as if it was in the vicinity of this building alone. Ignoring my better judgment, I continued on up those stairs, but a tremble sent me sideways and I found myself hanging on to the banister for dear life. I almost dropped my Tranter at this point, but managed to keep a grip on it long enough for the 'quake to subside.

I raced up the next few steps, which was yet another mistake – as my foot crashed through the rotting wood of one. I scrabbled to haul myself out of this fix, for I would be no use to Holmes if I broke both my legs coming to his rescue. The rattling of the house appeared to have died down for now, so I crawled up to the top of the stairs, to the darkened landing. There was light coming from one of the rooms, through the gaps between the frame and the door itself. A blue light, as if the room beyond had suddenly become submerged.

As I crept closer, I detected that now familiar scent of vanilla. If that wasn't enough to spur me on, then the noises emanating from behind the door were the final straw. Voices, but also a banging and clattering; definite sounds of a struggle. I knew that at this moment, Holmes was facing an unspeakable menace and I had to help. I tried the door and found that it was locked. No, not locked, merely jammed. For, as I put my shoulder to it, the barrier gave and suddenly I was inside the room, staring at more sights that shouldn't have existed.

No skinless men this time, but on a par with it. Four figures illuminated by the blue light coming from – through? – the walls, especially from one large rent in the back one. The first, and closest, figure was the largest of the four. Clothed in a vest and trousers, he was well-muscled but there was something very wrong with his head – perhaps some sort of birth defect, I wondered, akin to that of poor Joseph Merrick, the so-called Elephant Man? His head resembled a closed hand ready to strike, so I silently named him: 'Fist'. There was a woman, pale with ruby lips, dressed in a corset and skirts, brandishing a deadly whip. She, I labelled 'Madame'. A third looked to me like he was suffering from every kind of malady known to man! He had been disfigured by some form of flesh-eating affliction, which had destroyed his nose. 'Plague' I named him. But it was the final figure, dressed in some sort of religious garb, including a flowing black robe, that was the most bizarre – for he had what looked like the remnants of the window I had caved in downstairs embedded in his neck and head. 'Glass' was the moniker I gave to this individual.

They were clearly members of the Order of the Gash. They wore their – more than likely – self-inflicted wounds with pride, like military medals. What on Earth kind of organisation were we up against?

My eyes found Holmes last, bare-chested, bloodied from their attentions and held fast by hooked chains that had torn through his arms and legs. He was doing his best to appear defiant, but I could tell he was in agony.

I fired a warning shot into the ceiling and everyone turned to look in my direction. I demanded that they let my friend go, struggling to keep the hitch from my voice. I was confused, petrified and angry all at once.

Glass – who had more than an air of their leader about him – glared at me as if to say, 'How dare you interrupt?'

"I said –" I began, but was swiftly cut off.

"This is not for you to witness. It is none of your concern," the man told me. "Leave, before you make it ours."

"My friend is being tortured! That is what makes this my concern."

"Very well," he said curtly, nodding at the largest of the figures.

"S-stay where you are! I'm warning you." But the deformed man paid me no heed. Could he even hear me? Now Fist was only a few feet away, leaving me no choice, so I fired two bullets.

Nothing happened. At this close range I couldn't have missed, yet he did not stop advancing. I went for a headshot, but nothing happened again. He just kept on coming.

I moved away from the door, immediately regretting the fact that I'd sacrificed our only escape route. Now Plague lunged at me, but I shifted my weight to the side and backed off – having enough wherewithal to understand that one touch from him would be lethal. Indeed, hadn't I spied amongst Holmes' wounds one on his chest that looked like a bubbling patch of diseased skin? Not to be left out, Madame directed her whip towards me. I ducked, losing my bowler hat in the process, firing at her and Plague with the last of my bullets. These had no effect either and I tossed my empty pistol in their direction.

One thing I did notice, which encouraged me somewhat, was that this distraction had allowed Holmes to complete the unenviable task of pulling out those hooks and freeing himself.

I did not have long to rejoice, however, because the members of the Order were converging on me. How long now before I myself was the victim of those chains and hooks?

Crawling backwards, I reached around for something – anything – I could use as a weapon. It was then that my fingers found it: the box

I brought it around in front of me, mesmerised by the gold leaf on the black, lacquered ornament. It was our murder weapon from those earlier crime scenes, it had to be: the Lament Configuration Lemarchand had spoken of; the means to make control easier. A distant part of my mind realised Holmes must have solved the puzzle of this box, and that was the reason all this was happening, but I did not have much time to ponder such thoughts, because Glass said, "No – put that down."

It broke me out of my reverie, and I held the box up before me. "What, this?" It was obviously important to them, my new trophy. Perhaps I could use it as a bargaining tool? Getting to my feet, I brandished it and the figures nearest backed off, as if I were holding a hand grenade. Maybe that was it – did this have some sort of explosive capacity?

"Watson…" said Holmes. "Be careful."

Still, I used the box to clear a path to my friend.

"Let us go!" I demanded. "Or… or…" To be honest, I did not know what I would do. In the end it was of no consequence, because I felt something wrap itself around my wrist tightly and yank. The box flew out of my grasp, and I looked down to see the end of Madame's whip curled around my forearm; squeezing hard. Quickly, Holmes untangled me from its grip before it could do any more damage, then pulled me by the coat-sleeve into the fissure in the wall before any of the others could react. With the deformed man still barring our way to the door, it was our only means of escape.

"This way, Watson!" he urged me, though I had very little choice.

Then we were in a secret passageway much like the one back at Monroe's; a stony corridor stretching out in front of us. I heard laughter coming from behind. Glass spoke once more, the words echoing after us.

"By all means, explore. We will find you. Then we shall spend an eternity exploring your flesh!"

I glanced across at Holmes, who didn't even register the words; he was too busy driving us forward. Too busy pulling me along for the ride, as always. But where were we? Where were we going?

The answer to the first question was too impossible even to contemplate, but I would have to come to terms with it eventually.

You see, we were in Hell.

We were both in Hell.

CHAPTER SEVENTEEN
The Hound

SHERLOCK HOLMES WOULD have been lying if he'd said he was not happy to see his old friend again.

It didn't matter that he'd sent the man away to try to keep him out of all this; Watson had been pulled back. And his timing had been impeccable, as always – both good and bad. (But hardly a coincidence, surely? Drawn together at that precise moment – had that been the reason the box hadn't responded to his touch more quickly?)

Now, here they were, running down dusty, old corridors that should not even exist, arches opening left and right, junctions, turnings which they took with no notion of how they might retrace their steps, trapped in the place those four figures had originated from. The place they called home.

They had been running, half-stumbling, for some time, in an effort to put as much distance between themselves and the members of the Order when Watson pulled up sharply. "Holmes?" he said. "Holmes, enough. I need to stop for a moment."

He was holding his wrist where the whip had caught him, reminding Holmes of the wounds he himself had endured back in the room; his back raked, his chest poisoned – though the further away from that diseased creature he was, the less its effects were felt – the hooks in his arms and legs. The niggling sensation of pain was returning, but he beat it down.

"Here," he said, "let me have a look."

He took his friend's arm and turned it over. The cuts were quite minor, thankfully. It could have been a lot worse – what if their leader had decided to slice off Watson's hand with that glass blade of his, to get the box back? It did not bear contemplating.

"I think I should be the one saying that," Watson replied, nodding at Holmes' afflictions. But there was more wrong with the good doctor than these slashes to his wrist, Holmes could see that now he had the time to look. Watson appeared drawn, fatigued.

"Watson, what happened to you in France?"

"Malahide," was all he would say.

"You went back then, even after I specifically told you not to!"

"Yes, I went back, Holmes. My conscience would not allow me to look away while people were being treated so contemptibly. The same conscience that would not leave you here to the mercies of... I waited for you to get back in touch with instructions, but –"

"I was occupied," Holmes retorted. That was partly true, but he could have sent another telegram to make sure his companion didn't go off on some damned fool errand that could get him killed.

"Yes, I can see that." Watson looked up, and the hurt was immediately apparent. "And look where this obsession of yours has brought you." Watson snatched his wounded arm away and waved his hand around. "Brought *us!*"

"You're right," Holmes admitted. "But it was never my intention to involve you in this part of it, Watson. In the endgame."

"No, you sent me away – probably because you knew I would

have talked you out of... whatever it was you were planning on doing."

"Actually I..." Holmes shook his head. No amount of explaining would make any difference. Watson was in no mood to listen to the reasoning behind his being 'banished'.

"What *were* your intentions anyway? To find the box, to recreate those crime scenes – try and draw the attention of the Order? Well, I'd say you succeeded, judging from the state of those people back there. I mean, Holmes – did you see them! Did you see what had been *done* to them? What I suspect they may have done to *themselves*? This is not some ordinary criminal organisation or cult we are dealing with."

"Once more, you are correct. They are anything but ordinary – and I'm not sure you could classify them as people, either."

Watson frowned. "What are you talking about?"

"Look around you, Watson," said Holmes, sighing. "You cannot ignore the evidence of your own eyes, no more than I can."

"It's another one of those secret passages, like Monroe's. Like the one I discovered Malahide had under his institution, where he kept the patients he experimented upon. It is where I would still be, if a friend hadn't returned to rescue *me*."

"What friend?" asked Holmes.

Watson shook his head. "It's not important. The point is, we need to bring in the cavalry. This is all getting a bit beyond us."

"It is certainly... beyond our experience."

"Stop talking in riddles, man!"

"Watson, none of this should be here! There was no room in that old house for one secret corridor, let alone this many. No hidden space where they could possibly be! How is it even lit? There are no torches, no electric lights... And those members of the Order back there, how could they have had all that done to them and still be alive? How could they have withstood it? Before today, we would have said such things were impossible. But now, all evidence points to the contrary."

"This is nonsense, I –"

"Watson, I fear I may have done something rather ill-advised in my pursuit of the truth. Because of my, as you call it, obsession with this affair." It wasn't very often Sherlock Holmes admitted he was wrong. "I underestimated our enemy, and for that I sincerely apologise."

"Holmes, I... I still do not fully understand."

"Sadly for me, everything is starting to slot into place," the great detective said wearily. "On my travels I came across mendicants who spoke of transcending our reality. Of reaching other dimensions, other worlds."

"Holmes, this is Verne and Wells territory. The kind of thing readers of their stories might –"

"I am not talking about reaching the stars, Watson. About exploring the oceans. But travelling via..." Holmes tapped the side of his head. "I had assumed that even if it were possible, then it would be the mind – the spirit – that would undertake such a journey. Not the body. And yet..."

"This is preposterous! We are both suffering from fatigue, from the after-effects of drugs, of poisons. Shared hallucinations, the result of mental and physical abuse... I know I have seen some strange things, but none of them could possibly be real."

"No? Then how do you explain the pain you're feeling in that wrist? The fact that you were out of breath from running. Watson, we have to face facts: it is my firm belief that we have crossed a bridge to... somewhere else. Just as one might open a door and step through into another room, the box –"

"The Lament Configuration."

"– opened a doorway to *here*. To them, the members of the Order. Just as it did for Francis Cotton, for Mrs Spencer and Mrs Thorndyke's husbands, for Monroe and Kline... The Gash came for them, brought them back here either before or after they'd killed them. It is the only possible explanation given the circumstances and what we already know."

"Good God," Watson breathed.

"I do not think that God played any part in this. You remember the kind of material Monroe was obsessed with. The pictures, the books."

"No," said Watson. "No, it can't... But we –" A low-pitched rumbling interrupted the conversation. Both of them looked up and down the tunnel, but it was impossible to tell which direction it was coming from. Watson regarded his companion. "Another earthquake?"

The sound transformed into not so much of a rumble as a growl. A long, drawn-out growl, one that they both recognised. "I don't think so, no," said Holmes.

"The... the Hound? But that's..."

"Not possible?"

"No. We killed it, Holmes. A large dog, yes. But not *the* Hound."

Holmes cocked his head. He knew as well as Watson that the animal they had encountered on the moors, the one that had slaughtered poor Sir Charles Baskerville, was no more. But now came a howl, and that set the seal on it as far as Holmes was concerned. His expression told Watson as much, but the Doctor still shook his head in disbelief.

However, when the shadow of the creature appeared ahead of them on the wall, followed swiftly afterwards by the thing itself, there was no denying the resemblance. It was the Hound they had both witnessed, glowing once more. Yet something had been done to it, the beast shorn not only of its fur, but also its skin in places to reveal the muscle and bone beneath. It was strapped up here and there with black leather, including at the collar, and across the eyes, rendering it blind. Drool cascaded from its jaws. It was as if someone had taken the Hound and made it even more nightmarish. It paused to sniff the air with its slit-like nostrils, and turned its head towards them, wagging a stumpy tail.

"W-what do we do, Holmes?" Watson said, as the creature padded towards them. "Keep still?"

The Hound drew closer, clawed feet tapping out a staccato beat on the floor.

"We..."

"Yes?"

"We... we..." Holmes grabbed Watson's arm and pulled him back slowly. "Watson, we should..."

"Yes?"

"I think we should... run!"

It was sensible advice, and both turned at the same time to begin sprinting back up that corridor, with the Hound in pursuit. At one of the junctions, Holmes pointed and they skidded to turn left. The Hound behind them attempted to stop, but couldn't get a grip on the stone floor and ended up sliding past the archway. It only gained them a few moments, however, as the creature soon righted itself and dragged its lumbering frame through.

"It... it doesn't matter... how far... we run... Holmes... or if we hide... the beast will still find us," Watson panted as they made their way towards another arch. "That blasted sense of smell!" What they needed was some way of fighting the thing, but there was nothing to hand – the walls pitifully free of any adornments, just smooth stone that apparently went on forever.

Watson rounded yet another corner, but in so doing stumbled and fell. Holmes was already a few feet ahead of him before he noticed and turned back, but by that time the Hound was bearing down on the Doctor. "Watson!" called out Holmes, but there was nothing he could do.

Watson looked away from the Hound, screwing up his eyes and waiting for the inevitable. The Hound blew out a jet of air through its nostrils, which ruffled Watson's hair. Then it moved away from him, looking up towards Holmes.

"Hoi... Hoi there!" Holmes began shouting, waving his arms.

"Here – I'm here!" He needn't have bothered, for it was obvious who was the real target when the Hound began moving off at a trot in his direction. "It's me he wants, Watson."

"No!" Watson called from behind, standing and running after the Hound. He caught up and leapt at the great animal, grabbing it.

"Watson, don't be a fool. Run!"

But Holmes' companion wasn't listening; and with a flick of its hips, the Hound threw Watson into a wall, where he slid to the ground.

"Watson!" cried Holmes, but he knew he couldn't go and see whether his friend was all right – it would simply lead the animal back to him. No, Watson had bought him a head start and he had to lead the thing away.

Sherlock Holmes began running again, until both he and the Hound were out of sight.

CHAPTER EIGHTEEN
A Vision of One War...

As we fled from the Order, up one secret corridor and down another, I grew fatigued and eventually had to pause for breath. My arm was aching where the whip had caught it, though by comparison to Holmes' wounds it was a mere trifle. There had been little time for a reunion while we were fending off the Gash, and only now did we speak of what had happened. There was no sign that Holmes was happy to see me – nor a hint of gratitude that I had just saved his life. Indeed, I got the distinct impression that he was angry at me for returning – and that only increased when he found out I had revisited to the Institute and been captured myself.

"You went back then, even after I specifically told you not to!" he said to me, shaking his head. "Oh Watson, it was never my intention to involve you in any of this."

No, his aim was to keep me in the dark, not include me in his final move – that of securing the box and replicating what Cotton, Spencer and the others had done, using himself as bait, no matter what the dangers might be.

It was at this juncture that the conversation took a turn for the surreal, with Holmes talking about other realities and dimensions.

I'm afraid to say I railed against this even after everything I'd seen and experienced. The alternatives I laid out were shot down, but why not put the blame on drugs, on the abuse our bodies had taken, on some form of hypnosis – yes, I kept returning to that one. Better that, than facing the truth of the situation.

"I do not think that God played any part of this," Holmes told me emphatically, only for our 'discussion' to be interrupted by a rumbling noise. And then, as incredible as it might seem, a creature that looked for all the world like the Baskerville Hound was before us! But it had been horribly changed – shaved, skinned, strapped up in leather, and blinded.

We managed to evade the beast, tricking it at first one turn then another, but eventually it caught up – not helped by the fact that I tripped and made myself easy prey. As its fetid breath blasted into my face, I turned away and closed my eyes, knowing this was the end.

But it did not want me; it had been following Holmes' scent all along. Trained, just like the original Hound, to be directed at one individual. I tried to stop it, jumping on its back as it bounded after Holmes, but the monster threw me off and into a wall, winding me.

There I lay for some time, trying to work up the energy to clamber to my feet; thinking that if I just closed my eyes and opened them again, I would wake up (only not in that chamber back at the Institute – please God, not there). I would wake in a time before Holmes had even heard of Moriarty, back when our friendship was firm and I knew exactly where I stood with him. Before he 'died' and came back aloof; before our encounters with the box and the Order of the Gash. A time before skinned men and flayed priests with glass sticking out of their faces, or fists for skulls, or diseased flesh or...

Of course, when I opened my eyes, everything was still there. The hardness of the stone floor, the bleakness of the corridor, the strange blue light which illuminated this hellish place.

When I struggled to my feet, I ached in places I did not even know I had; 'old' wounds from my time with Malahide were flaring up again, my body in no shape to be tackling vicious animals. I placed a hand against the cool wall for support and slid myself along it, towards the direction I'd last seen Holmes and the giant dog heading off in. When I got to the next junction, I could see no sign of them – and there were three options now ahead of me to choose from.

I let out a resigned breath and plumped for the middle tunnel, stumbling up it for want of any better plan. I was already lost, hope dwindling of ever finding either Holmes or a way out. But I would not just lay down and die. I didn't survive all those times on the battlefield, nor my adventures with Holmes, to shuffle off my mortal coil there.

Just when it seemed like the passageways would go on indefinitely, I found an exit – but quickly wished that I hadn't. The corridor opened out onto a platform or balcony of sorts. I hobbled towards the edge, but swiftly pulled back when I saw the drop before me. Looking out over this new landscape I saw the corridors and arches from a very different perspective, and from a distance now – all interlacing and making up the many levels of this confusing place. The whole thing was a complex labyrinth, a network of streets and roads that wove in and out of each other, so many times it made my head spin. The levels I could see, for I felt sure that it reached down lower still – possibly into some sort of pit – were vast, stretching out for miles and miles (I tried to push away thoughts of Dante wandering through his circles). At the same time, I couldn't help thinking that the surface looked a little like a giant chessboard, like the patchwork countryside in one of my favourite books from childhood.

There was no way I could deny that I was in some other... what, world, dimension? That's what Holmes had called it when he was trying to get me to see we had stepped through a breach into somewhere else.

I *was* Alice at the bottom of the rabbit hole, on the other side of the looking glass – but this was no Wonderland. Far from it. The dizzying sight of it all chilled me to the bone. Especially when, here and there, I caught shadows flitting about along those corridors, framed against more arches; some recognisably human in shape, others not. But it was what I saw when I looked above the maze that frightened me more.

Something huge in the distance, hanging above it all – suspended. At first it was quite far away, then it was suddenly very near. Each time I blinked, it seemed to change its appearance. One moment a geometrical shape, gem-like, the next a huge monstrous creature with many tentacles, like something ancient mariners might speak of in hushed tones: a Leviathan. Then it more closely resembled the box that had brought us here. In every incarnation, it was spewing out something: black jets of what I took to be liquid – possibly oil, or perhaps smoke? Then I remembered what Mrs Spencer had said about that summerhouse, about what she'd seen just before her husband had vanished (had been taken here?).

The black light.

To begin with it was aimed away from me, but the huge shape's gaze soon found me. Seconds later, so too did that blackness, rotating like a lighthouse beam in my direction and striking me before I could do anything about it.

I think I screamed then as the tendrils of evil found their way inside me.

Screamed like I had never screamed before.

THE NEXT THING I knew, I was somewhere else again.

Back on the battlefield, in Maiwand, our regiment being attacked by the Afghans. Soldiers – my friends and comrades – were being slaughtered left, right and centre. There was blood... so much blood. My own screaming was being drowned out by theirs.

"*No!* Not again – *please!*"

I was dreaming; some part of me recognised the fact that I was back in my nightmare, facing my greatest fear of being in the midst of battle. Soon it would be my turn to be shot. I didn't even see the bullet that caused the damage, that would later in my life still cause me so much pain – especially in damp weather. Just felt the blasted thing as it tore through my leg, looked down and saw the gaping hole and the blood pumping freely from it.

I was vaguely aware of someone strapping up my wounded thigh, and bundling me on a horse, to travel back to the Army hospital in Peshawar, where I would begin my slow recovery. As I was loaded onto the animal, I do remember seeing something... a figure in white robes, walking amongst the men. Bending and shaking its head – *her* head – as she examined the wounded and the dead. Some kind of nurse? An angel? Come to bring peace in their final moments, to help them on their way?

Everything blurred, and I was in another time, facing another enemy. Now I was in a trench with people I did not recognise. It was night-time and explosions sounded all around me. I ascended a ladder and risked a peek out onto this other battlefield. It was a desert of churned up earth and barbed wire, where dozens of men wearing tin hats were shooting at each other. A shell landed not too far away, throwing me backwards. Body parts rained down from the sky: a hand here; a foot there. Infantry shredded by the might of modern warfare.

I did not know it at the time, but I was being shown a war that was less than two decades away, and which would claim seventeen million lives – with as many more again horrifically wounded. One of the most appalling and deadliest conflicts in human history, and I was being given a preview of it against my will.

After I had regained my composure, I looked up over the lip of the trench again – to see that the woman in white had returned.

She was drifting through the bullets and muck, bending and placing her hand on the fallen soldiers to ease their grief, shaking her head. I saw now that she was not wearing robes as I had first thought, but some sort of long, flowing nightgown.

I waved at her to try and gain her attention. "Get out of there! Can't you see how much danger you're in?" She did not even look in my direction.

Another mighty blast and this time I was thrown clear of the trench. I landed and shook myself, realising that the scene had shifted a third time – and I was in a city, with oriental-looking people rushing around me, pointing at something and screaming. Men, women and children, all in a state of turmoil.

Then I saw why.

A huge cloud in the distance, I can only think to compare its shape to that of a mushroom. A bomb, unlike anything I had seen before, or since, had been dropped. Moments later, the people around me were blown apart as a wind ploughed through them. All that was left in the thing's wake were shadows cast upon the walls, the outlines of people. And there, in the distance, walking through the carnage, was the woman in the nightgown – walking slowly and looking from side to side.

"Wait!" I called out, running after her. "Please wait!"

But she did not, rounding a corner and vanishing. When I reached the spot myself, I skidded past. As I turned the corner and ran on, I found myself in a jungle – trailing men dressed in green. They were holding rifles that looked more advanced than anything I had ever seen, and when we suddenly broke cover, I was confronted with strange flying machines. Much smaller than airships, and with some form of propeller on top, these were landing – waiting for the soldiers to climb on board. A sneak attack came from the jungle, flashes of gunfire tearing into the soldiers, ripping them apart before they could fire back. Another future war, and there was the woman in white again, bullets not even grazing her. I realised now how ridiculous my warnings were; she was in no more danger of being hurt than I. So, trying to ignore the bloodshed as best I could, I ran after her again, ran past the metal machines that were taking off, running so fast I barely noticed that I'd stepped on something: a landmine, which blew me several feet into the air.

When I landed with a thump, I was in a more urban environment, where the warfare had spilled out onto the streets.

Explosions shattered storefronts and as they had in that other cityscape, people were scattering in every direction, but it was doing them just as much good; they were killed on the spot by flames and... chains with hooks. I frowned, puzzled. For the perpetrators of this chaos were not soldiers this time, but what looked like members of the Order of the Gash.

No, *not* the same as the others. I could not quite put my finger on it, but these were different somehow. As amazing is it sounds, they looked more haphazard, as if not as much care had been taken over their appearance. Like they were copies... They acted differently, as well. Much less controlled, but at the same time directed. Maybe they were foot soldiers? I glanced around for the general orchestrating this 'invasion', and, yes, sure enough, I spotted him. At first I almost mistook him for Glass, as he wore a similar kind of crown and skirts; carried himself with the same authority. It was not glass in this one's head, however, but a crown of something altogether more disturbing – something akin to those fetishes back in Monroe's quarters...

"John!" I turned, and there she was, walking away from me, beckoning me to follow.

As I ran after her, I tripped and fell... only I did not land on the ground. I was falling for the longest time – twisting over and over, blackness and stars all around me. Something whizzed past, another flying machine making its way through that space – only this one was more like the rocket from that famous George Méliès motion picture which would astound audiences in a few years' time. This particular rocket was engaged in a battle with lots of others. Different-coloured lights shot from cannons mounted on those rockets. When the beams hit something, they destroyed it completely in a big ball of fire. In the distance was a larger vehicle. No, more like a train station in the sky, where the rockets could land, docking as ships might after a long journey on the waves. I'd only been watching this display for a few moments when that too exploded. It was a pretty sight, but no less devastating for those who must have been on board the structure.

I was left there floating through space, nothing but silence surrounding me, when I felt someone behind me, heard my name called out one last time. "John... Turn around, John."

I managed to manoeuvre myself until I was facing the lady I had been chasing through one war after another. Part of me had known who she was all along. Who else could it have been? If I was dreaming of my time abroad, then it followed that I should also be dreaming about her. Indeed, the nightgown she had on was the one she had been wearing when she died in that hospital bed. Now restored and smiling, fair hair flowing behind her, she looked as beautiful as the day I had met her and given her my heart.

"Mary," I said.

She nodded. "Yes, my love. It is I."

We drifted towards each other and then I had her in my arms again. Oh, how I had missed holding my dear, sweet wife. Words cannot express the joy! I pulled back and kissed her. I thought my heart might just burst, such was the strength of feeling I experienced. I was crying when I broke off that kiss, and Mary brushed my cheeks with her thumb.

"No tears, John," she said to me. "Not here." I couldn't help it. If this was a dream, then I did not want it to end. As if reading my thoughts she said, "Oh, you're not dreaming, sweetheart. Not really. I wish you were."

"Then how...?"

"Your memories of Afghanistan, they provided the raw material for your visions. It was their deity, John."

"Deity?"

"You saw it, and it saw you. It looked *into* you, used those recollections. For a vision of one war, is a vision of all wars. Past, present and future."

"I... I don't understand."

"There is a war coming, John. A battle which you will play an important part in. But I will be with you; I will always be with you."

"A battle..." I still didn't understand, but then how was I supposed to? I did not yet have all the information at my disposal. As Holmes once said, one cannot make bricks without clay.

"If that monstrosity back there is the Order's god, then where exactly am I?"

"I think you know the answer to that question already. You're just not ready to admit it."

My mind flashed back to those representations in Monroe's chambers and I shuddered. "And the others? Cotton, Spencer...?"

"They are all here, in their own private purgatories. It was their choice, John. Nobody forced them. Would you like to see?"

Before I could answer, Mary waved a hand and the stars around us vanished: replaced with a chamber, a dungeon room that looked very much like the one I'd been held captive in back at the Institution. I recognised the man we were looking at as Francis Cotton, for he bore more than a passing resemblance to his brother. He was on his knees, pounding the floor. A group of women entered the room and encircled him. All were in various states of undress, enough to make me blush; writhing and moaning and coaxing him with crooked fingers. Francis wasn't blushing, he was gazing up at them with lust in his eyes – and when he stood and reached for one, she disappeared, as insubstantial as mist. He turned and tried to touch the others, and the same thing happened again and again, until there were none left. At that point he fell to his knees once more, ready for the whole performance to repeat itself.

We moved on to the next victim, Lieutenant Spencer – who was wearing his Army uniform. He was being treated to a succession, not of women, but bloodied and wounded men – paraded before him, arms hanging off, bandages wrapped around their heads. Not his comrades in arms, but all the people he had ever killed brought back to haunt him. I wondered if such a fate might await me, as well.

Monroe, now, and he was being made to watch his parents' death – him as a teenaged boy slitting their throats as they slept. Grinning at the time, with the thought of inheriting their money, the grown up Monroe who bore witness to this never-ending scene was less than entertained. A man I imagined must be Thorndyke was being put through the horrors of watching his little girl wandering around in the darkness, terrified and calling out for her father. "Where are you?" she kept repeating over and over. "Please come, Daddy. Please, I need you!" But every time he ran to her, she would shift position and the whole scenario would play out again. As for Amelia Kline, she was being put through the torment of watching her partner, Miss Summersby, being stoned to death by a crowd, shouts of "Bitch!" and "Trollop!" ringing in her ears.

"Enough, Mary! I've seen enough." She halted the sights immediately. "It doesn't mean a thing. You could *be* one of those apparitions, conjured by their god. Or... or my mind could still be making all this up. I could still be dreaming or –"

She took my hands. "Oh my love, you are not. This is as real as anything you have ever experienced. Perhaps even more so. *Please* believe me."

"But... but if this isn't a dream, how can you be here?"

She sighed. "I'm not. Not really. I am just an echo – a shadow."

I thought back to that mushroom cloud, the remains of those people left behind; I looked down, more tears escaping. So this Mary was no more real than Cotton's women? She felt real enough. Perhaps that was to be *my* punishment? I only raised my head again when Mary continued. "I am allowed to be here because of my link to you – and my link to someone else."

"Holmes?"

Mary shook her head again. "No. Not Sherlock. But someone who is known to you both."

"Mary, please tell me what is going on. I think... I think I'm going insane."

She looked at me then with eyes that held so much love, and I knew deep down inside she was no illusion. This was my Mary all right, echo or no echo. "If you'll indulge me one last time, husband. Perhaps it might be better if I showed you," she said.

And the scene around us changed one final time.

CHAPTER NINETEEN
The Engineer

SHERLOCK HOLMES HAD somehow managed to throw off the beast that had been trailing his every step. He'd glanced behind him at some point during the chase, only to find that it wasn't there anymore, though he felt sure it wouldn't be long before it caught up – the one thing he couldn't really do was mask his own scent. If anything, the sweat pouring from his skin would make him even easier to find.

Nonetheless, he was free of the damned thing for now. The *damned* thing... just one more damned thing in a place chock full of them. Holmes realised now the enormity of what he'd done, cracking open the division between his world and the one the Order occupied. He'd accepted the truth of it much more easily than Watson, and that surprised him a little. Holmes wasn't a particularly religious soul, and up until now had been no great believer in the supernatural – but he trusted logic and the evidence of his own eyes. As he'd once said, "Once you eliminate the impossible, *whatever* remains, no matter how improbable, must be the truth."

What happened, though, if the truth turned out to *be* the impossible?

Then, by that token, the impossible *became* the possible. The Order of the Gash, no matter how incredible their existence had seemed before today, were real. Hell was real. He did not subscribe to Watson's theories about drugs, hallucinations or mental collapse. This place was as authentic to him as anything he had ever seen or experienced. Those mutilated creatures back there, as solid as anyone he'd ever come across, client or villain. That Hound in pursuit of him, though it should not still be alive, in this place it was. In this place, death had no dominion – or at least not in the way human beings had always subscribed to.

It was as he mused about all this and turned the next corner that he realised his mistake. The Hound had not broken off its pursuit at all; it had merely completed its task, played its part to perfection. And that role had been to manipulate him into coming here, to this large stone room.

That much became apparent when the hooks and chains flew out of nowhere again, more than before: so many more. A dozen at least, embedding themselves in his limbs, his torso; there had been no hope of avoiding them, even with his superior reflexes, so Holmes let them have their way, shutting out what his nerve endings were telling him about the pain. He breathed in and out slowly, compartmentalising the distress, like the Tibetan monks had shown him. This was easier said than done when the chains pulled taut and lifted him off the ground, pulling his body into a star shape.

"*Gah!*"

There was someone, several someones in fact, here in this room with him.

"Show yourself," Holmes managed. "I think we're beyond games, don't you?"

There was movement, and one of the figures stepped forwards into the blue-grey light. Pale-faced, and dressed in the apparel of the Order, this thing in front of him was, nevertheless, a newcomer. Its deformities and lesions were unlike any Holmes had witnessed before, parts of the creature having been replaced with clockwork and pistons. Steam escaped as the 'man' shambled forwards, pipes coiling around his neck and into his skull. Both eyes were red-raw, bloodshot and gaping as if only just awakened from its deathly slumber.

Another figure emerged on the other side of the room, similarly tampered with, except a whole arm had been replaced with machinery; wheels and gears, cogs that were visible beneath the surface of the skin, leading up to a shoulder-plate that would not have looked out of place on a suit of armour. Tubing and pipes snaked around its waist and legs – running down, in and out, the whole length of them.

A third figure slunk from the gloom, and the most startling thing about this one was that its head was a patchwork of flesh and metal; squares of copper and steel bolted on to it here and there. It wore goggles, but removed these to show that its eyes were uncoordinated – rolling wildly. The creature that came around the side of Holmes, from behind, had no legs at all, and was propelling itself along with its forearms, its hind-quarters two metal wheels. It turned and looked back at Holmes, and he could see that this one was a female – or had been. Tubes flowed from the back of her head in lieu of hair, each pipe pumping out thick gouts of smoke.

None of them spoke. All of them had the same vacant expressions. Toys, puppets, but belonging to whom? Holmes fancied he had a good idea.

"Finally. You," he said, speaking into the darkness still at the back of the room, "must be the Engineer, sir."

There was a throaty laugh which bounced off the walls. "And you are Mr Sherlock Holmes. Your reputation precedes you, even here."

"And what, pray tell, do they say about me?"

There was a pause before the answer came. "That you stand apart. That you are unique – and that you have no equal. But you and I both know that is not correct."

Holmes' brow furrowed. "Show yourself! Stop hiding behind these 'inventions' of yours. I wish to see your face, *Engineer*."

"By all means."

Then came the true madness. The moment when Holmes really did think he might be losing his mind.

The monster that revealed itself was – like him – suspended. Except it wasn't being held aloft by chains, rather by thick tentacles made from meat and bone. Four of them to be precise, which disappeared beneath the long, flowing leather coat he was wearing – it looked like they were attached to his sides, between his arms and his legs. Where they were coming from was unclear, but they were supporting him and under his command, as he glided confidently towards Holmes. He had once described this individual as a 'spider in the centre of a web' and at no time was this description more accurate than now, for these glistening tentacles made it look like he had eight limbs. Apart from his pale blue face now adorned with metal piercings and chains, he looked practically the same: protruding forward from those rounded shoulders, forehead dome-shaped, sunken eyes, an angular nose and thin, pursed lips. He also wore a top hat, perched at a jaunty angle. The collar of his black shirt was up, his tie a mess of muscle and tissue carved out and left to flop down from the top of his throat.

"Hello again, Holmes," said the man.

Holmes shook his head, then thought, but why shouldn't *he* be here? Had he not already seen the Hound's 'resurrection'?

What better place for one such as him to end up, but in Hell? Moriarty. Professor James Moriarty.

In spite of what Watson might have thought, Holmes would have given anything for this not to be so. He had been willing to sacrifice his own life so that the world would be rid of this fiend – little realising that another world would claim him for its own, welcome him back like some kind of prodigal son. Promote him and give him his own supply of raw material to work on and revel in. An engineer indeed, constructing new nightmares out of old.

"I know exactly what you're thinking," he said, drifting close. "How easy it must have been for me. Well, you're quite, quite wrong. I had to prove myself, Holmes. Prove myself worthy of being included in the ranks of the Cenobites." When he saw Holmes' eyebrow twitch, he smiled. "Ah, you haven't come across that name? It's what they... what *we* call ourselves. To some, demons. To others... something else."

"Something vile," Holmes breathed out.

"Something *glorious!*" corrected Moriarty, opening his arms wide. Out of the shadows more came, reconstituted beings, as much mechanical devices as humans now. "Do you like my handiwork, Holmes? My own personal creations, no two the same. Oh, I'm so glad you're here – you have no idea! There are so few who would be able to appreciate all this." It was at that moment a clicking sound caught Holmes' attention and, at last, the Hound came in to join them. It growled when it saw Holmes, but wagged its tail when Moriarty called to it. The tentacles eased him down so he could pat the creature's head. He produced a chunk of raw meat from somewhere inside the folds of his coat. "Good boy. Here's a treat for you. Nice touch, don't you think, Holmes? I thought you might appreciate being welcomed by a familiar foe. Wasn't easy to find, but, well, I specialise in getting what I need, and getting what I want."

Holmes hung his head. Moriarty had engineered this whole affair!

"I warrant you thought you'd seen the last of me? At the Reichenbach?" Moriarty shook his head. "I always had a plan. An escape route."

"The box," said Holmes, grimacing. It had taken him so long to solve and yet apparently Moriarty had completed it plummeting to his death.

"Oh no, not the Configuration. I didn't have time for that."

Holmes let out a breath; at least that small victory hadn't been taken away from him. "There are other means, other routes to this place. Did you know, for example, that the Vatican guards a secret code in a theological work that enables the user to travel here? That the Marquis de Sade was reported to have been in possession of a particular and singular origami exercise that would do the same; he traded it for paper to write his famous *The 120 Days of Sodom*... The key can be anything, Holmes: a word puzzle, a piece of music, brush strokes on a canvas, a simple knot puzzle on a piece of string. But no, I needed something that would expiate my journey, and that something was the solving of a mathematical equation – my speciality, if you'll recall. The mouthing of the solution, something I'd been holding back for a good while, allowed me passage. Allowed me to survive our encounter... after a fashion.

"But those who willingly come here do not have an easy time of it, my friend. You have had a taste of their 'delights', have you not? I wasn't welcomed with open arms. I suffered – oh, how I suffered! Time works differently here, you see. Minutes are like hours; hours like days. Days like an eternity. And for what seemed like forever I belonged to those you have already met. I was ripped apart and pieced back together again more times than I care to remember. They made my nerve endings sing to their tune.

"Eventually, my potential was finally discovered. Their god saw what I had the capacity to be, if I were allowed my freedom. It is not dissimilar to a criminal organisation, Holmes. Ambition and planning is key, and ideas of course. They positively *thrive* on ideas in Hell. So, I was plucked from my lowly position and promoted, 'invited' to join their ranks – my memory wiped, or so they thought – and it was here I proved my worth. They had never seen such quality work, such imagination."

"Your work on these poor unfortunates," spat Holmes.

Moriarty shook his head. "Once again, you misunderstand,

Holmes. No – these are not my victims. There is very little of those left to speak of. Soon you will see first hand for yourself what I am capable of in that respect. In any event, when the position of fabled Engineer became vacant, I was the obvious choice as replacement. I *made sure* I was the obvious choice."

"And doubtless ensured there was a vacancy in the first place," Holmes muttered.

Moriarty cocked his head. "It is a powerful position and allows me a little more... leeway. A little more privacy."

"But you are still not the one in charge, and – knowing you as I do – that must rankle."

"I serve their god, Holmes – for now. It suits my purposes to do so. But, just as it has its favourites, its trusted seconds, so too do I." Even more figures stepped out of the darkness to take their place at his side. One of them looked like he belonged in a different age – white-faced and wearing a wig, he carried himself as if he might have been royalty once but his glory days had long since passed. The others he vaguely recognised as associates of the Professor's. One in particular Holmes knew immediately, in spite of the fact he now had what appeared to be a small spyglass embedded in his left eye-socket.

"Moran?" whispered Holmes, recognising the final member of Moriarty's gang to be rounded up upon his return to London. Holmes had heard rumours that the man had died in custody, but now he knew exactly what had happened to the former sniper. As if on cue, the telescopic site in Moran's skull zoomed out and then in again, powered by miniature motors.

"Indeed," said Moriarty. "The loyalty of my men has never been in question, and still isn't. They are helping me to achieve my full potential, just as they did before. They would die for me. Actually, they all have." He laughed. "As for these others you spoke of, they are my burgeoning army of lost souls."

"Lost souls?"

"Lost, tortured... Those who slipped through society's cracks without being noticed. You have spent so long searching for a handful of missing people, Holmes – but do you have any idea how many just disappear each day without a trace all over the world? People who have no loved ones, people nobody cares about? *I* know. And I have given them purpose, here at my table."

"You're even more insane than when we last met. Hell does not become you, Professor!"

"Oh, but it does! I've waited a long time for this, Sherlock. To face you again, but on my terms."

Holmes set his jaw firm in defiance. "Do your worst!" he told Moriarty.

More hooks shot out of the darkness, embedding themselves in his face – stretching the skin, pulling it taut, and causing him to clench his teeth. "Oh, I will," Moriarty replied, floating in closer, spittle flying from his mouth.

"Don't you worry about that, Holmes. I will."

CHAPTER TWENTY
True Pain

WHAT MARY SHOWED me was my friend's ongoing torment.

Holmes, held fast by a multitude of hooks and chains, being carved up by a member of the Order of the Gash (or, as Mary termed them, Cenobites). A creature with thick, pulsating tentacles feeding into its back, wearing a long-coat and hat, giving the superficial appearance of a gentleman.

Watching this display were a crowd of monstrosities, all disfigured in various ways, but with cogs, mechanical workings and steam powering them.

"Imitations: pseudo Cenobites," explained Mary. "They're foot soldiers, *his* creations."

"Who?"

"You'll see," Mary assured me, and not long after that I did.

The monster turned to one side, and my mouth fell open when I recognised it as none other than Professor James Moriarty. He had somehow survived the Falls and found his way here. He had been manipulating Holmes all along, guiding him – *luring* him to this place. I recognised some of the other creatures as Moriarty's colleagues: Colonel, Moran, who I'd last seen taking pot-shots at a facsimile of Holmes in Baker Street; and that had to be the aristocrat, the one I'd returned here by shooting him myself back at the Institute.

"The messenger," I whispered. "So that's what Malahide meant when he said I hadn't killed the skinless man."

"Malahide has been in league with the Professor for a long time," Mary said. "Trafficking souls. Funnelling bodies to him, so he could build up his followers. And he is not the only one."

"Lord have mercy."

"There is only one lord here, John. And it is not a lord of mercy, I can assure you of that."

"We have to get Holmes out of there. Before –"

"You would be slaughtered before you could remove even one of those hooks." She looked down sadly. "This is something he must bear. Something that he has to undergo."

"No! There *has* to be a way."

She squeezed my hand. "Just wait, John. Please wait."

I did as she asked, though it did not sit comfortably at all. My friend was a mess of raw meat and blood, sliced up so much I could barely recognise him. Flames were used to inflict agony and also to cauterise the wounds, leaving him blackened and crusted. He did not scream once, though we had not seen the half of it yet.

"I know how much all this hurts, especially now. You were always so keenly aware of everything, Sherlock – but never as much as you are at this moment. We have ways of heightening the senses, of using them to our full advantage. Are you enjoying yourself yet?"

Holmes said nothing, just took everything Moriarty could throw at him and more. The Professor grinned through it all; 'A Devil', as Mrs Hudson had once described him. Unfettered, unbound.

"Mary, I don't know how much more of this I can stand," I said, and felt guilty immediately. My only torture was to observe.

"Give me your pain!" Moriarty demanded, but still Holmes refused.

"There is a reason for everything," Mary said, putting an arm around my shaking shoulders. "Trust me, my love. Trust me."

I did. In spite of the fact I was still unsure as to whether she was even here or not, I trusted her. I would have trusted her to the ends of the Earth – were we there.

It was only after all this, only after Moriarty had finished with Holmes physically, that the real torture began.

"Very well, you have forced me to take these measures – just remember that." Moriarty floated away from Holmes, turning his back on him. I saw my friend raise his head as best he could, for he was still secured by hooks and chains. "Enola," said the Professor. I saw Holmes twitch at this, but it was soon followed by a succession of other names. "Alcorn, Cunningham, Green, Storey, McColl, Lyons, Willett, Taylor, Dawes, Angus, Porter..."

I gasped as I finally understood what was happening.

"Hilton," Moriarty went on, "Brunton, Roylott..." He was listing all of Holmes' failures. The deaths at his hand, or by his failure to act; the mysteries he had never been able to solve. The people he had let down. Moriarty eventually ended with, "Phillimore, Cotton, Spencer, Monroe, Thorndyke and Kline." One of those names at least solved something as far as I was concerned; to be included in that company must have meant that the disappearance of Mr James Phillimore, who vanished after stepping back into his house to retrieve his umbrella – never to be seen again – was due to the Order of the Gash. And the mention of those others only served to remind me of what I'd seen of their plights, reiterating that the traumas in this realm were not solely reserved for the body, but also the mind. That was what Moriarty was doing now, plucking at a different set of nerves, reminding my companion of all his shortcomings.

He finished with the greatest taunt of all. "Watson."

"What... what is he talking about?" I asked Mary, but she would not answer.

"You failed to keep him safe. Failed in your duty to your best friend, just as you did with your sister." I wasn't even aware Holmes had a sister, but that was a matter for another time. For now I was allowed to see what Holmes saw, a vision of me lying in that corridor after the Hound had thrown me, battered and bloodied, still unconscious. Then hooks and chains appearing out of nowhere, digging into me and dragging my body off into the shadows. A lie, for that is not what happened, but how was Holmes to know otherwise?

It was only now, upon seeing this, that he screamed: long and loud. "*Nooo!! Damn you, no!*"

Moriarty grinned, for he was already damned. "There. Now isn't that better?"

"Mary, I'm going to him," I told her, regardless of the fact I didn't even know where he was being held.

"Wait John. You *must* wait."

"For what?" I yelled, tears in my eyes.

Then I saw the quartet of original Cenobites that had appeared when he first opened the box were suddenly back.

It was Glass who spoke first, pointing to the Professor's prisoner. "What is this?"

Moriarty eyed the interloper with obvious disdain. "What does it look like?"

"His soul is ours. He summoned *us*."

"Yet he found his way here. That makes him mine."

They were arguing about him like he was a piece of fruit at a market stall to be bartered over. "Holmes," I said softly. "Holmes, I'm so sorry."

"You dare to –" Glass began, but was swiftly interrupted.

"Oh, I dare, favourite son. I am the *Engineer!*"

Glass' lip curled. "You were never fit to claim that title." It was clear there was history between these two. "You were never really more than my plaything."

"Not everyone saw it that way. Surely you are not arguing with our master's decree?"

Glass fell silent. He nodded at Madame, a silent command, and she set off towards Holmes. I wasn't sure he'd be better off in their hands, but at least it would get my friend away from Moriarty... for now.

"Leave him!" roared the Professor. "I will only warn you once. You and your mollisher over there!"

Glass bared his teeth, furious. His other two aides were slowly flanking him.

"Ah, excellent," said Moriarty. "A fight. Something else I have been looking forward to, for a long, long time."

"If you thought your suffering and pain were excruciating before, I assure you that was as nothing compared to what awaits you now... Engineer."

"Pain?" said Moriarty. "*Pain?* You know nothing of true pain, maggot. Let me show *you* pain!"

Hooks and chains flew in every direction. Moriarty's pseudo Cenobites launched themselves at Fist, who cleaved one of their number in two, and lifted another over his head – bringing the underling down over his knee. Plague turned and grabbed the aristocrat by the throat; in mere seconds the man was shrivelling, turning first to bones, then to dust.

Madame's whip lashed out, incapacitating three of Moriarty's monstrosities, before reaching Holmes with an aim to finally freeing him. The Hound, meanwhile, had pounced on Glass, jaws clamping onto his arm. With a heave, he threw the animal off; then, as it came at him again, he directed several lengths of hooked chains at the beast, into its mouth and down its throat. Glass ground his teeth and, with a silent command, the chains were wrenched back, hooks ravaging the Hound and turning it inside out. The whole disgusting lump flopped to the floor and was done.

Moriarty grimaced at the loss of his pet.

"I'm waiting," said Glass, gesturing to his Cenobites who were dispatching the Professor's minions. Madame used her whip to slice through the chains that held Sherlock, and caught him before he could fall. "Waiting for you to show me this so-called pain of yours."

"If you insist," said Moriarty, holding his hands out wide and throwing back his head. Something was building inside him. When it came it spewed forth from his mouth, his eyes, from lesions in the palms of his hands. Night black energy leaped from pseudo Cenobite to pseudo Cenobite, waking them and strengthening them. It also reanimated the Hound – now nothing more than jellied meat – and brought the aristocrat's dust back together into the form of a man. The tendrils of dark power took hold of Glass, gripping him just as the chains and hooks had done with Holmes. The Hell Priest struggled, lashing out with his glass blade.

But it was over. Glass was pulled in every direction, bursting open, ripped to shreds – utterly destroyed.

His companions gaped at the place where he had been standing only moments before, as the blackness retreated back inside Moriarty. More of his followers were emerging from out of the shadows now, to face the leaderless trio of Cenobites. They were clumsy and undisciplined, but there was strength in numbers as I knew all too well.

Plague took charge, telling Madame and Fist to flee. "I will hold them as best I can." He did not buy them much time – spreading boils here, rashes and scales there – before one of the mechanised men came up behind him and brought together the long blades that were his arms, decapitating Plague. His head rolled away, his body toppling sideways, landing with a thud – turning to putrid liquid as, without his consciousness to keep them at bay, the diseases that raddled him did their worst.

It had been enough of a distraction, however, for his comrades to make their escape – with Holmes in tow. I saw Moriarty realise this and scream, "After them!" But that was the last I saw of what happened there, the scene fading around me.

"No... Holmes, we need to go to –"

Mary cut me off. "Our paths will cross soon enough. They will come to *us*, John. And he will need you by his side more than he's ever needed you before."

I had no choice but to believe her, she had been right about everything so far. "That... energy Moriarty was using. It was black light, wasn't it?"

Mary nodded. "That is what you call it, yes. He has been siphoning it off, a little at a time, until..."

"And that thing didn't even notice?" I pointed over the vista in the direction of their god. "What is it, anyway?"

"It is not for me to say," Mary replied sadly. "But I can tell you how powerful the Engineer is becoming. John, if he succeeds with his plans... The Cenobites only cross over into our world when they are called, but Moriarty... well..."

"He has never been one for following rules."

"If he breaks down the barrier between this reality and ours –"

"Then it will be Hell on Earth. What can we do?"

Mary paused before answering. "It is being done, John. We just have to wait a little longer."

"This connection, the reason you're here. If it's not Holmes, then it must be –"

Mary nodded. "When Sherlock... In his will, Moriarty left instructions that you should be punished, my love, as Holmes' closest associate. The Colonel was the only one of his men still at large, and so he took it upon himself to carry out those final wishes. He was going to kill you, John, by poisoning – you might recall the day, when we were about to take tea at Simpson's and you had to rush off to see one of your patients. It was that tea which was poisoned, my love; a slow-acting, practically undetectable poison."

"I remember," I said with a sigh. "You were already in a coma when I reached you at the hospital. We never even got to say goodbye."

Mary sniffed, tears welling. "Moran decided to leave you alone after that, for he could see how the grief of my passing had affected you so. As could I, but I was powerless at the time to do anything about it. When you travelled here... The link between you, me and Moriarty allowed me to..."

I clapped a hand to my eyes. "I should have known it was... I should have been able to tell, to have found a cure. An antidote for –"

Mary held my shoulders, looking right at me, crying. "There was nothing you could have done, sweetheart. I was already dead."

I'm ashamed to say that I was filled with a terrible rage then. That and a thirst for revenge, which I knew Holmes must be sharing. Not only him, but probably the Cenobites who'd just seen Glass slain right in front of them.

"And so is he," I said to Mary finally. "I swear it. Dead – for good this time!"

CHAPTER TWENTY-ONE
Broken

SHERLOCK HOLMES WAS broken; his body, his soul, his spirit. He knew that others had tolerated far more for much longer in this place; the Cenobites had mentioned eternity when he'd first encountered them. Had he not also been told by Moriarty that time worked differently here? He may have only been under the scrutiny of the Professor for minutes or hours, but such was the level of agony, that it seemed like he'd been abused for millennia.

And he'd been able to withstand most of it. Everything he had exposed himself to, from diseases and poison to blows, burns and incisions, had been leading up to this.

But then came the other tortures. The naming of all those he'd failed, often because he hadn't seen them as people to help, but mysteries to solve. He had been able to understand motivations on an academic level, but not experience emotions, such as love and jealousy... at least not in the same way others did. What had been the chink in his armour, and Moriarty knew that more than most, was his ineffectuality; his inability to fix every problem, solve every puzzle in time; falling short in his efforts to keep not only clients safe, but his friends and family. Especially his family... And he counted Watson in that category. He owed them debts he hadn't been able to repay, yet worse than that he was made to feel everything they'd ever felt *because* of him.

That had been the last straw, that is what had broken Sherlock Holmes. The sight of Watson had hurt him the most; the friend who he'd placed in harm's way, not only by sending him to Paris, but by dragging him into this mess in the first place – and for that he would never forgive himself.

So, there he was, a sad excuse for a human being – not that far removed from those lost souls Moriarty had surrounded himself with.

Except... when Holmes thought all hope was gone, imagine his surprise at seeing the quartet of Cenobites in the chamber! Come to take him back – and he was actually grateful for the fact. Nothing they had in mind or in store for him could have been worse than the suffering he had already endured.

Only there was unfinished business between Moriarty and his own torturers; those who had come when he was falling towards the rocks; those who had taken him back with them, not knowing that at some point he would make a play for the Engineer's position. A post that, as far as Holmes could determine, was separate from anything they did. Was perhaps even separate from this god of theirs? Had that entity underestimated Moriarty's resourcefulness, his ruthlessness and ambition? Saw potential in him, but not fully understood it? After all, Moriarty had obliterated the leader of the Cenobites. 'Hell's favourite,' the Professor had called him. Holmes had no idea what it took to kill one of those creatures, when bullets had as much effect as flea bites, but he suspected it was a lot. What was even more terrifying was that he also suspected Moriarty had only used a fraction of the power at his command to do so, revitalising his fallen troops at the same time.

He recalled the interview they'd conducted with Lieutenant Spencer's wife, the mention of black light, a power source here. One Moriarty had clearly tapped into.

The others appeared completely bewildered by what had happened – which only confirmed to him that Cenobite deaths did not happen often, if at all. The female, who had freed Holmes from his bonds, paused to scoop something from the floor and hide it beneath her skirts, while the diseased Cenobite remained behind to stem the mounting tide of clockwork soldiers.

And then they were hurrying through corridor after corridor and when they could run no more, the female Cenobite turned and looked behind her. "Carnivan!" she cried, warning her remaining associate, the largest of them, who spun around. Moriarty's followers filled the tunnel and Carnivan threw himself into the fray. For the first time since he'd opened the box, Holmes began to wonder if the Cenobites had always been this way, if they had always been here. He knew, from Moriarty's horrific change that, in exceptional circumstances, human beings could be transformed into these things – if they had the inclination and a certain something that had obviously been spotted in the Professor. If so, what or who had this Carnivan been before? He reminded Holmes of some of the bare-knuckle fighters he'd seen in the pits, even fought against himself when he was undergoing his training. Perhaps that was it; the flesh of his head moulded to more closely resemble what he'd once been?

Carnivan rammed into the pseudo Cenobites, crushing them against the wall with his bony head. The corridor rocked, and the female dragged Holmes back along it, reluctantly leaving her brethren behind to be swamped by the Engineer's creations.

She continued to half-carry, half-drag Holmes along, through corridor after corridor.

"W-where are you taking me?" Holmes said, though she didn't reply.

The pseudo Cenobites must have finished with Carnivan because they had renewed their pursuit.

The female dropped Holmes and unfurled her whip, gripping

it tightly. Holmes watched her swing it around her head several times, but it wasn't the clockwork monstrosities she was aiming for. She struck the ceiling, dislodging masonry. A huge stone dropped onto an advancing pseudo Cenobite, crushing it; not even Moriarty's magic would be able to resurrect the creature.

The female Cenobite struck the ceiling again and the tunnel collapsed behind them, completely cutting off their enemies.

As she lifted Holmes and hurried him along the tunnel once more he asked, blood bubbling from his mouth, "N... n-name... What... what is you... your name?"

She paused, before answering: "Veronique. They call me Veronique."

"T-thank you, Veronique."

Veronique continued to ferry him along, and at various points Sherlock Holmes passed out from his traumas, but when he opened his eyes one final time they had arrived at their destination. The corridor opened out onto a spacious landscape, a stone platform overlooking more of the network that made up this section of Hell.

And there, standing not far away, were two figures; one of whom Holmes recognised immediately. If he could have, he would have run towards the man, but his legs would not carry him any further.

"*Holmes!*" shouted Watson as he hurried over. A woman in a white dress slowly followed, floating just above the floor.

"Watson," Holmes whispered. "Is... is that really you?"

"Why, yes old fellow."

"I thought you dead."

"A deception. I am very much alive."

"Watson... Watson please forgive me... I am so, so sorry."

"No need, Holmes. No need." There was sadness in his companion's eyes as he looked over the detective, bending and reaching out a hand, then withdrawing it. "My God – look at the state of you."

"I... I fear not even your medical attentions will aid me this time, my friend." He paused, then rasped one word, "Moriarty."

"I know. Mary showed me."

"Hello Sherlock," she said, and Holmes suddenly realised who she was. "It's good to see you again, although I would have preferred it to be under much better circumstances."

Before he could say anything, Veronique cut in, "What are you doing here, ghost? You don't belong in this realm."

"There are... no such things... as ghosts..." Holmes heard his own protest and couldn't help laughing.

Watson ignored Holmes' statement and said, "Moriarty. He has to be stopped."

But Holmes' attention had strayed past Watson and Mary, to the giant shape hanging above the labyrinth. "W-what...is that?"

Veronique followed his gaze. "The one I serve. That is *my* god. The god of pain and desire."

Holmes coughed. "Lucifer?"

"No. Not the Fallen One. He is but a legend here."

"Then take me to your god, Veronique."

"Holmes, are you quite sure that –"

"Watson, *please*," he implored, grabbing the Doctor's hand with his own shredded appendage as best he could. "I need to do this." Then, to Veronique once more. "Your world is broken," he wheezed. "And I wish to broker a deal."

CHAPTER TWENTY-TWO
Knowledge is Power

MARY WAS RIGHT, of course.

They did come, though by the time they reached us there was only Madame and Holmes left. My friend was a mass of cuts, deep punctures and burnt flesh, leaving a blood trail behind him as he was hauled along by the Cenobite. I rushed over to him, distraught, though there was little I could do for his injuries, as he warned me himself. Holmes seemed happy that I was alive, but I feared he might not be for much longer.

"We have to stop Moriarty," I said to change the subject, though I had no idea how my friend would be of any assistance in this, especially now. I couldn't see how Holmes might ever recover from such terrible wounds.

Then came those dreaded words, "I wish to bargain with your god."

I tried to stop him, but it was clear that Holmes was clawing back some of that irritating stubbornness I hated and admired in equal measure. The Cenobite, whose name I discovered was actually Veronique, agreed and off they went to see the 'King of Hearts'.

"What now?"

245

"Now," said Mary, "there is a place we must visit."

As I followed my new guide, my Virgil if you will, I began to think about something Holmes had said during our brief conversation back on the platform. Holmes had asked Veronique if their god was Lucifer, and I wondered why I had never thought to question this myself. But if this was Hell, it wasn't the one we had learned about in Sunday School. Why, then, should it be presided over by Satan?

Hearing my inner thoughts once more, Mary said, "It's complicated, John. There are different kinds of Hells, as you have seen for yourself. Different parts making up the whole. All you need to know is that if the Engineer is set to break down the barriers to our world, he will not stop there. He will go on a rampage that might see Hell fall completely. Others have tried before and no doubt will do so again, even if we succeed."

"But why should we care about that? I mean, home – yes. But Hell... Surely we'd be better off without such a horrible place and its inhabitants?"

She turned and gazed at me. "There must be balances and checks, my love. Without darkness, light cannot possibly exist. It is the age old struggle. Ah, here we are..."

We had arrived at an arched door made from antiquated-looking wood, covered in knots and ridges. Mary opened this, then held out her hand for me to cross over. I was staggered by what I saw. If I'd thought the libraries of the Cotton residence and the Diogenes were impressive, they were as nothing compared to what lay before me now. The shelves were so high I could not see to the tops of them, running so long I could not see their ends. The layout of the stone corridors might have been confusing, but the rows of books here gave them a run for their money.

"What are we..." I began.

"Knowledge, John. Knowledge is power. And this room contains all the knowledge we will need to fight Moriarty."

I looked back at her. "Then I'm surprised he hasn't had the place razed to the ground."

She shook her head. "It would have tipped his hand too early to try. Besides, it cannot be destroyed. It is between worlds, and protected by forces more powerful than him."

I nodded, not really understanding and knowing that even if I asked her to explain I would probably be more confused than ever (I was – again – feeling more and more like that bumbling oaf I was later portrayed to be). I examined some of the spines of those musty old tomes, which had dates on them, the numbers reaching higher the further in we went.

"This is the Scribe's records section," Mary told me. Ledgers then, just like Mr Cotton Sr kept, but infinitely more detailed. I pulled one of the books off the shelf at random, dust causing me to cough and sneeze. I opened it up and saw accounts of what had happened to a Scottish fellow named Johne Duncansone from the early 16th Century: beginning with his childhood, flipping forward to the meeting of the woman who would become his wife, the birth of his children and finally his death; it was all written like some sort of story, pages and pages of it. As a writer myself, I couldn't help but be impressed. The narrative revealed his innermost thoughts and feelings, some of which he certainly would not have wanted anyone to know. These were records of anyone whose life had intersected with this realm.

"Are there books about me in here, Mary? About us? About Holmes?"

Mary took the huge volume from me and placed it neatly back on the shelf. "This is not what I brought you here for," she said.

She walked away and I followed, a little uneasy about the fact that my every step might be written about, recorded and kept somewhere in the library.

Mary led me to a section, where I could see a book in an illuminated glass case. Writing was appearing on the pages as if by magic, some of it in languages I did not even understand.

"What is it?" asked I.

"Every library has an index, John," Mary said. "It will tell us what we need to know – we simply have to ask."

"And what *do* we need to know, exactly?"

"How to defeat someone who is becoming a god," she said.

I THOUGHT I knew a lot about warfare, about battle tactics and troop movement, but I came away from that library feeling like I'd been the worst student ever of such things.

After we had 'asked' the great book what we needed to know, it replied by pointing us in the direction of various sections. One was devoted solely to the art of combat. It was a strange thing, but perusing these tomes I felt the information flooding into me. If I'd had access to books like these about the human body, it would have made my medical exams that much easier. I would certainly not have needed to spend the time learning anatomy by rote.

Siege tactics, heavy force, human wave attacks, turning manoeuvres... I became intimately acquainted with them all; enough that I felt sufficiently able to engage the Professor and his troops on a battlefield. I was given more information about the battles of Vienna, Yorktown, Waterloo, Cajamarca, Hastings, Antietam, Leipzig and so many others than I actually knew what to do with. The basics, though, came down to strategy and cunning – which Moriarty, I was all too aware, had more of than anyone.

It would also take a decisive leader to employ such techniques.

Next we paid a visit to the sections on ancient magicks, where we intended to gather arcane knowledge that would aid and protect us, as I would definitely be in over my head facing the Engineer's pseudo Cenobites. I was hesitant, but Mary once again managed to persuade me I was doing the right thing, for the greater good. But if that was the case, why did it feel so very wrong? Probably because all this went against everything I've ever believed in and stood for. It is not so easy to ignore such misgivings.

As our research continued, I felt Mary stiffen beside me. "John... we are not alone."

I looked up. "I can't see anyth –"

But yes! I could sense it now: the strongest feeling that we were being watched. "There's definitely someone in here with us," I said.

She nodded. "Agents of the other side."

No sooner had she said this than the attack began. Moriarty may not have been able to destroy the library, but he could certainly stop people leaving it with vital information. Moriarty's soldiers this time were arachnid in nature: spider-things almost as large as the Hound. Part organic – with human limbs as legs – part mechanical, they were the most hideous creatures I'd seen so far. And there were at least four that I could count... maybe even more waiting in the wings.

The nearest one shot out a web, which looked to be made from strands of black light. I pushed Mary out of the way, as the webbing struck a bookcase, sending broken shelves and tomes flying. I wasn't quick enough the second time, however, and a web struck Mary, pinning her to a bookcase; ghost or not, it was hurting her! As I went to help, two more spiders leapt at me – one scratching me down the side of my cheek with a sharpened mandible. What could I do? The only weapon to hand was the book I'd been reading, which I used to club the thing and send it flying. The second spider reared up in front of me, kicking me back into more shelves and winding me.

I slid down, waiting for them to advance again – then rolled sideways out of the way, so they'd hit the shelving themselves. Books from above were dislodged and dropped onto the spiders, trapping them. I narrowly avoided being hit with another strand of webbing, kicking out at the spider who'd fired it and sending it spinning over and over. Breathing hard, I made my way over to Mary, only to find the final spider suddenly in my way. It rose up, ready to launch its web, when suddenly something wrapped itself around the monstrosity, tugging hard.

The wrench caused the thing to split in two, pus-like ooze flowing from its body. I looked over in time to see Madame Veronique, aiming her whip at the webbing that was holding Mary, freeing her with a series of precision strokes. My wife fell and I caught her in my arms. "Are you all right?" I asked, and she nodded.

I glanced across in time to see the spider I'd kicked about to leap on the Cenobite. "John... the magick," said Mary. "Use your magick!"

There was no other option; I mumbled the first words I could call to mind, held out my hand and closed it into a fist. The spider curled up into itself, mangled into a tight ball by my spell.

I opened my fingers slowly, amazed by what I'd just done.

Veronique turned, looked down at the mess, and nodded. As much of a thank you as I would get from a servant of Hell. Hugging Mary close, I said, "I... I thought you said this place, these books, were protected?"

Then I looked again at the devastation Moriarty's beasts had wrought, to find everything in its rightful place. The books that had been destroyed were back on the shelf, as were the ones that had fallen on those spiders who attacked me.

We joined Madame, who was examining the dead Cenobitical spiders nearest to her. "Lucky you happened to come along," I said.

"It was no coincidence. I was sent to fetch you both at my Lord's behest."

I sighed. "What does your god want with us now?"

"Not my god," Veronique explained. "My Lord and Master. The being that was once known as Sherlock Holmes."

CHAPTER TWENTY-THREE
Born Again

DYING WAS HARD.

However, what followed was the most painful thing Holmes had ever experienced. Inside that great machine he'd been slowly unpicked, piece by piece, until there was only his essence left. He was confronted not only with his failures, but the fact that his existence had been insignificant compared with the future that awaited him. Yet something kept drawing him back to that moment at the Falls, grappling with Moriarty, losing his footing and tumbling over and over – losing sight of the Professor, but seeing *something* as the man fell away from him. The opening of a door, a gateway unlocked by the solving of a mathematical puzzle. A gateway through which he'd seen something; through which something had seen *him*.

The sight had instilled in him a desire to find out more, and the nagging feeling that something terrible was going to happen that he needed to prepare for. That moment had led to him finally being mangled himself by his arch-nemesis, who'd escaped and suffered at the hands of the Cenobites, only to claw his way to the top of the ranks and operate behind their god's back. A god that now needed Holmes' help, that was prepared to heal and transform him so that he could finally put an end to Moriarty's schemes.

This was how they were made, he'd been told – how they always had been since anyone could remember; unique individuals chosen to fulfil a certain set of duties. A constant stream of servitors to do Hell's bidding. Something of the previous character would always be retained, however – reflected in the dress or what was done to the flesh. Holmes' coolness, his aloofness, should have stood him in good stead during and after his conversion, if it hadn't been for the Engineer's heightening of his senses. Consequently he'd felt *everything*, not just the pain but every single moment of his being, good and bad. Every kind of emotion bombarded him at once, so many that he thought he was going to explode.

However, his alteration was different to those who had gone before. Their god had handed over as much of its power as it was able, enough – hopefully – that he would be able to stop Moriarty. He would be himself, but at the same time its vessel.

It would take a god to fight a god.

So he was pieced back together. Born again. Organs, muscle, bone and skin. All much stronger than before, his outer-layer bearing the markings of his transformation: blue flesh patterned with redness. Then clothed in the traditional leathers, the finishing touches added. A worthy general to command Hell's forces.

As he stepped out of the 'womb', she had been waiting for him. Veronique, who had escorted him to parlay with a deity, who had saved him so that he could take the place of her beloved.

Her reaction was... unexpected. Mouth gaping, hands trembling, she fell to her knees in front of him, swearing her fealty. He doubted the others would be so quick to do the same, some would take greater persuasion – but in the end they would see it his way. There was a war coming and he needed soldiers.

But first, he needed his best friend.

He needed Watson.

*   *   *

WHEN VERONIQUE RETURNED from the library with the man himself, accompanied by his late wife, the Holmes Cenobite was standing and looking out at the view.

Now he knew every single corridor of Hell, knew where each archway led. He could even find his way to the heart of the maze; and he admired the simple complexity of it all, the beautiful contradiction. He was also aware now of every single member of the Order, had already sent out a call to them. A call to arms; a summons stronger than any opening of the box, than any solving of a knot or code or origami exercise.

But Watson, well he'd had to send for him the old-fashioned way. Veronique had been all too willing to oblige, obeying her first command with delight. She'd known, even as she was carrying him to make his pact, that this was the only way to ensure Hell's survival. That he was the key to the Engineer's downfall, and subsequently, her revenge.

"Here they are, my Lord. They were under attack when I found them."

He did not turn, not yet ready to see the horror in his friend's eyes.

"Holmes..." Watson began, and he could hear his footsteps. "Holmes, what have you –"

Holmes finally faced his old companion. "Only what I had to do," he replied. But instead of horror, he saw yet more sadness there. The kind of sadness that comes with grief at the loss of a loved one. "What was necessary."

"Oh Holmes," was all the Doctor could muster. "Surely there must have been some other way?"

"If there was, I remain at a loss to see it," he admitted. "You and I both know what is at stake here." Once again, he had sacrificed himself – a means to an end. The same means to an end, in fact: to rid the world, *both* these worlds, of Professor

Moriarty. "Have you yourself not crossed a line, also?" he said. "I can smell the dark magick on you."

Watson hung his head. "So," he said when he looked up, "you have done what you have done. You are their leader now, you have an army of Cenobites at your disposal. Why do you need me anymore?"

Holmes placed his hands on Watson's shoulders. "You think I don't need you?" he said. "I need you more than I have ever done before. You are my right arm. You are my constant companion. You are my friend... And you are my Major. It is not just my army to command – it is *ours!*"

Watson stared at him, searching a face that he knew and yet didn't. Then he looked back over his shoulder at Mary, who smiled. "Very well," he said, turning back and nodding. "What happens next?"

"I would seek your counsel, Watson. There is much preparation to do before we meet our enemy on the field of combat." Holmes waited a moment or two then finished with, "And our army will need to be armed."

CHAPTER TWENTY-FOUR
Hell's Armoury

BY THE TIME Madame Veronique had led us to Holmes, I'd worked it out.

I knew by the way she now referred to him – her Master; her Lord – that whatever deal he had done with their god, it had put him in charge; Glass' replacement as Hell's favourite son. I had to hope it was only temporary, although when I saw him standing on the edge of that precipice, surveying his new kingdom, I began to wonder if it was. His stiff demeanour had returned after the rigours of his time with Moriarty. His clothes – that dress, the leathers of his trousers and cape – mirrored the outfit that I had seen him wear so many times, on so many adventures, but it was only as I called out a greeting and he turned, that I saw exactly what had happened to Sherlock Holmes.

His pale face was covered in markings – his flesh tattooed with symbols from the box, grafted not just onto his countenance but also visible on every inch of exposed skin. The scarification looked red raw, but Holmes showed no sign that he was in pain. However, it was his eyes that most startled me, not totally devoid of white, but cloudy and swirling, as if full of the black light that had so empowered the Professor.

"What have you done?" I asked him.

"Only what was necessary," came his reply. Yet, the more I looked at him, the more we talked, the more I sensed the true Holmes beneath it all. The one I had so wanted to return to me ever since his... since his death. How ironic that it had taken his actual death, that it had taken being turned into one of them – one of the Order – for this to happen. His very survival dependent on his dying first. And how strange that after all the disguises I had seen him don over the years, I found this one – a Cenobite, and a Cenobite general at that! – the least convincing. Nevertheless, it appeared the most permanent.

My shock at all this would have to wait, though. As Mary had said, and Holmes confirmed, he needed me now more than ever and what forces were his to command were also mine. But first, before we could talk about how we were going to fight Moriarty, I would need to see what kind of weaponry Hell had to offer.

If anything, its armoury – which Veronique took us to next – was larger than its library. Knowledge might well be power, but one would have been able to rule entire continents with only a fraction of the arsenal in that place.

"I've... I've never seen anything like it," I admitted. And I never would again. If you took all of the weaponry from all of the wars I'd been taught about, and placed it together, then you still wouldn't have any sense of the cache that had been amassed and stored here.

There were swords and axes, so sharp they could cleave stone in two; maces I couldn't even lift, that would cave in a skull proficiently if wielded by expert hands; spears forged from gold and silver, decorated with jewels – although whether they were for show or to cause more damage, I could not say. There were scythes that would have made the Grim Reaper green with envy; bows and arrows and crossbows I was assured, when used, would penetrate even the toughest of armour. Defensive weapons too – shields of every size and shape, polished and gleaming. There were rifles and pistols that would never run out of bullets; shells so large that they could probably destroy an entire building. I picked up several of the handguns, testing their weight in my hands and finding each one perfectly balanced.

All of this on top of the supernatural powers that were already at each Cenobite's disposal.

"What's behind there?" I asked Madame, pointing to a huge metal door that had a padlock on the handle.

"Our most dangerous array."

"More dangerous than all this? Is that even possible?" Poor choice of words, I know, for none of this should actually have been possible. Part of me was still waiting to recover from whatever drugs or hypnosis had been used on me. But all I could really do was play along and hope for the best. If the fate of the world, *my* world, rested on what happened next, whether this was real or not, I had to give it my best shot.

"Yes. Staffs of power, magical hammers, amulets, wands and stones... They are locked away because they are the items that are potentially the most harmful to us. That can do us the most damage."

"Forgive me for saying so, but I think right now we could do with all the damage we can get our hands on, don't you?" I looked from Mary to the female Cenobite. Veronique thought about it for a moment or two, so I prompted her. "Holmes did say *all* of this was at our disposal."

Finally, she agreed and opened the door with a key while mouthing a series of incantations. "I... This is not right," she said gazing into the vault.

Mary and I peered around her, but all we could see was blackness. "There's nothing in here."

"The weapons have been stolen!" shouted Veronique.

"If I was still a betting man, I would put quite a considerable amount of money on who has taken them."

Mary closed her eyes and nodded. "You would not lose that bet, John."

"Then the situation is graver than we thought."

"And if you're going to arm the Cenobites, you need to do so quickly," Mary added. "Because it is about to start. The Professor is gathering his troops together. Soon they will march and then..."

"Then," I said, "then you will have your war."

CHAPTER TWENTY-FIVE
Hellfire with Hellfire

THE MAN WHO had once been Sherlock Holmes stared out over the congregation of Cenobites below, armed and as ready as they'd ever be, laid out like pieces on a chess board.

His father would have been proud that he commanded such an army, though probably not what they consisted of, nor the way he had come by his new rank.

(And he knew he was fortunate that he was even able to retain those memories; none of the other Cenobites had... apart, of course, from the Engineer, by way of trickery.)

"Sherlock," his father had once said, "it does not take courage to send men into battle. But it does to *lead* them into battle." Those were words he intended to honour. He would not hide behind a wall of bodies until the fighting was done. No, he would lead by example.

His gaze swept over the figures in black, metal glinting here and there in the cobalt luminescence of Hell. Still, there were not nearly as many as there had once been – and now he knew why. The secret vault of the armoury had been accessed, the most lethal weapons of all taken; used, a few at a time. Moriarty had been building his own creations and simultaneously whittling down the number of true Cenobites, knowing that this day would come. One step ahead, as usual.

One step ahead until he'd let Holmes escape from his clutches, that was; a move which had forced his hand, escalated things somewhat. He might have gone on, destroying servant after servant, draining off more and more black light until his victory was all but assured. And then... well, who knows what would have happened once Hell was under his control? What might *still* happen...

It was a powerful drug, the light. Even now he felt it coursing through him, strengthening him; more potent than anything he'd ever taken, more toxic than any poison he'd ever fed himself. Part of him couldn't blame the Professor for wanting more, for wanting so much he would elevate himself above all other Cenobites, so much he would practically *be* a god himself. If the amount he'd 'borrowed' made Holmes feel like this, how would it be if it was all inside him?

But it wasn't his to take, to own. It belonged to some*thing* else. His new father and mother combined, who had granted him this form. Who would ordinarily have winked him out of existence just as quickly for such thoughts – if it hadn't needed him so badly. As badly as he'd needed Watson's support himself.

Time ran differently here, but it could still run out, and they'd only just had enough to confer about the best course of action, broaching ideas about the strategies that might win them this war, eventually coming to an agreement on one plan – and with another little surprise up their sleeve from Holmes. Something, hopefully, the Professor had not anticipated.

It was how they'd always worked best, Watson asking those niggling little questions and forcing Holmes to think harder, to be on top of his game; to doubt himself, but to finally break through to a solution. Oh, Holmes masked it all the time, the doubt which was always there, but knew Watson suspected the truth.

He looked over at Veronique, who had substituted her skirts

for leather breeches and was now preparing to lead her own troops: a squadron of Amazonian-looking Cenobite women, some – who were holding bows already primed with arrows – having cut or cauterised their breasts in order to obtain a better aim. Holmes knew they had enjoyed this process of scarification, the ladies being Cenobites after all. Also amongst their number was the winged Lilith, first wife of Adam, seductress and child-murderer; Eve, who many still believed to be the first woman and was often blamed for original sin; Cleopatra the Alchemist, originally from the 3rd Century AD and not to be confused with the famous Egyptian Queen, she had actually been one of the few who possessed the knowledge of the Philosopher's Stone; Joan of Arc, who had been influenced by her countryman Gilles de Rais and took part in rituals to bring forth demons to help the French fight the British, creatures who had eventually 'saved' her from the fire after recognising her potential; and the woman who had once been known as Elizabeth Báthory, who had bathed in the blood of her hundreds of victims, and was now permanently red and slick with the stuff...

Veronique herself was armed not only with her whip, but with the weapon she'd stooped to snatch up when they were escaping from Moriarty's lair: her former leader's glass blade. She must have felt Holmes' eyes upon her because she looked up and saluted. Holmes nodded and returned the gesture.

Holmes looked out over his army. Even the most rebellious Cenobites had rallied to his call now he had been so transformed. One, called Tomain, had such tiny pin-prick eyes it was a wonder he could see anything. Another had several bulging, bloodshot eyes that stood out on its shaved head. He was known as The Watcher. One Cenobite had skin that looked paper thin, almost translucent. His mouth was damaged, flesh ripped away to reveal ragged teeth, and his eyes glowed red in his skull. This was Vestimenti, one of the oldest and wisest of those gathered below; Holmes was lucky to have gained his support.

Holmes' gaze came to rest on The Ravisher, whose eyelids and lips had been wrenched back by hooks; more a lover than a fighter, even so he had answered the summons. As had The Confessor, with his jaw stretched obscenely wide, to accommodate his many writhing tongues. Not far away was the Cenobite known as Our Lord of Quarters, a demon obsessed with wealth and the striking of bargains, his finest hour had been in Constantinople many centuries ago. Coins formed the irises of his eyes, and were embedded in his gums, flashing whenever he grimaced. And who could forget The Gardener, usually found in the centre of his own maze of foliage; his body alive with branches, plants and vines.

One Cenobite stood poised to strike, with a six inch knife in one hand, a curving blade in the other, shrouded in a cloak of darkness. He was still known only as 'Jack', even in Hell, but Holmes was now privy to his true identity – had once helped Inspector Abberline pursue him, London's most notorious killer – and it at least cleared up the mystery of where the villain had disappeared to. He wasn't at all surprised that the man had been added to the Order, given his penchant for slaughter, his talent for inflicting pain. Holmes never dreamt they'd ever be on the same side.

Umbra favoured rope as his method of self-harm – or self-pleasure, as it was here – and they had been wrapped around the Cenobite with the skill of a seaman. Some were so tightly wound the muscle on either side was grossly swollen. Then there was Gamont, whose skin had a rough, rock-like texture. Meanwhile Harrigad's frame more closely resembled that of a scarecrow, but instead of straw it was sharpened wire he'd been 'stuffed' with. Cassandra's flesh looked like melting wax, her features shifting with each movement, bare arms and legs hardly able to retain their shape, her torso barely contained by her leather corset. Flourret, meanwhile, looked like he had just come from an abattoir; a magnificent super-butcher complete with apron, and with a slab of meat slung over one shoulder, he held a massive cleaver which dripped with blood.

Perhaps the most disquieting of all, however, was the Cenobite who had a metal spike rammed right through his head, dried blood caked around the sides, a helmet helping the skull to retain its shape. It was as if he'd been the victim of some sort of train derailment, and had no business being up and about, let alone in the ranks of their crude army.

On and on, no two alike, so many variations, plucked from different places, different times. Holmes saw some costumes that resembled Samurai dress, others that were more like the knights of the Middle Ages or gladiators of classical times, while still others looked like pirates, complete with eye-patches and cutlasses. There were those who'd been snatched from more modern conflicts, holding their rifles and pistols, but would it all be enough? Holmes had to hope so, had to claw back some of that lost – broken – hope Moriarty had ripped from him.

There was no more delaying, the great bell was tolling, signalling the approach of their enemy. Holmes reached down and picked up his headgear, placing the black deerstalker on his head and snatching up his cane before making his way down to join his soldiers. Mycroft had often told him when he was younger to make the best of things, to take advantage of all situations and see them as a way to learn. Maybe he was doing just that now, but he doubted it.

What he was doing was settling an old score.

The rumbling started across the way as he descended the steps from the balcony. He'd ordered several of the arches across the plaza to be demolished, hindering the progress of the enemy, funnelling the Professor's troops in one direction, so they could be picked off as they struggled through. And, as they started to emerge, the monstrous Hound leading the way, it seemed like that plan was working.

The first of the Engineer's clockwork monstrosities ventured through and were met by Holmes' initial line of defence, hooks and chains flying into them, pulling them in every direction. Holmes might have felt sorry for them, had he not come to terms with the fact that they were giving them a sweet release, granting them their ultimate freedom... as long as Moriarty didn't reanimate them.

The strategy seemed to be working, but seconds later, there was a massive bang followed by flying masonry – some of it hitting the Cenobites at the front. Other explosions followed, clearing the blockages and allowing more of the Engineer's foot-soldiers free passage. Even Holmes balked at their numbers. It was only now that he could see what had caused the blasts: one of Moriarty's men had a cannon fixed to his chest – no, in fact it *was* his chest, firing discharges of pure black light into the crowds Pieces of stone erupted into the air where the blasts hit, taking Cenobites with them, raining down debris and body parts alike.

There was no sign of the Professor; he was obviously letting his troops clear the way before showing himself. But that wasn't going to be Holmes' way. Climbing into the back of a chariot attached to a skeletal steed, he took hold of the reins and urged his vehicle forward. A path opened up, Cenobites moving aside so he could make his way to the front.

"Charge!" he cried at the top of his voice.

Holmes gripped the reins with one hand and brought his stick to bear with the other; attached to the top was a large round object that looked a little like a magnifying glass. He let loose a bolt of black light, focussed by the glass: fighting fire with fire. *Hellfire* with *Hellfire*. It sprayed the pseudo Cenobites, scattering them. But there was another wave coming immediately behind: more of those mechanical human-spiders that had caused Watson problems back in the library.

He couldn't help it, even as he led this fight against the enemy, Holmes' thoughts turned to his friend, wondering how he was faring, hoping at least that part of their plan would work.

CHAPTER TWENTY-SIX
Best Laid Plans...

It was a variation of the strategic envelopment manoeuvre.

That's what Holmes and I came up with after conferring about the best way to proceed. It wasn't easy, let me tell you – after all those times in his study, mulling over cases, while he smoked his pipe or we drank brandy; to see him like that, to be *around* him in his new guise. Soldiering I understood; I didn't much care for it after everything I'd seen and experienced, but I at least understood it. This... this was beyond any comprehension. Yet I persevered and, once we had gone through all the options – including the possibility of using flanking, pincer or encirclement manoeuvres – we settled upon a variant of the tactic Napoleon often favoured (ironic, given who we were up against). Holmes and his forces would face the enemy head on when they came, trying to bottleneck their advance by blocking off certain routes. Myself and another group would skirt around the back, attacking from the rear.

"It's risky," I told him, "but it could work. If he's ploughing most of his number into a full frontal attack, which Mary insists he is, then they won't be expecting us to come at them from behind. It might also be where they're hiding the weapons they stole, so if I can take those out of the equation as well…"

I could tell Holmes would have felt more comfortable if I had remained with him, to offer support and strategy in the midst of the battle, but it would take someone who knew what they were doing to time it just right.

Holmes shook my hand before we headed off, wishing me luck. "They will follow your orders to the letter," he assured me, gesturing to my small squadron.

They were bizarre, freaks to a man – and woman – each as monstrous as the next, and I couldn't repress a shudder of disgust at their appearance. One of them looked like the living embodiment of a jigsaw puzzle, his flesh made up of sections that had been slotted together; the grooves thick with dried blood. One of the female Cenobites was covered in scales, a forked tongue flicking in and out of her mouth. Then there was the Cenobite that had two huge cuts for a face – no other features, just the titular gashes of the Order – one running vertically, from domed head to chin, and one where his mouth should have been, resembling an inverted cross. There was even one creature that looked to be three Cenobites in one, wound *into* each other: triplets perhaps? I'd seen conjoined twins before, but never anything like this, attached as they were by the legs, the waist, and their heads; most of their disfigurement thankfully covered over by copious amounts of leather.

It almost made me sick to look at them, worse than anything Bosch could ever have conceived of, and yet we would have to rely on each other wholeheartedly. Thankfully I would have Mary by my side. Part of me wanted to keep her away from any of the fighting, but then – as she argued – nowhere would be soon safe.

"John, my love – it is too soon to be parted again," she had said, and I concurred. I never wanted to let her go again, if the truth be told.

Concealed about my person were a variety of pistols, and I'd donned a sturdy breastplate. In my hands I held a rifle, which I had been told could fire repeatedly without having to be cocked after each shot. How much of an effect it would have on Moriarty's playthings remained to be seen, even if it had come straight from Hell's armoury.

I'd experienced warfare before, killed men I did not know, merely because they happened to be on the opposing side. Perhaps they had deserved it, yet I'd always regretted the loss of human life – how could I not, given that I had also trained to preserve it? This, though, was an altogether different kettle of fish. The tortured souls that the Professor had used as raw material for his puppets, I had to believe, would welcome the chance to be free again; for their spirits to go wherever they were destined, before he got hold of them. This thought made it somewhat easier to fight them – and did nothing to quell my hatred of the person who was really responsible for all this; for the death of my wife, as well. I know Holmes had his own axe to grind, and had suffered so much at Moriarty's hands, but I really hoped I would get a chance to have my own revenge upon the Engineer.

Our goodbyes said, we set off then down the winding corridors. It did not take as long as I thought to reach our destination, having benefited from a few short-cuts known to Mary and the Cenobites. We were behind enemy lines, closing in on our targets: those making up the backbone of the Professor's forces. We proceeded quietly, pressing ourselves up against the stone walls and sliding along until the mechanical pseudo Cenobites were in view. Then we waited, and waited...

"The Engineer is mounting his first attack," Mary whispered. "It is time, my darling."

I nodded, and held up my hand to my troops. I was just about to drop it when I felt fingers around my throat. Shocked, I turned awkwardly to see Mary, face contorted. "It's... it's not me, John," she said through clenched teeth.

Her grip tightened, and her voice changed, becoming deeper. "I thought I felt someone poking around in my mind. The thing about connections like ours, Doctor, is that they work both ways!"

Mary flung me across the corridor and into the opposite wall. Moriarty was controlling her, just like he was controlling his own people.

"Men!" Mary cried in that same deep voice, shouting out a warning – or an order – to the pseudo Cenobites. The row of soldiers spun around, and we were just as suddenly facing as much trouble as Holmes and his band out there on the front.

The best laid plans had gone awry in the space of just a few moments.

A couple of the Cenobites lunged at Mary, perhaps thinking – too late – that they could silence her. "No!" I screamed, for she was not responsible for her own actions. I needn't have worried, for my spouse stuck the first across the jaw, then shucked the other one off her when it tried to grab her arm.

"John," she pleaded in her own voice, but I wasn't sure what I could do. And we had other problems. The pseudo Cenobites surged towards us. The Cenobite who had only cuts for features, soon added more to his collection as a mechanical warrior with a rotating blade arm drove this into his 'face', splattering blood everywhere. The snake-woman ducked, shrugging off one of her attackers and lashing out with a huge tongue that wrapped around its neck so she could draw it in for close combat. Sadly, another pseudo Cenobite grabbed the tongue with both hands and pulled in opposite directions, ripping the thing in two. The snake-woman stumbled backwards, clawing at her mouth. Jigsaw seemed to be faring better, for whenever he was struck his flesh would open up and then knit itself together again as hooked chains flew in from every direction, ripping apart his opponents.

I rose and fired into the mob, but no matter now valiantly we fought, it was clear we were hopelessly outnumbered.

Our plan had quite spectacularly failed.

CHAPTER TWENTY-SEVEN
The Rush

SHERLOCK HOLMES HAD never felt such exhilaration, such a rush. This must have been what it was like during those great historical clashes – kings fighting shoulder to shoulder with their countrymen to drive back the enemy. They were hopelessly outnumbered, of course: Moriarty's hordes continued to flow through the gaps in the walls, reminding Holmes of what had happened to Carnivan; ants swarming over a hill. He watched as one of the Professor's creatures unfurled a huge scorpion-like stinger before burying the tip into a Cenobite's skull. The combatant – a tall, rake thin Cenobite known as Brakis – was lifted into the air and battered against walls and pillars. His cries could be heard even above the fighting as he was cast down into the waiting abyss below.

A centipede-esque pseudo Cenobite, made up of dozens of the lost souls welded together, powered through Holmes' ranks, winding in and out to knock combatants clean off their feet. One of Holmes' best warriors – Matadin, who was an overweight individual with rolls and rolls of fat – had unleashed a hook and chain to snag the beast, using his weight to anchor himself and direct it off course; while Jack had climbed up on its hind quarters, kicking away a multitude of hands as he cut into leather and metal alike, making his way to the front to shove a blade so far into the creature that the whole muddled mess unravelled. He just about had time to spring off – losing his hat in the process – before the pseudo Cenobite came to a halt at the base of one of the pillars. His grimace of satisfaction soon changed to one of despair as the individual lost souls that had made up the creature scampered their separate ways to continue the fight.

Above the battle, huge moth-like creations soared through the air, spewing gouts of black light that exploded amongst the Cenobites below. Though he should have felt dismay at the carnage before him, Holmes realised that this was the perfect opportunity to reveal his surprise. His troops could sense it as well, for they were huddling together, trying to lure the flying aberrations towards them. Nearer and nearer, waiting for their mouths to open again and –

Suddenly his troops ducked, drawing out polished shields, slotting them together to form one massive barrier that reflected the black light right back at the winged monsters, incinerating them with their own blasts of energy. Having tackled these, Holmes' troops turned and angled their shields to face the oncoming horde, deflecting the blasts from the huge cannons mounted in the chests of the pseudo Cenobites, turning their deadly discharge back on the enemy.

Moriarty was using so much of his own power to keep his men going, that Holmes hoped he was beginning to spread his resources too thinly, and they could keep his troops at bay long enough for Watson's squadron to have some kind of impact on the other side.

Holmes ducked just in time to avoid a metal claw. A pseudo Cenobite had thrown itself at Holmes' chariot, but that had turned out to be a distraction, as a javelin was tossed into the spokes of the wheels, causing the vehicle to upturn. Holmes was pitched forward, landing awkwardly on a nearby group of enemy soldiers. He rose up, his cane held aloft, turning in a circle and completely obliterating his assailants with his black light beam.

Cenobite warriors were dropping all around him, riddled with bullet-holes... But these were no ordinary wounds, caused, as they were, by small pellets of rock; pieces of sacred stone, one of the weapons stolen from the armoury broken up. Holmes looked up and across, tracing the trajectory of the unusual bullets. He'd known even before his eyes found the man that it had to be Colonel Moran, camped out on a high balcony and hunched down over a rifle that was pumping out round after round.

"Veronique!" shouted Holmes, and gestured up towards Moran. She nodded, signalling Lilith to join her. There was a brief exchange, after which Lilith picked Veronique up and unfurled her wings. They rose rapidly, narrowly avoiding a collision with one of Moriarty's moth-creatures, which Veronique shredded with her whip.

Moran saw their approach and trained his rifle on them, letting off two shots in quick succession. Lilith banked and the pellets fell just short, but it drove home that they couldn't wait any longer. Lilith let her living payload go and Veronique's whip was out again, the sentient barbs digging into the edge of Moran's perch. He leaned over, aiming for her, but the angle was too acute this time, and, seconds later, Veronique had swung up to wrap her legs around the sniper's neck, twisting and causing him to tumble forward into thin air.

Holmes let out a sigh of relief as he saw the man plummet towards the ground, but it was short-lived when he witnessed another of the winged creatures swooping in to catch him. Below, another wave of pseudo Cenobites flooded in and submerged his troops. Holmes could only watch as Gamont was pushed to the edge of the precipice and shoved over, dropping much further than Moran had with no hope of rescue; not even Lilith could reach him in time, even if one of her wings hadn't just been damaged by a spear thrown in her direction. She spun downwards, and careered into a group of enemy soldiers, knocking some of them over the edge in the process. It was a bitter triumph given the circumstances and the fact that, bit by bit, Holmes' army was being eradicated.

Still there was no sign of his true enemy. Where was Moriarty hiding? But, perhaps more importantly:

"Watson, where are you?" Holmes shouted, dodging another blow – this time from a ridged saw that stood in place of one poor unfortunate's forearm. He brought his cane down and relieved this particular lost soul of his weapon, before sweeping the soldier's legs out from underneath him, staking him with the bottom of his cane.

"Where *are* you?" he repeated, and surveyed the scene of devastation.

CHAPTER TWENTY-EIGHT
Darkest

WE WERE ON the verge of defeat, I don't mind admitting. Our darkest hour without doubt, and certainly mine since this whole sorry story began.

I could do nothing to help my comrades – such as they were. Monsters themselves, and perhaps deserving of the end that was coming to them, they were, however, all that stood between us and the fall of this second front. My bullets were finding their marks, but against such odds our chances of survival, let alone success, seemed pitifully low.

And that was *before* an old adversary announced himself, appearing as little more than a cloud of dust at first: the aristocrat, who had been all but destroyed by the Plague Cenobite back when Holmes had been freed from his Moriarty's grasp. He could now slip easily into mouths and ears and eyes, felling my troops from the inside.

It was then that he spotted me. "Ah, what have we here? *Le soldat!*"

I fired off a number of rounds, but of course these did nothing. He wasn't solid, held together only by the wicked determination of the Engineer. A raucous laughter filled the corridor, bouncing off the clammy stonework. "This time you miss, I think."

The aristocrat flew at me, and I knew I only had moments before he was inside me. Panic setting in, I recalled words I'd read in the library, a spell that might just save my life. Speaking the incantation, I opened my right hand. There was a high-pitched scream as the aristocrat's body dissipated, strewn in every direction with no chance of reassembling itself; I'd seen to that.

I stared at the space in front of me, thinking then that maybe there *was* hope.

There was a sudden flash of yellow light. It took a few moments for my eyes to adjust, but when they did I saw that the band of Cenobites who'd been closest to me, ten or so at the last count, were now gone, vanished by that luminescence. But what had caused it?

Then I saw that one of the pseudo Cenobites was wearing a medallion, the source of that blast. More were stepping forward, wearing similar accoutrements, and still others had staffs and sticks, wands: the weapons Madame Veronique had spoken of back in the armoury. The approaching figures could easily wipe out the rest of my squadron, not that there were many left.

I'd failed Holmes totally: failed to make a dent in these forces; failed to flush out the Professor.

Just as it seemed all was lost, the ground shook and a hole appeared in a wall not far from those pseudo Cenobites. When the dust cleared, I could see that the aperture had been made by none other than Fist. I had thought him dead, though he was anything but, stomping through the enemy, razored knuckles tearing into them before they could even bring their weapons to bear.

The distraction was sorely needed, but I still didn't have a clue how to turn things around. Thankfully someone else did. I'd lost sight of Mary in all the confusion, had last seen her raining blows on Cenobites under the control of the Professor, but now I heard her voice again.

"John... John, where are you?"

"I'm here," I replied, then spied her slumped against a wall. I hadn't been the only one who'd lost track of her, it seemed – Moriarty's influence had worn off. I rushed over. "Oh Mary..."

"John, there's no time. The connection."

"I know. It wasn't your fault."

She shook her head. "We can use it against *him*. Take my hand. It might only work for a little while, but it will be time enough – I hope. Now close your eyes and concentrate."

"On what?"

"On Moriarty."

I focused on the last time I'd seen him, when Mary had shown me the vision of him torturing my friend. The anger I'd felt at what he'd done to my wife, the instructions he'd left to have us both killed. "Yes, that's it. We're getting through!"

I could feel myself looking out through his eyes. He knew we were there, but it was too late. Through him, we were able to reach out to his troops surrounding us.

I opened my eyes, watching as the pseudo Cenobites ahead of me turned their weapons upon themselves, amulets and wands; even a bejewelled hammer brought down on a fellow trooper. Fist paused, stepped back, then lumbered over to us. It was a sight to behold, and we were joined by the rest of my surviving troops, looking on in astonishment.

All of a sudden everything was quiet.

Mary leaned against the wall and smiled at me. "We did it."

"We certainly did, my love," I said, brushing back her hair. I looked at each of the remaining Cenobites in turn – the triplets, Jigsaw, snake-woman, Fist – and said, "Moriarty will have no option now but to move forward, because he knows what we have done, what we are capable of with those weapons – and he knows we are right on his heels. He will have no choice but to come out of hiding... To finally face Holmes once more!"

CHAPTER TWENTY-NINE
War is Hell

IT WAS CHAOS.

Bodies covered the landscape, some hanging from precipices, some littering the lower levels, nailed to archways by hooks and chains, just like the butcher, Flourret, who was hanging amongst them, almost unrecognisable. Unlike Watson, Holmes had never served in the Army; never fought in a war. It was nowhere near as glamorous or exciting as some writers made it out to be; this was dirty and bloody and unpalatable. *War is Hell*, he thought, and nowhere was that more appropriate than here.

But it was also necessary; to stop a madman's plans, to prevent him from taking over this dimension, and elsewhere. Holmes shuddered at the thought of a Hell populated by Moriarty's puppets, of an Earth where he ruled supreme. Here, now, they had a chance; still had a glimmer of hope while the last of them remained standing against the mass of clockwork demons. Like the men at Rorke's Drift, they would stand firm even though the odds were against them.

Morale was waning, though, even Holmes could see that. The Cenobites who were still up and fighting – including the female archers, and 'Spike' headbutting another foe – were close to exhaustion. The mechanical beings thrown at them didn't need to rest, didn't care about fallen companions, they simply kept coming. Not far away, Holmes saw one of the Samurai Cenobites – Hukatu – cleave a clockwork Cenobite in half with his razor-sharp katana, only to have the two separate pieces beset him; Bathory, slick with blood, was leaping onto backs, biting necks, tearing away flesh and motorised workings alike with her pointed teeth... until she was hauled off by three pseudo Cenobites who proceeded to trample her until she was merely a stain on the stone floor. Cassandra, her malleable flesh gumming up the workings of the lost souls she was fighting, came to the aid of Harrigad, who'd had most of his wire-like innards already ripped out. All this while Veronique provided covering fire using the weapon Moran had abandoned up in his nest.

Enough was enough Holmes decided.

"*Engineer!*" he hollered. "Show yourself, coward!"

The only response was from some nearby pseudo Cenobites who zeroed in on Holmes. He obliged them by blasting each in turn with black light, sending body parts flying.

Then, suddenly, he was there. Floating out on those hideous tentacles, grinning madly as he surveyed the scene, parting the chains that criss-crossed in front of him. "I am no coward, Holmes, as you well know from our previous encounters." Moriarty locked eyes with his nemesis.

"And I am no longer at a disadvantage, as I was the last time we met," spat Holmes.

"I like the new look. Very fashionable." Moriarty's grin widened. "I was wondering who our 'Lord and Master' might select now as his champion. I never in a million years imagined it would be you. That you would willingly choose to turn yourself into a monster simply to... I *am* honoured, Holmes."

"You were a monster long before you came here. So, shall we

just get on with this? Formalities seem somewhat redundant, do you not think?"

"If you insist," said Moriarty, and shot a bolt of black light from his palm.

Holmes ducked, glancing back at the smoking hole the bolt had made in the floor. When the Professor attacked again, Holmes retaliated with a focussed beam of his own, relishing the look of surprise on Moriarty's face as he did so; the Professor clearly didn't know that Holmes had been loaned such power. Then the two streams met, sparks crackling. Holmes gripped his cane with both hands and pushed, forcing the Professor to retreat. They went on like this for a few moments, each gaining ground and then losing it, both becoming drained with the effort. The pseudo Cenobites flagged as a consequence, granting Holmes' troops a much needed pause in the fighting.

A mighty blast sent both parties reeling. The immovable object had met the irresistible force, but something had to eventually give. Holmes flew backwards, skidding to a halt as he landed just shy of the edge of the abyss.

Moriarty, for his part, was wilting, sagging almost to the ground, the hat tumbling from his head, before he roused himself and rose again.

"Holmes!" came a cry, and the former detective looked over to see Watson with Mary and some of the members of the squadron he'd taken, as well as Carnivan, last seen being buried by a mound of rubble. They were carrying what looked like wands and hammers, the lost weaponry from Hell's armoury, and they were losing no time putting these to use against the pseudo Cenobites. Watson himself, however, had a pistol in each hand and was shooting at the enemy – Holmes couldn't help thinking that the more things changed, the more they stayed the same.

Watson was making his way across the field of conflict, attempting to reach Holmes, when Moran appeared again. He was on the ground now, and had a pistol levelled at the Doctor. "Watson, look out!" cried Holmes, but his companion had already seen the danger – just not quick enough to avoid being clipped in the arm, a shot which spun him around.

Holmes was about to move in his direction when a blast of black light struck an area just off to his right, sending him sprawling. Moriarty was drifting towards Holmes, palms ready to dispense more of his deadly power. But he was just as prepared, rising and firing a blast before the Professor could shoot again. It struck him with full force, crackling around his body. At the same time, Veronique had leapt down from her position above, glass blade and whip in her hands, landing on the one remaining mechanical moth and steering it towards the Engineer. When she got close enough, she slit its throat and jumped off, bringing the ends of her whip down across Moriarty's tentacles, severing two in the process.

He shrieked in agony, but she was already finishing the job with her glass blade – separating him from the appendages that were holding him aloft. Moriarty dropped heavily, dark liquid pumping from his back and spraying from the tendrils as they flailed across the floor. Veronique didn't have long to celebrate, though, as the Professor sent a single, concentrated bolt of black light coursing towards her, which rammed into the Cenobite's chest and carried her out of sight. Holmes watched her go as he tried to rise, weakened by his own efforts.

Moriarty was staggering to his feet, holding up his hands... but nothing erupted from his palms. Both parties were practically spent.

It was only now, as the Professor looked like he was about to give up, that he reached beneath his waistcoat, pulling out an amulet: the last of the Cenobite-killing weapons from the armoury.

And it was pointed right at Sherlock Holmes.

CHAPTER THIRTY
Lost and Found

FOR A LONG time I thought we were lost, hurrying down stone passage after stone passage, but eventually, we broke free – into the very heart of the war. Bodies were strewn across the floor ahead of us, and pseudo Cenobites still engaged Holmes' forces... what was left of them. Immediately, we started to pitch in. I had not seen any sign of Moriarty on our travels, but then I saw why. Holmes was indeed facing his mortal enemy, black light pitched against black light, both combatants looking as if they had seen better days. A burst of energy crackled and blew them apart, Holmes almost tumbling into the abyss, but managing to stop himself in time; the Professor slumping with the effort of it all.

I shouted across to him. When he didn't respond, I started to make my way over – and heard him call back just as I saw Colonel Moran, out of the corner of my eye, level his weapon and fire. I remember spinning, the whole panorama swirling around me. I lost consciousness, and when the darkness cleared, and I sat up, I was back on the battlefield – not of Hell, but of Maiwan.

Bullets were whipping by me, men crawling on their bellies to try and escape the Afghans. The fear had returned, that I would not get out of there alive, that they would do to me what they were already doing to many of my comrades.

"John? John, my love."

"Mary?" I looked around, but there was no sign of her.

"John, where are you?"

"I'm... I'm here. I'm in the war."

"John, you're lost. It's Moriarty again. Don't let him inside your head. Come to me, find me. Follow my voice. You're in grave danger!"

I clambered to my feet, my shoulder aching and pouring with blood, just as an Afghan was about to attack me. I blinked, trying to focus.

"My voice, John. Concentrate on –"

There was a sudden flash and the Afghan transformed into Moran, getting ready to shoot again, determined to finish the job. I stumbled sideways and more through luck than judgement dodged another of his rounds.

He was taking aim when something suddenly protruded from his chest, a large spear rammed through at speed. Moran looked surprised, head tilting to get a better look at his wound. "I don't think we've been properly introduced," someone said from behind him. Then, as he fell, revealing the person who had done the damage, she continued, "I'm Mary Watson and you killed me. Allow me to return the favour!"

She gave a satisfied nod, and I couldn't help smiling. There couldn't be many murder victims who had been allowed their revenge from beyond the grave – certainly none that Holmes and I had come across before.

"Found you," I said then.

"You did," she replied.

There was no time to rest on our laurels, however, as I looked across to find Holmes, and saw that Moriarty had been separated from those tentacles he'd been attached to – separated by Madame, no less, who had now been shot with black light for her trouble. So there they faced each other, Holmes and Moriarty, on equal footing once more. Both had evidently drained their reserves of energy, and Moriarty was losing navy-blue blood, through the gaping holes in his back.

He wasn't done yet, though. As I watched, I saw him reach into his clothing and produce an amulet. It was one of those I had seen in action back in the corridors, like those we had brought with us: lethal to all Cenobites, including my friend.

There was no time to reach him, or even call out a warning – much good it would have done anyway. Pure instinct took over and I began mouthing incantations, reaching out with my hand to cast one final spell.

The amulet pulled sideways, but was attached to a chain around Moriarty's neck. So I closed my fist again, issuing more strange words. The amulet folded in on itself, crushed beyond use. I'd done my bit.

Now it was up to Holmes and Holmes alone.

CHAPTER THIRTY-ONE
Familiar Ground

MORIARTY GAPED AT the crushed amulet, confused.

He looked at Holmes, as if he had the answer, then gave up searching for one altogether. The Professor bent and scooped up part of a broken staff, a stick to match Holmes' – which was already raised and waiting.

"Well, this is familiar ground at least," Moriarty said.

"Indeed," admitted Holmes.

The sticks clashed, in a series of moves that were part baritsu and part fencing. These eventually brought the two men together, each clutching the other, until they shoved against one another and parted.

"Admit it, Holmes – you've missed this!" Moriarty was smirking, only this time it was tempered by the considerable pain he was in; though, Holmes suspected, it was nothing compared with what the Cenobites had originally put him through. "No other foe has ever come close, nor ever will!"

Holmes said nothing, he merely came at his opponent, stick twirling, wood clacking against wood. Moriarty swung his weapon, smashing the glass top of Holmes' cane. Even if he could muster any black light, Holmes had no way of directing it now. He blocked a blow to the head, but in doing so forfeited surer footing. Then Moriarty dealt him a strike to the torso with his free hand.

The former detective bent double, only to have Moriarty's knee driven into his face. "I'm... I'm more than ready for you this time," boasted the Professor, in spite of the defeats he'd already suffered at Holmes' hand.

He drove forward, bringing his weapon down again. Holmes blocked it, dislodging it from Moriarty's grasp – only to lose his own in the process. Holmes grabbed Moriarty around the waist. The Cenobite brought a fist down on Holmes' back in retaliation, but there was no real strength there. Holmes brought up the back of his head, losing his deerstalker, but catching Moriarty under the chin. It felt wrong to be brawling like this; Hell's finest and best. But it was the only way they would settle things.

They took hold of each other again, wrapped up in more moves that were countered, blocked and parried – each anticipating the other's blows as if seeing them in their own minds before they actually happened. There was really only one way this could end.

Holmes went in for a final attack, fully expecting it to be fended off, and when it was, he hooked Moriarty's arms around his and pulled backwards, letting gravity do the rest. There was a resigned look on the Professor's face as they fell, as if he'd been expecting this.

Tumbling over and over into the abyss, the two old enemies regarded each other. Moriarty shifted, removing his arms from the lock they'd been placed in. Holmes reached out, but couldn't hold on. His mind flashed back to the Falls, to that other drop – when Moriarty fell away from him and solved the equation to enter Hell. That wasn't an option this time, he was already here. Holmes remembered the chink of an opening; Hell not only taking Moriarty, but staring through *into* him. Everything had been leading up to this, when he'd had to face the Professor's army, face the Professor again – and sacrifice himself a third time to defeat him.

Nothing had been left to chance, nothing ever was here.

The Engineer continued to fall. Holmes watched, puzzled – wondering why he'd suddenly stopped falling himself. He was aware of something wrapped around his waist. A rope of some kind? No, a whip, the ends moving of their own accord, tightening their grip.

Then he was rising, back towards the edge of the precipice. Holmes continued to stare down, to witness the long fall of the Professor. Until he himself reached the top, pulled up not only by a badly injured Veronique, but by others who had come to her aid: Spike, The Confessor, Carnivan… Mary and Watson, no less injured himself. They rolled him back onto the platform, just as a bright burst came from below – a jet of energy signalling the end of the Engineer, and his coup. It flared upwards, whatever black light that remained being sucked back into the shifting body of their god, hanging patiently above them all.

The pseudo Cenobites were dropping too, falling now that their strings had been cut.

"Holmes? Holmes…?" It was Watson's voice he could hear now. "Are you all right?" He attempted a nod, but the effort was too great. So instead, his friend asked, "Is it over? Is it really all over?"

But that question Holmes refused to answer.

For he knew it was only just beginning.

CHAPTER THIRTY-TWO
The Aftermath

ALL I COULD do was observe as Holmes battled his nemesis one last time.

The fight was evenly matched, and transpired in a similar fashion to that of the altercation at the Reichenbach, except that this time the finale saw both of them going over the edge. My heart was in my mouth when they fell, and both Mary and I made our way over to the edge, even though we knew there was nothing we could do to help.

Fortunately, Madame had crawled back across and managed to unfurl her whip over the edge, and by the time we got there, she was being helped by some of the other Cenobites. We got him safely up onto the ledge, just before the explosion erupted from below – a rush of black energy which meant that Moriarty had to be no more.

I hoped.

His minions were falling, the conflict over. We had won! Yet I couldn't help feeling that we really hadn't. The cost, to Holmes especially, had been so great. But I did not know the half of it back then...

I recovered from my wounds swiftly enough, for it transpired that the Cenobites were just as good at knitting people together as they were at tearing them apart. Mary didn't leave my side the whole time I was being tended to, holding my hand, making sure I was comfortable; the same way I had when she'd fallen into her coma. My return to health gave me hope that what had been done to Holmes could be reversed. Of the man himself I saw very little during this period, but I assumed he was occupied. I did hear that Madame Veronique was to be appointed the new Engineer, though in light of her extensive injuries, she would need to be radically altered before she could take up her promotion. As much as I hated to admit it, Hell would be in very capable hands.

By the time I was fit enough to be on my feet again, the clean-up operation was underway – of the damage, of the pseudo Cenobites and other creations that Moriarty had concocted to fight his war (their long-suffering spirits now granted the peace they should have had in the first place). All the Cenobite-killing weaponry was recovered and locked away again. There really had been no rest for the wicked.

Mary gave me a tour of Hell and I relished the time we spent in each other's company, regardless of the circumstances and location. One might have thought we were strolling through an English meadow in springtime rather than the corridors and balconies of such a foul dominion.

"Our time here is almost at an end. You will have to leave soon, John," she said to me eventually. "And so will I."

"Together," I said hopefully, though my stomach was churning as I waited for her response.

"You know that is not possible. I wish that it were. I do not belong in your world; no more than you belong here."

"But Mary, I... I can't lose you again."

"Oh John, I'm already lost," she said sweetly, taking my hands in hers. "Moriarty is gone, the connection broken. I'm starting to fade." It was true, her grip wasn't as strong as it had been.

"No, *please* no. It's been so lonely without you, my love."

She touched my face, wiping my cheek. "No tears, remember? You will always be able to find me sweetheart – in here." Now she placed a finger on my temple. "And in here." Mary put her hand on my chest.

"It's not the same, I –"

"You will not be alone for long. I promise," she said, planting a kiss on my lips. I closed my eyes, savouring the taste of her, but when I opened them again she was gone. "Goodbye, my darling," I heard her whisper.

"Goodbye," I said back, a catch in my voice. "I love you."

I assumed she had been talking about Holmes, when she said I would not be alone for long, but when I finally spotted him, issuing orders to a group of workers, and broached the subject of returning to our dimension, all he could do was look at the ground.

"I am sorry, Watson. My place is here."

"How can you even... Holmes, you've done as they asked. You stopped the Professor in his tracks; you've done more than enough for them. Far more than they deserve."

"Watson, please. This is difficult enough without –"

"Without what?"

He looked directly at me. "It was part of the arrangement. The deal I brokered. I said I would not only do my best to prevent Moriarty's advancement, but also aid in the rebuilding after he was gone."

"Why on Earth would you agree to that?" I shouted, red-faced.

"In exchange for your safe passage home. For immunity. For Hell never being able to darken your doorstep."

I did not know what to say.

"Who knows, maybe it is all for the best. I might even be able to do some good here. Change things for the better? Make a difference?" Holmes placed a hand on my shoulder. "I *am* sorry,

Watson. Truly I am. You have always been a loyal friend to me and I shall miss you greatly."

"Holmes, no. Don't do this. Mary is gone and I –"

But it was already done. Holmes did not vanish, as Mary had, but I did. I found myself transported in the blink of an eye back to our study at Baker Street, confused and more than a little disorientated, weak in the knees. When I had steadied myself, I screamed at the top of my voice, so loudly it drew the attention of Mrs Hudson – who burst in.

"Oh, Dr Watson, it's you! I didn't hear you come in. What in Heaven's name is all this shouting about?"

I met her gaze. "Nothing. Nothing in Heaven's name, I'm sad to say."

She frowned, then asked, "Did you... did you manage to find any trace of Mr Holmes?"

I opened my mouth to answer, then shook my head. Better to leave it at that than say he simply would not be back. She had mourned for him once before, as had I. And it wasn't as if he was dead in the traditional sense this time – just... missing in action. She asked me if I would like a bite of supper and I declined, telling her that it had been a tiring time of late and I would retire to my bed early.

Instead, I made use what was left of the whisky and brandy we had in those chambers and reluctantly fell asleep in the armchair.

WHEN I WOKE the next morning, I was even more disorientated, imagining everything to have been a hideous nightmare.

I was awake now, though, like Alice.

Indeed, I wondered if perhaps everything since Holmes' return disguised as that bookseller had been a fiction? A vision? Perhaps he had not come back to me in the first place, perhaps we had never investigated those missing persons cases? I had not gone to France, nor had Holmes opened the puzzle box –

and as for our adventures in Hell... Too fanciful to contemplate, even with my writer's flair for romanticism, for 'colour and life'.

However, the calendar told me that it was 1896, and when Mrs Hudson knocked to see if I wanted any breakfast, she confirmed that I had been searching for Holmes since my return from Paris. It did not mean that the whole affair in 'Hell' or whatever you wanted to call the place had happened, but it made it that bit more possible.

As the days and weeks passed, I began to turn to the drink and gambling. I even found myself looking over to Holmes' Morocco case every now and again, thought about opening that particular box and experimenting with the other drug he relied on a little too heavily; the only thing stopping me was my experience at the Institute. Mrs Hudson's fussing did little to shake me out of my mood, just annoyed me to the point where I found myself shouting at her to leave me alone. Summons to Scotland Yard to help on cases went unanswered, as did those from Mycroft Holmes. Pleas from clients went unheard, my poor patients were once again neglected. And I did not dream – not of Mary, not of the war (any of them), and not of Holmes.

But I did grow increasingly obsessed with the idea that we had been cleverly manipulated by something infinitely more fiendish than the Professor. If their god was so powerful, surely it should have had some idea as to what Moriarty had been up to – what he would become when he was given the role of Engineer? If so, perhaps Hell had a different endgame in mind all along? To lure Holmes there, to use him? Perhaps there was never any hope of him changing things, of doing any kind of good with his newfound position. He had been tricked, just like so many who had opened the box before him. Moreover, it troubled me greatly that, in the end, we had both been as much servants of Hell as anyone else.

This had never been about control of London at all; there had been much greater things at stake. I had misunderstood Simon

Lemarchand, the box had purely been a means to ease their passage into our world.

However, more than any of this, I simply *missed* Holmes. Mary had promised I would not be alone, and yet here I was. What made matters worse was that even though he had been changed physically, I felt – when I saw him after that transformation – like the *real* Holmes was back, not the preoccupied one I had spent time with over the last few years. Yet there was nothing I could do now. It was beyond my power to bring him back.

Or was it?

I was a loyal friend and I could not just leave him there in that place for all eternity; I had to protect him, save him, just as he had tried to do with me. I started to think about how Malahide had returned the aristocrat – and that phrase, "The blood is the key." It would be another gamble, but maybe – just maybe – there was a way of breaking Holmes out of Hell. I returned to that now abandoned hole where he had opened the box (the object itself was long gone, of course – almost certainly recovered by the vagabond), bringing with me a vial of my own blood. This I poured over the floorboards where I had seen Holmes spill his own – the *real* trace of him – watching and waiting for something... anything to happen.

Nothing did, and I convinced myself then that it *had* all been a nightmare; that my mind had made it up to reconcile the fact that he had gone missing, just like the people we had been brought in to help. Or, if it had transpired, their god was not about to let him go so easily...

Then it happened, not quite as it had back at the Institute – and certainly more graphic. A body piecing itself together out of nothing, feeding on the blood I had supplied until it had all been mopped up. I gaped, open-mouthed, at this sickening display; as organs appeared, juices slopping over nerves until a basic outline of a man was left writhing on the floor in agony. It was Holmes, I knew it was... but there the 'birth' halted.

"M-more," was all the shape could manage.

I wasn't sure what he meant at first, but then I nodded – for I would have done anything I could just to have him back. I won't go into the details of how I brought him all the way; there isn't the need, and I feel I have said too much already in this account that might turn people against both Holmes and myself. Suffice to say, I managed to wrestle him from the clutches of Hell, knowing full well that there would be no retaliation because of his deal. It was on my head alone.

They weren't the only ones who could play tricks.

(I often think also about how and *why* their god finally let him escape – and that perhaps Holmes had served his purpose; that there might be another Hell Priest lined up to take his place. Maybe the one I'd mistaken for Glass, who looked like the African fetishes?)

Anyway, Holmes was where he belonged.

Alas, what I got back was not the man – or even the Cenobite – that I had left behind. He was a poor imitation of his former self, haunted I suspect by the things that he had seen afterwards – or something else. I could never really get him to open up about it all. The stories from that point onwards, though most happened, are as I have said, by necessity, embellished, designed to satisfy the appetites of readers who had grown used to a certain kind of Sherlock Holmes tale. There were only a couple of adventures where I felt he was almost back to his old self, the first an investigation that forced him to finally confront the monster that resided within...

But there is no time for that now, I grow weary and will soon put my pen down. I think it has helped a little, to recall these events, to set them down – even if no-one will ever read these words. And nor should they. Most would probably call them the ramblings of a senile old fool if they did! However, I can't help thinking back to those visions of war Mary gave me, and how true the first one turned out to be. The one where all those men died in the trenches, so much fodder for Hell, during and afterwards. More lost souls. I think about how we're now occupied by the next one, how that mushroom cloud explosion I bore witness to might be only just around the corner.

I can only hope I am gone by then, for once was quite enough.

And I can't help thinking of something Holmes kept repeating when I returned him to this world. About how all this had happened before, how it would do so again.

I didn't know quite what he meant back then, and still don't.

If I am honest, I am not even sure I want to.

EPILOGUE

THE BLOOD HAD brought him back.

Just a small amount had been enough, but it had returned the man to her. In the months since he had been 'declared' dead, Juliet Cotton had found herself being drawn time and again up to that attic room where Francis had disappeared. It was silly, she knew, but she felt like she was closest to him up there. No-one had been able to tell them what had really happened, and she still held out hope that one day he would be back in her life – just as she had longed for since their time together; prior to her wedding to the increasingly dull Laurence.

They had fired that wretched housekeeper, Williams, Juliet had made sure of that. The thought that she might have been with Francis at some point in the past was enough to turn her stomach, let alone having to look at her each day. However, that had just left her and Laurence in the house together, alone, and she had grown more and more disgusted by his touch, his adoring glances; the way he would trail after her like a puppy dog and keep asking if she was all right. Juliet was as far from that condition as was possible. She was becoming distant with him, and couldn't help it. Her thoughts, more so now than at any other time during their sham of a marriage, were with Francis. His tousled hair, that lean body of his.

It was why she kept taking herself away – up to the attic room, a place she'd insisted they leave just as it was, in spite of Laurence's arguments that they could turn it into a second office. She just wanted to be alone, with her thoughts of Francis. But, of course, Laurence had not allowed her that time to 'grieve'. (Was that what she was doing? It certainly didn't feel like letting go.) He would continually follow her up, and then, one day, in a rare display of bravado after she had piqued his anger he had stormed in with the intention of dragging her back downstairs with him. He could not even get that right, catching his hand on the ruined doorframe and opening up the back of it.

Laurence had turned grey immediately, clutching the wounded hand, looking away and shambling towards her. "Is... is it deep?" he'd inquired, his voice immediately shrinking. "You... you know I cannot abide the sight of blood."

Sighing, she had taken him downstairs to wrap the hand in cloth and call a cab, which would take them to the hospital.

That night, when they had arrived back after Laurence's hand had been stitched up, she found herself climbing out of bed and returning again to the attic room, perhaps to finish what her husband had not let her do earlier that day; to think about Francis. What she had found in the darkness had been both repulsive and exciting. Something scuffling, which at first she took to be rats, but then she'd known – actually felt – it had been *him*. Or part of him at any rate.

"Do not look at me!" he'd insisted, but she couldn't help herself. Yes, he was disgusting, only partially formed, but he was still Francis. *Her* Francis. When she had heard Laurence stir below, she'd left the creature but vowed to return – something she had done many times after that, but only when Laurence was at his work.

Francis had explained about the box, the tortures he'd

endured, the Cenobites – and how, while their attention was fixed elsewhere, he'd been able to escape. The spilt blood had provided a means by which he might slip through and be with her once more. It was an incredible story, but one which she was willing to accept if only because it had brought Francis back.

"But I need more, Juliet. And I need you to get it for me. Then we can be together again. You'd like that, would you not?"

She'd nodded, for she would do whatever it took to make Francis whole. So she had gone out, using the charms she'd developed over time to lure her prey back to the house – one a gentleman called Patrick, in London from the Midlands on business; another a family man called Sykes who'd had second thoughts when he returned with her. Juliet had told them she was lonely, and they'd believed her – but she knew her lonely days would soon be over. Fuelled by thoughts of being in Francis' arms again, she had fed these pitiful fools to him, looking away when he devoured them to put more flesh on his bones; telling herself that the blood they spilled would make him stronger.

Juliet had almost been caught once, when Laurence returned home from work unexpectedly, and she'd had to feign illness to keep him away from the attic room; to keep him from discovering her secret. She'd play the dutiful wife role a little longer, then she and Francis would leave and nobody would be any the wiser.

Except Laurence had told her then that he'd made arrangements for his daughter to finally come and stay with them, for a short while at first and then maybe permanently. Plans expedited by the fact *he* was probably lonely, with only Juliet for company.

"We can be a real family," he'd said, beaming – the idiot. Little realising that Francis was already plotting to take his skin and complete himself, something he had only just informed her of. If it was the only way, then it was the only way.

This time, when they were almost caught, it was by Kirsten. Fresh-faced and over in this country for the first time, she was more woman now than girl. And, Francis had managed to convince her to begin with that he was Laurence, in spite of the way Laurence's skin only just fitted at his hairline and around the eyes. For her part, Juliet had balked at the way he was looking the girl up and down, but dismissed this – if *Francis* now wanted them to be a family, then there was a chance they could make the situation work.

It was only when he said to her, "Come to your father," opening his arms, that Kirsten had realised he was not who he claimed to be. She probably did not know exactly what was wrong, but something told her to run; to get away from that place. Which she had promptly done, wrestling herself out of Francis' grip, and practically diving out through the front door. This made her dangerous, a threat to their future life together. What if she told the authorities, what if the Cenobites or their agents on Earth caught wind of it? Francis would be taken back and all this would be over.

That was not tolerable. But Juliet would find a way to fix all this – to fix what was broken. She'd promised Francis, and in turn he'd promised to be with her for an eternity.

It was all she cared about. It was all she would *ever* care about.

This was not over yet. In fact, it was only just beginning...

ACKNOWLEDGMENTS

THANKS TO JONATHAN Oliver and the Solaris team for taking a chance on this book, and seeing the same potential in the crossover that I could. A huge thank you to Mark Miller at Seraphim and, of course, to Clive who not only put his full support behind this project but graciously offered some excellent insights – even down to suggesting I change the names of the original clients to Cotton, to foreshadow later events; something we did elsewhere in the book as well, as you'll have seen. A big thank you to Sam Gretton for the superb cover, and to Christian Francis for his input. Thanks to Charles Prepolec, Holmes expert who published my first ever Sherlock horror story, for taking a look at the manuscript before I sent it in, and fellow Holmes author Mark Latham for not minding my niggling questions. A big thank you to Barbie Wilde, not only for the introduction but for allowing me to use some of her kick-ass female Cenobites from her SST collection *Voices of the Damned*. And thanks to Sarah Pinborough, Simon Clark, Tim Lebbon and Nancy Holder for doing the same with 'The Confessor', 'The Lord of Quarters', 'The Gardener' and 'The Ravisher' from *Hellbound Hearts*, plus Gary Tunnicliffe for allowing fan favourite 'Spike' to cameo.

The same goes for Nancy Springer, who kindly gave permission for me to use the name of Enola Holmes – Sherlock's little sister – from the excellent YA mysteries that she writes. Thanks also to everyone who has kept the *Hellraiser* mythos alive for thirty years and have been such an inspiration, especially people like Doug Bradley, Pete Atkins, Stephen Jones, Ashley Laurence, Simon Bamford, Tony Randel, Nick Vince, Dan Chichester, Tony Hickox, Ben Meares, Rick Bota, Phil & Sarah Stokes and the *Leviathan* guys. Lastly a big-words-are-not-enough-thank-you to my lovely family and especially to my wife Marie, who not only offered support and encouragement during the writing of this one, but also truly wonderful edits. Love you sweetheart.

ABOUT THE AUTHOR

Paul Kane is the award-winning, bestselling author and editor of over sixty books – including the *Arrowhead* trilogy for Abaddon (gathered together in the bestselling *Hooded Man* omnibus, revolving around a post-apocalyptic version of Robin Hood), *Ghosts*, *Monsters* and *Nailbiters*. His anthologies include the *Hellraiser*-themed book for Simon & Schuster, *Hellbound Hearts*, *The Mammoth Book of Body Horror* for Constable & Robinson and *Beyond Rue Morgue* for Titan, while his popular Holmes stories 'The Greatest Mystery' (*Gaslight Arcanum*) and 'The Case of the Lost Soul' (*The Mammoth Book of Sherlock Holmes Abroad*) have been well received and critically acclaimed. He has been called 'the resident *Hellraiser* expert' by Clive Barker himself and 'the world's leading expert on the *Hellraiser* films and their mythology' by Peter Atkins (who wrote *Hellraiser*s II-IV), while Pinhead himself, Doug Bradley, said in the introduction to the bestselling *The Hellraiser Films and Their Legacy*, 'It would be, perhaps, facile of me to say that he has such sights to show you, but the simple fact is, he has'. Paul also designed his very own puzzle box, 'The Scribe Configuration', for the Pyramid Gallery complete with its own mythology.

He has been a Guest at Alt.Fiction five times, was a Guest at the first SFX Weekender, at Thought Bubble in 2011, Derbyshire Literary Festival and Off the Shelf in 2012, Monster Mash and Event Horizon in 2013, Edge-Lit in 2014, plus HorrorCon, HorrorFest and Grimm Up North in 2015, as well as being a panellist at FantasyCon and the World Fantasy Convention. His work has been optioned and adapted for the big and small screen, including for US network television. His latest novels are *Lunar* (set to be turned into a feature film), the YA story *The Rainbow Man* (as P.B. Kane), and the sequel to *RED – Blood RED*. He lives in Derbyshire, UK, with his wife Marie O'Regan, his family and a black cat called Mina. Find out more at his site www.shadow-writer.co.uk which has featured Guest Writers such as Stephen King, Neil Gaiman, Charlaine Harris, Dean Koontz and Guillermo del Toro.